Beyond
the Goat Trails

Beyond the Goat Trails

ISBN-13: 978-0998463827
ISBN-10: 0998463825

3 Pooches Publishing
3poochespublishing.com

Printed in the United States of America

For the always elusive and endlessly available spirit of creativity and Buddy Cyrus.

2001-2016

Evoke the Magic of Writing

For the always elusive and endlessly available spirit of creativity and Buddy Cyrus.

2001-2016

Evoke the Magic of Writing

CHAPTER 1

A BIG WHISKEY NEAT

"Do you see the woman in the red dress at the bar?" the man in a bespoke gray European suit asked the waiter.

"Why, yes, Dr. Matson, everyone in the room has noticed her," the waiter said. The waiter poured a glass of sparkling water for the doctor.

A mischievous smile etched across the doctor's face. "Do you know if she is part of the private group for tonight?" Dr. Matson asked the waiter. His gray eyes locked on his prey.

The waiter did not hesitate for another look at the long legs wrapped around the bar stool and said, "I don't recognize her as a member of your group, sir."

Most unfortunate, Dr. Matson thought to himself. "Order her another drink, and let her know it's from me." His fingers tapped the white linen tablecloth.

"Very well, sir. Will you have your usual tonight?"

"Yes, but make sure it is without ice. Last time I ordered the drink 'neat' and instead received a miniature glacier in my drink," Dr. Matson said. He was curious if the woman at the bar was alone.

"My apologies, sir. The owner hired his nephew with no bartending experience," the waiter said after he realigned the silverware on the table.

Dr. Matson picked up a knife on the table, his finger running along the edge of the blade. "Did the owner keep him as a bartender?"

The waiter noticed a scowl on the doctor's face and hesitated before he answered. "Yes, but he is not scheduled to work tonight, sir."

"Good, Jimmy. The other patrons and I can enjoy our drinks tonight,"

Dr. Matson said.

Most the wait staff avoided Dr. Matson because of his lack of generosity despite his demands and expectations of impeccable service. Tonight the waiter had the misfortune of waiting on Dr. Matson. His name tag did not have "Jimmy" printed on it, but he did not bother to correct the doctor about his name.

Why bother? After three years he does not care to learn my name, the waiter thought to himself.

Dr. Matson observed the woman straighten her posture and flick her hair. Her eyes lingered for a moment in his direction. Her long black hair shimmered from the accent lights on the bar in the upstairs private dining room.

The guest speaker walked toward the podium as the guests in attendance clapped for him. Dr. Matson caught one last glimpse of the woman as she set a lipstick-smeared glass on the bar before the wait staff closed the privacy curtain.

Dr. Matson fidgeted and lost interest in the guest speaker after the first slide. The expensive whiskey and gourmet meal did not hold his interest either. Dr. Matson could not resist the woman's allure. The sirens of antiquity beckoned him to their island. He stood up in the middle of the lecture and did not bother to excuse himself from the table. His heart beat faster in anticipation of what waited for him as he walked toward the bar. A waiter held open the privacy curtain for him and unleashed the caged animal. Dr. Matson felt free to stalk his prey. His gray eyes scanned the empty room. Disappointment usurped the thrill of the hunt.

"Hey, baby," Dr. Matson said as he plucked an olive from the garnish tray from behind the bar.

"Yes?" the bartender said. She suppressed the annoyance in her voice as she turned around to face Dr. Matson.

"Honey, do you know what happened to the woman in the red dress?" Dr. Matson asked.

"I think she went downstairs to dance. A famous DJ from Europe performs in half an hour," she said. The bartender twirled a lock of her blond hair. "May I get you a drink, sir?"

Dr. Matson did not recognize the bartender, but he enjoyed what he saw. He smiled, touched his gold watch and said, "Call me Dr. Matson, but I'll pass on the drink."

"Are you sure, Dr. Matson?" She leaned in close to him. "I have excellent bar-side manners," she said.

He breathed in the smell of her perfume, but his thoughts lingered on the woman in red.

"Tempting, but no," Dr. Matson said. He turned away to leave the room.

"Too bad, you won't have me to yourself for much longer," she said. She reached for another martini glass on the top shelf.

"Why is that?" Dr. Matson asked as he turned around toward her and admired her figure.

"After the dinner talk this place turns into a private VIP area," the bartender said as she sliced lemons for cocktail garnish.

"Velvet ropes and bouncers don't deter me," Dr. Matson said.

"You know where to find me," she said.

Dr. Matson increased his stride in his polished Italian dress shoes to catch up with the woman in red. "Hey, gorgeous," he said with excitement.

The woman paused and resisted the urge to turn around. Instead she continued across the empty dance floor. She felt the stares from the staff setting up the DJ booth as they drifted into fantasy land. Dr. Matson's hand curled around her sinewy, caramel-colored arm toned by hours in the gym. She winced when he touched her and turned around to face him.

"Hello, did you enjoy your drink?" Dr. Matson asked. He held onto her arm, enthralled with her sultry green eyes and black voluminous hair. She looked at him with a tinge of anger, and he let go of her arm but felt entwined in a trance.

She caught his eyes wander over the curves of her form-fitted red dress, and she bit her lip to set the hook in his imagination.

"Yes, thank you for the club soda," she said as she rubbed her arm where he touched her.

"Club soda?" he asked in disbelief. "Please allow me to buy you a drink to match your sophistication."

"Thank you for the drink, but I must go," she said. She tossed her hair and turned away from him.

"Why leave before the music?" His warm hand touched the exposed skin on her lower back.

"I am bored, and no one talks to me," she said.

"Join me for a drink, and when the DJ performs we can dance. My name is Dr. Matson," he said. Aware of the lecherous stares from the other men in the room he pulled her close to him and enveloped her petite frame. He smiled as their heads and shoulders slumped in defeat when she did not resist him. He claimed his possession. She turned around to face him and pushed him away after he held her for a moment.

"So you're a doctor?" she asked. She surveyed the impeccable details of his wardrobe. "One more drink and I'll give the evening another chance. My name is Lilia," she said as she extended her dainty hand toward him.

Her Latin accent lashed his mind with lascivious thoughts. His nostrils filled with the scent of lavender when he kissed her hand with French-tipped fingernails. "A pleasure to meet you, Lilia. How about a martini or a few?" he asked.

"No, I prefer tequila. It makes me do naughty things," she said.

"I bet it does," he said. His arm slithered around her petite waist and pulled her close to him. He resisted the urge to explore other parts of her body as he led her toward a private table.

She ignored her intuition and held on to his hand as they crossed the crowded dance floor to the restaurant exit. She enjoyed his charm and rent was due next week.

"Sir, did you enjoy yourself tonight?" the valet asked Dr. Matson as he admired the young woman who shivered next to the him.

"Hurry up with my car," Dr. Matson said. He noticed the valet's eyes traced the symmetry of his young companion and he pulled her close to him. She clung to him for warmth in the cool San Diego evening as the pain throbbed in her feet from her six-inch heels. She ignored the furtive stares of the men and the frowns of the woman who entered the club. A car with a V12 engine approached the front of the restaurant and she was no longer the center of attention. *Does he own this car?* she wondered as she read the license plate.

"Your car, sir," the valet said. He held the door open for the doctor.

Dr. Matson ignored the valet as he scrolled through the emails on his cell phone. The valet shut the door, disgusted he did not receive a tip from the driver of the exotic sports car, and walked toward the valet stand.

"Excuse me! Do you only open doors for the driver?" Lilia asked.

The valet stopped, turned around, and saw the attractive Hispanic woman with her hands on her well-shaped hips and pursed lips glare at him.

"Miss, your boyfriend is a terrible tipper," the valet said.

"He is not my boyfriend," she said in defiance. "You got what you deserve because you did not bother to open the door for me," she said.

The valet held the car door open for her and enjoyed the sight of her toned legs in heels sliding across the leather seat. He glanced at the doctor, engrossed in his cell phone and oblivious to his companion. The valet thought, *What the hell, I'll take a chance.*

"Please allow me to make it up to you, Miss. I valet on the side but own a gym in town. Stop by the gym and I will provide a custom work out plan for you," he said. He handed her his black and gold business card. "You're not a priority in his world, but I would give you all the attention you deserve."

She noticed the valet's cheap watch. "You can't afford me," she said. She ignored his card and slammed the car door shut. "I thought this car belonged to you," she said to the doctor. She stroked the rich leather interior with her dainty hand.

"How did you know this car belonged to me?" Dr. Matson asked. He slid the cell phone in his jacket pocket and revved the engine. He enjoyed the attention he received from the onlookers in line who took pictures of his car while they waited to enter the restaurant-turned-dance-club.

"The license plate gave it away," she said. She kicked off her heels and plunged her toes into the plush floor mats.

"Does the plate offend you?" he asked.

"It is a bit over the top," she said as she opened the vanity mirror to apply some lipstick.

"The female form is my canvas, and I create works of art where flaws of nature incongruent with society's ideals of beauty exist," Dr. Matson said.

"So you're a plastic surgeon, huh? Boob Doc?" she asked. She considered the vanity plate with "Boob Doc" printed on it as an indication of too much money for his own good and found this more offensive than the license plate.

Dr. Matson turned his attention from the tight dresses in line for the club and enjoyed the sight of the seat belt across his companion. "Yes, one of the best in the world, but you don't need any of my help," he said.

She ignored his comment. "Please turn up the heat," she said.

"I can arrange that," he said as he squeezed her thigh.

"No, silly, the car heater—I am cold," she said. She brushed his hand away from her legs.

His hand returned to her thigh after he turned up the heat. She squeezed his warm hand in between her thighs. He leaned over and glanced at her chest, curious if she might be a patient but concluded a greater master than himself was responsible for those works of art. He tried to kiss her, but she moved her head away from his puckered lips.

"Ay Papi, thank you for the drinks, but I had other things in mind for tonight," she said as she reached for the door latch.

"Of course, check the glove box" he said. He slumped in the leather seat after he depressed the button to open the glove compartment.

She opened the glove compartment and reached for the envelope. *Rent this month and extra,* she thought as she thumbed through the stack of hundred dollar bills.

"Satisfied?" he asked.

"Ay Papi, you can have me all day tomorrow."

He would have paid more to listen to her Latin voice and explore her irresistible body. He revved the engine, accelerated out of the restaurant parking lot and merged into traffic.

"Let's go for a drive in the hills, and I want you to drive fast," she giggled.

"You are in the right car for speed." He weaved in and out of traffic until he reached the exit toward the secluded hills.

"So what do you want to do after our racing fun?" she asked.

He ignored her question while he lined up his car to cut the apex of the turn like he was taught at Laguna Seca Racing School. She allowed his hand to roam and caress her cheek while his Italian shoe increased pressure on the gas pedal. The acceleration pinned her into the luxurious leather seat and her hands covered her face while she laughed. She enjoyed the rush of adrenaline from the speed and acceleration of the sports car.

"I thought we would visit a secluded bed and breakfast on the ocean after our spirited romp through the hills," Dr. Matson said. He loved to carve up the corners on the rural roads of San Diego, and his buxom companion who enjoyed the thrill was worth the price of admission.

"I would like that very much, and I hope the walls are thin," she said. She held onto the door grab handle to brace her petite body before the car cut through the next corner.

"That is enough speed for tonight," Dr. Matson said. He double-tapped the left paddle shifter on the steering wheel to downshift before the last corner he took at high speed.

"Don't be a bore; I want more speed," she said. She unlatched her seat belt to lean in close to him.

"It is pitch black on these backroads; we can go fast in the morning," Dr. Matson said. His eyes strained to see in the darkness and avoid the loose gravel shoulders of the narrow road.

"These cars crave speed, and you need some motivation to satisfy the craving," she said. She slid the top of her dress to reveal a lace bra that struggled to contain her ample assets. He resisted her pleas for more speed so she set them free with a flick of her fingers.

She swatted his hand away. "No, no, no," she said as she licked her red lips. "You must go faster! This is the checkered flag," she said and threw her bra on the dash. He mashed the accelerator to claim his prize.

CHAPTER 2

WE WERE ONLY FRESHMAN

"I TOLD YOU WE SHOULD HAVE taken the last exit," Stephanie said. She crossed her arms in disgust and scowled as he fumbled with the GPS device on the center console. "Stop with the GPS. It has not helped us once on this trip," she said.

Josh glanced in the rear-view mirror at the young woman asleep. He removed his Dallas Cowboys cap, rubbed his bald head and avoided eye contact with the woman next to him. *A consistent nag for the past few years,* he thought as he slid the cap on his head.

"We could have avoided this mess if you would help with the navigation," Josh said. He struggled to keep his cool. "I can't watch for traffic, road exits and other hazards while you play on your tablet or sleep," he said. He reached for the open energy drink in the center console below the GPS device. "Hell, you insisted on the GPS despite the thirty-dollars-a day charge."

Stephanie uncrossed her arms and brushed a loose strand of red hair from her face. "It's always about money with you, Josh. We can't do this, we can't do that because it is not in the budget," she said. She contemplated the dark countryside devoid of any activity and the similarities with her own life. "I never would have suggested the GPS had I known your incompetence with such a device," she said under her breath.

"What, what did you say, Stephanie?" Anger and fatigue seeped into his voice. "If you have something to say, tell me!"

"Mom, Dad, stop! I have a headache because of your bickering," the young woman said from the second row of the minivan.

Josh adored the young woman in the rearview mirror and did not want to upset her. Memories of her in a car seat flashed through his mind. *It doesn't seem so long ago,* he thought. "Sorry, honey, did we wake you?" Josh asked. He opened the window to toss the empty can.

"Yes, can you please choose a subject besides your dislikes about each other?" she said, agitated.

"Ok, honey, one more hour until we arrive in San Diego," Josh said.

"Bull shit; you will screw it up somehow like you always do," Stephanie said. She reclined her seat and wrapped herself in her blanket to avoid an argument about the heater. "I should have taken my mother's offer to buy plane tickets for us, but your ego could not handle that gesture of kindness. We would be asleep in a comfortable bed if I hadn't listened to your plan to drive to San Diego," Stephanie said.

"Damn, Stephanie, see the red arrow on the display?" Josh gestured with a stick of beef jerky. "It indicates our direction is west, and once we reach the city I am sure your innate sense of direction for San Diego will kick in from the memories of fleet week at the naval base."

"I would enjoy a detour through those memories," Stephanie said. "With you it always leads to a dead end in Dullsville."

"Mom, Dad, stop," their daughter said. She removed her headphones and paused the song on her smart phone. "Mom, give me the tablet please, and I'll find a way to the interstate," she said.

"Here, sorry your dad woke you up," her mom said. She handed her daughter the tablet.

Their daughter opened a navigation app on the tablet and found their location. "Dad, in about a quarter mile go through the intersection, and five miles past the intersection make a left on the farm road and it will take you to the freeway entrance."

"Thanks, honey. Try to get some sleep," Josh said.

"Promise you will be nice to Mom?" his daughter asked.

"Deal, honey," Josh said. He smiled at her through the rearview mirror.

She closed the navigation app and glanced at the article her mom left open on the tablet. She savored the memory of winning the distinguished Yehudi Menuhin International Competition for violinists at fifteen. It was her chance at a college education and freedom from the small Texas town. She tapped the violin case next to her and handed the tablet to her mom before she closed her eyes to dream of her future in a big city symphony orchestra.

Josh cracked the window to fight the fatigue that seeped into his reflexes from the droning tires on the pavement and the shrill voice of his wife. He saw the green light above the road his daughter mentioned and scanned the intersection for other cars. To the left he saw a bright orb of light between the hills on a trajectory toward the intersection. *Who the hell would be out this late on the roads?* he thought to himself.

CHAPTER 3

THE RIDE OF YOUR LIFE

A FLURRY OF ACTIVITY filled the intersection. Red and blue lights from the highway patrol cars and other first responder vehicles illuminated the hills on the moonless night. An eerie glow from the road flares directed the trickle of cars around the carnage of the intersection.

The stretcher legs crashed against the frame of the vehicle and jarred Josh from his muddled mental state. Constricting pressure on both sides of his body prevented him from moving his arms and legs. Panic gripped Josh like a straitjacket. He struggled to raise his neck, but the thick cervical collar limited his field of view. His head swirled with pain. The pain increased in intensity the longer he kept his eyes open to the world. Some of the physical pain was relieved when he closed his eyes, but the accident re-played over and over in his mind.

He felt free of gravity as he slid forward into the open vehicle. The ambulance doors slammed shut and muffled sounds of the first responders in the intersection. Red and blue lights trickled in through the small windows and created a kaleidoscope effect on the overhead storage lockers. He did not want to leave the tranquility of the silence in the ambulance—his own sanctuary amid the chaos of the evening.

He kept his eyes closed to embrace peace and realized he did not swerve to save his family when the other car ignored the red light. Tears glistened around his eyes. He thought of every moral decision he had made in his life and how he always chose the easy path.

A putrid sensation crawled along his throat. He suppressed the urge to throw up as panic scattered his thoughts because he did not know the fate of his family. Both ambulance doors flung open and beckoned the chaos to re-enter his sanctuary. The emergency medical technicians climbed inside the ambulance and stowed their gear in the storage compartments. The technicians' presence inside the ambulance chased away the panic Josh felt and the tranquility of the space. He kept his eyes closed and listened to their description of the carnage at the scene of the accident. He did not have the courage to ask them about his family.

CHAPTER 4

BLOODY RARE

AN OCEAN BREEZE dispersed the smoke from Dr. Matson's cigar perched on a makeshift ashtray. Ashes covered a pile of sugar packets next to the empty container. Members of the club glanced with annoyed expressions when he spoke on his cell phone.

"Hello, Gregg," Dr. Matson said as he placed the cell phone on speaker to enjoy his cigar. "Yes, I am scheduled to meet him today at the club." He exhaled a ring of smoke from his Cuban cigar. The outdoor dining section of the country club did not permit smoking, but none of the guests or staff had the courage to mention the rule to the doctor.

"Yes, you advised me not to speak with him in person, and I respect your legal insight as my lawyer, but you assured me he would settle out of court," Dr. Matson said. "Gregg, I will speak with him today and resolve what your legal team should have accomplished." Dr. Matson ended the call. He scrolled through his messages and ignored the waiter who brought his lunch.

I would be on the PGA tour had I played the game in my youth, Dr. Matson thought to himself as he ogled the local college girls' golf team on the driving range. His thoughts lingered to his ex-wife and bitter divorce. He smiled when he recalled how he convinced her father to cover his medical school expenses and teach him the game of golf.

"Excuse me, sir," a woman said. Dr. Matson did not see the young manager of the restaurant approach his table.

"Hi, Stacy. How is your little dog?" Dr. Matson asked.

Stacy smiled because he remembered her little dog. "Doing better. The vet said he will make a full recovery."

"I am glad," Dr. Matson said. He ignored Stacy and turned his attention toward the women's golf team on the driving range.

"Sir," the manager stammered. "Doctor, your guest has arrived, and he does not have the proper attire for admittance to the restaurant," she said. She felt uncomfortable because of his unpredictable temper.

"Did you offer him the tweed jacket a stuffy community college professor might wear?" he asked in a calm voice.

"You want your guest to wear one of those hideous jackets with the leather elbow patches and club crest on the pocket, sir?" she asked. She suppressed the urge to laugh when the doctor did not respond. "He declined the jacket, made rude comments to the hostess, and he seems troubled. Is he a friend of yours?"

"Absolutely not! I avoid his type as much as possible. Have I ever brought other people of his ilk to the club before, Stacy?" His demeanor changed and his voice elevated with anger.

"No, sir," she said.

Dr. Matson exhaled smoke in the air. The ocean breeze blew the cigar smoke toward her.

"So why would you assume he might be a friend?" Dr. Matson asked. He put his finger to his lips, so she would not respond. "Stacy, please usher him to my table. He will not be here for long. And give us some space."

Dr. Matson's obese guest waddled through the dining room toward Dr. Matson's table. His disheveled appearance and uncomfortable demeanor contrasted with the urbane guests of the country club. His polyester polo shirt struggled to contain the fifty pounds of fat that clung to his mid-section. The dark circles under his eyes made him look depraved and ghoulish. Dr. Matson enjoyed the disgusted expressions from the other patrons as the outsider encroached upon their afternoon social.

Josh clenched his fist and whistled at the accommodations of the outdoor terrace. "So this is how the infamous doctor spends his day," he said.

"Hello, Josh," Dr. Matson said. He took a long draw on his cigar and exhaled the smoke toward Josh. The embers smoldered like the anger Dr. Matson felt toward Josh. "Why do you want to see me?" he asked.

"Your settlement offer is full of shit. I thought a rich asshole would have more compassion," Josh said with a raised voice. Josh's profanity drew more attention to Dr. Matson and his unwanted guest.

"Lower your voice, Josh, and lose the profanity. Do not spoil the other members' lunch by your uncouth outbursts again, or security will remove you from the club," Dr. Matson said.

"Screw you and your rich friends. You don't have the balls to remove me from this club," Josh said with a threatening look.

"Josh, if you don't remain composed security will escort you from the club and future conversations will occur through our attorneys. Please join me for a drink."

"I don't want a drink! I want Justice," Josh said. His calloused hands tightened around the top rail of the mahogany chair.

Dr. Matson glanced at the other guests in the room and lost his composure. Silverware clattered when he hit the table with his fist, and he leaned toward Josh. "Josh, sit in the damn chair!" The doctor's chiseled model face contorted with anger.

Dr. Matson's outburst and change in demeanor startled Josh. Fear displaced the anger he felt toward the doctor. Josh hesitated before he took a seat at the table and leaned away in his chair to place distance between himself and Dr. Matson.

"Josh, it is tragic what happened to your family and unfortunate the county lacked the skill to design a safe intersection or maintain the stop light. You should go after the county for justice and damages instead of me. They are the villains, not me," Dr. Matson said in a calm voice.

"Go to hell, Doc. I know you influenced the cops to change the accident reports," Josh said.

Dr. Matson took a sip of his martini to suppress his anger. "Josh, I hate to drink alone. How about a martini?" Dr. Matson asked. He tapped the glass with his manicured finger.

"I don't want a drink," Josh said. He had been sober for two months and the offer of a drink made him feel more disdain for the doctor.

"It has BJ Hookers Vodka, a damn fine spirit distilled in Houston," Dr. Matson said. "Have a shot of the vodka instead? You might like it, and on your salary it won't cause you to miss a meal."

"Screw you, Doc. You know I can't have any alcohol."

Dr. Matson enjoyed the pain he saw in Josh's eyes but changed the subject. "Josh, your daughter will not have to work again for the rest of her life. Once she graduates college, she will collect 50k a year for perpetuity," Dr. Matson said.

"50K! Doesn't cover her lost talent and anguish! You took away her gift to fill the world with beautiful violin music. Her talent would have taken her around the world."

Dr. Matson reached for a steak knife on the table and gestured at Josh with it when he said, "50k a year for life adds up to a tidy sum, Josh."

Josh looked away from the doctor and cleared his throat. "My lawyer said your offer does not adjust for inflation, and it does not include damages for my wife and me," he said.

"So that is the real reason—you smell a pay day, Josh," Dr. Matson stabbed his steak knife into the table. "You and your wife walked away from the accident with a few minor bruises! Why the hell do you need compensation for your reckless driving? Take my generous offer. Your wife wants to take the offer, but you're a greedy fool. I know of your gambling and other unsavory interests, and I would hate for your wife to find out, Josh." He removed the steak knife from the table and took another sip of his martini.

"You're bluffing," Josh said in defiance.

"Can you take that chance, Josh? Risk your reputation in the community? The head coach of your high school retires next year and you are on the short list for his position."

"What do you know about high school football, Doc?"

"Texas high school football is famous. It is a religion for some folks in that part of the country, and you are responsible for three state championships," Dr. Matson said. He cut a piece of the succulent rare steak. "Take the deal, Josh. Go on with your miserable life, and collect your pension when you retire. Relish the adulation the small town heaps upon you when you become the head coach. You could be a god in that miserable town."

"Screw your offer. We will see you in court. You will not work again as a doctor. You will lose your license, and we will receive a generous settlement for your reckless driving and perversion of justice. You dodged the charges for the death of the hooker you killed in the accident, but you will be accountable for your actions."

"Josh, last chance. Lower your voice and take the offer," Dr. Matson said. He bit into the piece of steak with a savage bite.

"No, it's time the world discovers your true character," Josh said with a red face. "This member of your club murders hookers and destroys kids' dreams!" Josh shouted on the terrace.

Dr. Matson reached across the table and grabbed Josh by his nape. Josh's eyes bulged with fear, and he didn't resist. The doctor sensed capitulation and slammed Josh's head into the table. Other patrons in the restaurant recoiled in disbelief at the barbaric behavior. Dr. Matson did not care what they thought of him. It would be a good story for their pretentious friends over cocktails. Dr. Matson, scowled at a table of bankers who considered intervening on behalf of Josh.

"You threaten me at my club," Dr. Matson said in a hushed voice close to Josh's ear. "Kiss your coaching career goodbye along with your personal life."

Dr. Matson let go of Josh's neck and slid an envelope over to him. Dr. Matson waved away security as they approached his table to give him a minute.

"Open the envelope, Josh." Dr. Matson grinned while Josh's fingers trembled as he fumbled with the clasp on the envelope.

Josh, dismayed by Dr. Matson's speed and the strength of the attack, hesitated to peer into the envelope.

"Take your time, Josh. Last chance to take the deal," Dr. Matson said.

Josh did not respond to the doctor. He removed a photograph from the envelope. His face blanched when he recognized the picture. He slid the photograph into the envelope and avoided the other pictures. "How the hell could you have gotten those pictures?" Josh asked.

"I know everything about you and some things you don't know about yourself yet, coach," Dr. Matson said with malice. "You should have taken the offer. Security, remove this man from the premises." Dr. Matson motioned for security to approach his table.

Josh did not resist or argue with security. He clutched the envelope with a look of despair as he left the club.

"Stacy, come here!" Dr. Matson said before she spoke with security.

Stacy approached the table with caution. "Stacy, comp everyone's lunch because of this unfortunate incident, and tell them I paid it," Dr. Matson said. He wiped his mouth with the napkin and moved the plate with the unfinished steak toward the center of the table.

"Yes, sir," she said, surprised at his generosity. "Do you require anything else today?"

"No, Stacy. You have been a great help, but leave me alone." He smacked her on the butt when she turned to leave the table. Dr. Matson breathed in the ocean air on the outdoor veranda, snubbed out the cigar on the linen tablecloth and dialed a number on his cell phone.

CHAPTER 5

THE 19TH HOLE

SHE WALKED WITH CAUTION across the polished marble floor in her high heels. The cold air from the AC felt uncomfortable on her exposed shoulders in the early morning. She pulled the lever on a circuit breaker with the high voltage danger sign with one hand and held onto a stack of mail. She imagined she was a secret agent on a covert mission while she waited for the concealed door to open. The sound of metal cylinders unlatched and echoed in the empty hallway. The wall of fake electrical circuit breakers pivoted open to reveal a wrought iron staircase that twisted toward the fourth floor. The staircase resembled a double helix of DNA. Iron work shaped into outstretched wings from a staff encircled by two serpents provided the support for the hand rails. Light fixtures festooned with caduceus symbols illuminated the spiral staircase in an antiseptic glow of LED lights.

A red light flashed on the console of a sleek modern desk. Dr. Matson swiveled his chair to view a series of high definition screens with various camera angles of his office. A young woman in the restricted area came into view on a screen.

"I want the crate delivered today," Dr. Matson said. He zoomed in on the young woman with the security camera to relish her toned legs. "Yes, I am aware of the tenant at the address, and the contents of the crate are not your concern. End of discussion, Gregg. They can pick up the crate at my office," Dr. Matson said. He ended the call on his smart phone and imagined how the recipient would react when he opened the crate.

He set the piece of paper aside with his objectives and focused on the young woman in front of an armored security door concealed with a Borneo rosewood veneer. She fidgeted at the entrance to Dr. Matson's private office.

"Sean, I know you can see me on the security camera. Open the door. I have your mail." She glanced at her expensive diamond-encrusted watch on her petite wrist and wondered what surprises he planned for her birthday this year.

"Good morning, Tiffany." Dr. Matson's voice filled the stairwell from the intercom.

"It's about time. Open the door, Sean," she said. The heavy door opened to his private chambers. A frown replaced her smile the moment the violin concerto reached her ears. She felt depressed in the luxurious private office. Dr. Matson's strong arms lifted her off her feet before she sank deeper into sadness. One of her shoes fell on the marble floor. She breathed in the smell of his sandalwood cologne, absorbed the warmth from his arms and felt safe as he held her.

"It's good you're here before my staff," Dr. Matson said after he nuzzled his nose in her blond curls. She giggled when he spun her around the room. The mail scattered in every direction. He lowered her so her feet could touch the floor and crouched on one knee to retrieve her shoe. She wanted to run her hands through his hair while he adjusted her stiletto heel but she remembered his previous admonition. He caressed her calf and exposed thigh underneath her orange sun dress, but her coy demeanor pushed his hand away before it inched higher up her leg. Her hips swayed from side to side as she strutted toward the center of the room and collapsed on the designer couch. Her blond curls spilled across the plush cushions.

"Hungry for breakfast?" Dr. Matson asked.

"An espresso," she said as she scrutinized the room. His office occupied the entire fourth floor of his office building. The 4th floor contained a kitchen, bedroom, bathroom, putting green with real grass and various rooms for his unique hobbies.

"When can I decorate this room? A dash of color will stimulate the room unlike these black and white golf pictures," she said. Dr. Matson ignored her comment and left her espresso on the kitchen counter.

She entered the kitchen and noticed his attention on the smart phone instead of her. "Hello, over here," she said before she took a sip of espresso. I will go home if you neglect me again today," she said. Her southern accent plucked him from his smart phone trance.

"Follow me, I have a surprise for you," he said.

She took one more sip of the espresso. Her red lipstick left a mark on the porcelain cup.

"Sean, wait for me" she said. She struggled to keep up with his quick pace in her high heels and saw him pass the room with the golf simulator, where they had spent hours together. She remembered some of the golf lessons, but most of the time they devolved into other physical activities. She followed him into a cavernous room. "Want to go to the bedroom and play doctor instead, Sean?" she asked.

"After I show you my lab," he said.

"I'll be naughty in a lab coat in your lab." He ignored her comment. She sat on a swivel chair in the corner of the room and crossed her legs. The room contained work benches and machines she did not recognize.

"Why do you call this room your lab? This does not look like any lab we have at school," she said.

Her exposed thigh distracted him from her question for a moment.

"Since when did you become a lab expert? I tinker with exotic materials to create bespoke golf clubs in this workspace," he said. He picked up a cylinder of titanium and placed it on a lathe.

She wisely kept quiet and did not ask any more questions about golf because he would never shut up about the subject if she asked questions.

He enjoyed her statuesque figure—head held high with perfect model posture—but her posture wilted when she recalled the time they spent together in this room a few months after they met.

"I remember this room; you called it your art studio. The creative center of your practice," she said. Her head and shoulders slumped when the endless memories of the room washed over her.

"I hoped you would not forget this room. I painted your portrait in that exact spot," Dr. Matson said. He increased the volume of the violin concerto in the background from his smart phone. He could see the disgust on her face and wondered if she would lash out in anger or cry.

"Can you play some modern music instead of this classical crap?"

He detected anger in her voice and suppressed a laugh. For a moment, he considered the classical piece from her last solo, but instead he silenced the music.

She moved with determination toward an object along the wall and removed the sheet that concealed it. "What happened to your art studio?" she asked.

Dr. Matson smacked her on her firm bum when she walked by him. He breathed in the smell of her perfume before he picked up the painting she had uncovered.

"I have decided to move the studio to my home because this room does not have the proper amount of light for inspiration. The sound of the waves and the smell of the ocean will invoke the creative muse to help me paint," he said. He turned the painting around to reveal his masterpiece to her.

She looked away from the painting. *I have never seen his home,* she thought with pursed lips.

He enjoyed her dejected expression and refusal to look at his masterpiece—a reminder of her emotional pain. The only time in their relationship she had felt uncomfortable occurred in this room. His eyes lingered on her naked body with a deranged smile as the paintbrush touched the canvas. When she made love to him after he painted her portrait with the violin, the experience felt different. It reminded her of how she felt after a shift at her old job before she met him. She felt used, humiliated, an object for his pleasure; his tenderness and romantic nature replaced with an animalistic need to unleash his anger on her naked body.

"What will happen to the painting?" she asked.

"I sold it to the club where we met," he said.

The dim lights and music of the club made it difficult to see his face. Most of the time she did not have to dance for him and they would talk for hours. A welcome change from the drunk behavior, disrespect and foul smells she experienced with the other patrons.

His charm, funny stories and endless alcohol helped her forget the environment and her life.

He listened to her and was never disrespectful in the private rooms of the club. She did not hesitate to say yes when he invited her to dinner after a couple of months of exclusive visits to see her at the club. The expensive dress and shoes he sent to the club for her to wear on their date made her feel special. The free meal at a fancy restaurant also did not happen often.

She recognized him from the courtroom and screamed when she saw him at the chef's table. The monster who had destroyed her dreams visited her for months at the strip club and she did not recognize him. She suppressed her anger and ignored her intuition that night. Instead she had dinner with the man who had deprived the world of her gift.

"You better not give them that picture! I'll destroy it before it leaves this room," she said in anger.

The antiseptic glow of the florescent lights of the lab illuminated the picture and burned the image into her memory. The last three years of her life replayed in her mind: the acrimonious divorce of her parents because of the lawsuit; the alcohol and drugs that could not suppress the anger she felt toward her father after she discovered his infidelity; the pain in her mom's eyes when she discovered the man she married pandered child porn at his high school, which tormented her when she slept.

The lack of money to pay for her college education and her injury that denied her a career as a professional violinist was too much for her. She collapsed on her knees and sobbed with her hands over her face.

A grin crept across Dr. Matson's face as he picked up the painting and placed it in the crate while Tiffany cried. He lifted her chin when the painting was secure to reveal puffy red eyes and mascara-stained tears on her cheeks. He picked her up from the floor and held her for a few moments while he calculated the dimensions for an autoclave he had ordered for the room. He pushed her away to avoid another volley of tears on his dress shirt.

"I know the past three years have brought much misery for you because of the accident and your parents' divorce," he said, devoid of any emotion. "Here, for you," he said. He handed her an envelope.

"What did you get me?" she asked as the emotional storm subsided. She ripped open the envelope and savored the distraction. "I have always wanted to see this show!" she said. She pulled him close to her in excitement.

"I know; I do listen to you on occasion," he said.

"I know, baby. You helped me through these last three years, and thank you. I love you," she said.

"Pack your bags. We leave Friday for Vegas, and we will travel on my new helicopter," he said.

"Oh my god, you bought a helicopter? she asked. She danced with excitement in the center of the room. "I have to tell Amy about this; she will freak," she said. "Do you mind if Amy goes with us?" she asked.

"Your friend from the club I met?"

"Yes, it will be like Miami again, only better." She toyed with a strand of blond hair in her hand.

The doctor did enjoy himself in Miami with Amy and Tiffany, but only behind closed doors.

The inane conversations at the beach, dinner and when he took them shopping convinced him to leave them both in the city, but his real plan had yet to unfold.

"Sure, we can take Amy, but I wanted this trip to be special for you," he said as he caressed her cheek. "A chance to celebrate your transfer to a four-year university," he said. His hands slid aside the spaghetti straps on her shoulders.

"I know. Thank you so much for your help with tuition. Amy can go with us another time." She enjoyed his smooth hands on her bare shoulders.

"We can take Amy to see your new apartment at the University of Arizona." he said before he kissed the nape of her neck.

"Yes, perfect, and we can pick her up in the helicopter?" She did not stop his hands when they moved away from her shoulders.

"No, she can meet us in Tucson. Only special people fly on my helicopter." He pulled her toward him with a hungry look in his eyes.

CHAPTER 6

THE OCEAN AND YOU

"Sir, please fasten your seat belt before we land," the pilot said. Dr. Matson ignored the pilot's command.

"Good round of golf today?" she asked. The pilot's red hair unfurled around her head set.

"Join me for a drink when we land and I shall tell you all about my round of golf," Dr. Matson said. He closed the golf magazine and imagined her curves underneath her flight suit.

"Sir, you know I don't drink on duty."

"You're not in Iraq; you can drink with your boss. I would enjoy a conversation on how this bird compares to the attack helicopters you flew in the Army," Dr. Matson said. His cell phone interrupted her with a ring tone from a band Tiffany recommend. "Hello, Dr. Matson."

"Hi, Sean. We have not talked or texted in a while," Tiffany said. She tried to stay calm and composed on the phone.

"Hi, Tiff. How are your classes?" Dr. Matson asked. "Don't cry." It annoyed him when she sobbed on the phone because he could not witness the sadness in her eyes first hand.

"My dad, he...he...killed himself," she said.

"What? When did this happen?" Dr. Matson asked. He set the cell phone on the leather seat next to him to avoid the sound of her crying.

"My mom told me today," she said.

Dr. Matson picked up the phone and smiled as he imagined her red puffy eyes.

"Do you need anything, Tiff?" he asked. He observed the pilot line-up for the approach to the heliport.

"When can we get together? You promised me last month. Sean, I need you," she said.

Dr. Matson did not respond. Instead, he admired the helicopter reflection in the skyscrapers.

"Sean, my mom also told me something else."

"What did your mom tell you, Tiff?" Dr. Matson asked out of curiosity.

"Do you have the painting of me?" Tiffany asked. Her voice sounded concerned.

"Of course; I love the painting. Why the sudden interest in our painting?"

"My mom mentioned a painting she did not recognize at my dad's house," she said. Tiffany sobbed again on the phone.

"Did you see the picture?" he asked with anticipation.

"No, but my mom said she had never seen the picture either. The painting had a partially nude woman with a violin. The way she described it reminded me of your painting."

Dr. Matson stretched his legs and remembered the day he had painted Tiffany in his studio.

"It's creepy he would have a picture like that in his house," she said.

"When you have a break from class you should visit my home, and I will show you the new frame for our picture," he said. I hung our picture in the master bedroom so at first light I see the two most beautiful things in the world: the ocean and you." He suppressed a laugh and instead smiled with a depraved grin.

"Oh, Sean, that is so romantic! I can't wait to visit your house, and winter break will be perfect. Oh, one more thing, Sean."

Sean said nothing.

"Well, winter tuition is due next week, and I did not want to mention anything, but the deposit did not arrive in my account."

"Why didn't you tell me sooner?" he asked without genuine concern.

"I did not want to bother you, Sean, since I have never had an issue with the deposits."

"Did you speak with the bank?"

"No, I checked the balance online yesterday, and it will not cover tuition or books," she said.

"I deposited the usual amount last week. Call the bank and ask if there is a hold on the funds by mistake," he said.

"Thank you, Sean. I love you."

"I know you do. Stay focused on your grades, and save the partying until I visit."

"Love you, Sean; can't wait to see you," she said.

Dr. Matson ended the call and scrolled through the lists of names on his phone until he found the name "Daddy's Little Whore." He deleted the contact and blocked the number.

CHAPTER 7

COVERT OP

"Stacy, do you see the figure next to my cars?" Dr. Matson asked.

The afternoon sun reflected from the buildings caused an intense glare that made it difficult to focus beyond the painted "H" on the helipad. "Negative, sir. I observed no people on the roof or under the covered parking," she said as she adjusted the collective on the helicopter controls.

Dr. Matson squinted through his dark sunglasses and lost sight of the figure when his helicopter touched the ground. "There he is again, next to the entrance," Dr. Matson said. He leaned over the seat in the cockpit and pointed toward the only door on the rooftop.

"Sir, I don't see the person. How much did you drink on the course?" she asked.

He removed his sunglasses, reclined in his seat and rubbed his eyes. "I don't disgrace the game with alcohol," Dr. Matson said as he prepared to exit the aircraft.

The radio crackled with message traffic for the pilot.

"Roger, ETA in ten minutes. Sir, rain check on the drink. One of your VIP clients requested air service from her home."

The doctor snapped a golf tee he carried in half.

Helicopter concierge services for my famous clients sounded good in theory, but I have yet to see my pilot out of her flight suit, he thought to himself. The doctor leaned into the cockpit. "I'll take you to dinner tonight at the new French restaurant in town," he said.

"Not tonight, Doctor, unless you want to visit my parents with me," she said.

"Another time; enjoy your weekend." He opened the door of the helicopter and scanned the area for the figure.

"Sir, be careful as you exit the aircraft."

Dr. Matson gave her the thumbs up sign. The hot exhaust and dust enveloped him like an overcoat while Stacy gained altitude and left him alone on his heliport. For a few minutes his imagination conjured up images of a covert insertion into the mountains of Afghanistan for a clandestine mission.

He compromised his top-secret mission when he reached for the hair on his head, as it attempted to gain altitude on its own. He held his hair piece close to his head until the helicopter flew behind a skyscraper. He cursed. *Stupid city.* He adjusted his fake hair piece, concerned his new pilot had seen his bald spot.

Dr. Matson sensed movement on his periphery. A figure dressed in a black western-style trench coat clung to the shadows of the roof top garage and advanced toward him.

"Get away from my cars!" he shouted. Damn, he wished he had an M4 carbine rifle or any weapon. "Security will be here!" he yelled. The figure was undeterred by the threat.

Dr. Matson removed his phone from his pocket and dialed 911, but the conversation with Tiffany drained his cell phone battery. He lost sight of the figure and dashed toward the only entrance on the roof. He reached for the door knob before an ominous shadow cast across the door. He felt the presence behind him and lowered his shoulders. He turned the door knob, but a heavy hand on his shoulder spun him around before he could open the door.

Dr. Matson could not discern the figure's face because of the glare from the sun and a Spanish-style Córdoba hat with a wide brim pulled low over his brow. The figure towered over him, wearing a duster coat that concealed his build. *An odd wardrobe choice for the San Diego climate,* Dr. Matson thought. The figure reached into his coat with a gloved hand.

Dr. Matson felt an intense pain in his stomach and collapsed. The bright sun extinguished when he hit the ground. Dr. Matson rubbed his head, reached for his smashed cell phone next to him, and noticed a package. He sat up, looked around his private rooftop garage and checked to make sure his exotic cars remained. The windsock for the heliport fluttered in the breeze and the horizon embraced the sun.

He struggled to his feet and his head pulsated with pain when he picked up the package.

Alone on the rooftop, he leaned against the wall and looked at the dark crimson ink on the package. The color reminded him of fresh blood extracted during a venipuncture procedure. His manicured finger traced the ornate calligraphy on the package. *A rare embellishment in the digital age,* he thought. Dr. Matson clutched the package and staggered toward the door. He glanced over his shoulder for the ominous figure and opened the door to his building.

ATTENTION IN THE TOC

"SENTINEL 6, SENTINEL 6, this is Sentinel 5, over," the FM radio crackled to life on the dash of Colonel Yvette Askeri's armored vehicle.

"Roger, Sentinel 5," Colonel Askeri said. She removed her Kevlar helmet and waited for the Executive Officer's (XO) message traffic on the radio. Her tightly braided hair provided some relief from the unrelenting heat and dust, but she hated the field.

"Sentinel 6, be advised the VIP will arrive in your area of operations in fifteen minutes, over."

"Roger, Sentinel 5. Sentinel 6 out," the colonel said. She slammed the radio handset on the exposed metal console of the armored vehicle. "The battle update briefing did not mention a VIP visit, and I have to deal with a general in our tactical operations center (TOC) before a decisive operation today," Colonel Askeri said. She chewed on her worn fingernails concerned about the general's visit.

"Ma'am, the S1 personnel officer updated the staff and commanders on the general's review of our unit's training today at the battle update briefing last night," the major in the front seat of the armored vehicle said.

"Bullshit, Major. The briefing did not address the exact time and location of the VIP in our area of operation," Colonel Askeri said. "You will be responsible if anything goes wrong, Major." She tightened the chinstrap of her Kevlar helmet and adjusted the M9 pistol strapped to her leg.

"Roger, ma'am," the major said. He rolled his eyes behind dark wrap-around ballistic sunglasses and removed one of his gloves to send a text message to a West Point classmate. The classmate was the general's aide, and he hoped to buy Colonel Askeri extra time before the general arrived at their TOC. After spending six months with her in charge of the brigade, he discovered she did not cope well with change.

"Major, how long until we reach the TOC?" Colonel Askeri asked. Her voice strained over the sound of the diesel engine.

The major glanced at the digital map and did a quick mental calculation. "Ma'am, we will arrive in ten minutes," he said.

"Unacceptable, Major. I will not have time to inspect the TOC," the colonel said. She flipped through her green notebook with a list of tasks to accomplish and other notes about her unit.

"Ma'am, the staff and noncommissioned officers have TOC operations under control," the major said. He acknowledged a text from the general's aide and thanked him for the extra time he provided his unit before the general's visit.

"Driver, increase speed," Colonel Askeri said to the young private behind the wheel of the armored vehicle.

The private glanced at the S3 operations officer next to her in the vehicle. The major motioned with his hand to stay quiet.

"Ma'am, I don't recommend we increase our speed. The range control safety officer stated vehicles with trailers inside the training area will not exceed twenty-five miles per hour on unimproved road surfaces," the major said.

"I don't give a shit about range control or their speed limits. I will not be late for a meeting with the general. Driver, increase speed and get us to the TOC," Colonel Askeri said.

"Negative, driver. Do not increase your speed. Ma'am, the storm last night washed out portions of the trail and any increase in speed is dangerous," the major said.

Colonel Askeri gnashed her teeth and clutched her green notebook to keep her composure after a subordinate questioned her judgment.

The major glanced out the window and noticed a patch of terrain beyond the trail. "Ma'am, we could stop here and leave the trailer to increase speed. The private could return to retrieve the trailer once we are at the TOC."

"No, Major, we will not leave my trailer," Colonel Askeri said. She braced herself from the

impact of the deep ruts and washed out sections of the trail on the suspension of the vehicle.

The trailer contained the colonel's personal living quarters when the unit trained in the field. She refused to sleep in the same accommodations as her soldiers and sought creature comforts unavailable to others in her unit at every opportunity. The colonel's driver set up or stowed the equipment in the trailer based on the colonel's itinerary of the day.

Colonel Askeri ordered the supply officer to equip the trailer with a portable bed, wardrobe, shower system, generator, air conditioner, camouflage kit and an encrypted radio set to monitor unit frequencies before the unit deployment to the training center. The brigade motor pool warrant officer seethed with anger at the modifications and delayed the order of a portable air conditioner for the trailer until after the training rotation.

Colonel Askeri found out about the delay and had him replaced despite his exemplary leadership of the motor pool. She also tried to ruin his career with bogus charges of improper use of a government credit card.

"Ma'am, I suggest we turn left at Observation Post 34 and follow the trail around the terrain feature to avoid an accident on this treacherous section of the trail," the private said with trepidation.

"Excellent idea, Private," the major said. The major noticed the alternate route on the digital map would save them time without the need to increase the speed of the vehicle. "We will have extra time to prepare for the general's arrival today if we take the route the private suggested, ma'am."

"Driver, continue on our current heading," Colonel Askeri said.

The major swiveled the computer screen with the digital map so Colonel Askeri could see the route. "This is the route, ma'am," the major said. He picked up the stylus from the display to zoom in for the colonel to see the exact location. "We can coordinate for the general to visit the unmanned aerial vehicle command and control site here, before he arrives at the TOC," the major said. He drew a blue box around the site for the colonel on the digital map to further emphasize the point by indicating the distance from the TOC.

"The general's visit to the unmanned aerial vehicle site gives us thirty to forty minutes before he arrives at the TOC," the major said. The colonel did not visualize or accept new ideas often, but the major convinced her to change her mind.

"Hooah, Driver! Change direction at Observation Post 34, and Major, coordinate a visit for the general to see the unmanned aerial vehicle operations. Major, who is in charge of the unmanned aerial vehicle site, and what is the location of the captain in charge of overall unmanned aerial vehicle operations?" Colonel Askeri asked. She thumbed through her green notebook with the names of her soldiers in leadership positions to recall the name of the captain.

"Ma'am, the chief warrant officer is in charge of the unmanned aerial vehicle site and the captain is at an infantry battalion TOC," the major said. He slumped his shoulders in anticipation of her disapproval of the general meeting with a warrant officer.

"I only want the general meeting with officers, Major. Coordinate with the TOC and the infantry battalion to have the captain report to the unmanned aerial vehicle site to meet with the general."

"Ma'am, the battalion commander has coordinated with the infantry battalion to have the captain advise them on unmanned aerial vehicle operations. This was your guidance before the unit deployed to the training center. If we request a transfer for the captain back to our unit this will impact the infantry battalion's training objectives for this exercise," the major said.

"Bullshit, Major; why can't you execute my guidance and see the big picture?" Colonel Askeri said. She slammed her green notebook against the major's seat.

The major, accustomed to the colonel's outbursts, did not respond to the colonel and checked their position on the digital map.

"Private, after the last ridge turn left onto the trail, but keep the speed below twenty-five miles per hour," the major said. He checked the time on his military watch and noted they had plenty of time to reach the TOC.

"It's the same trail the First Sergeant took us on for the TOC recon," the driver said.

"You should consider Officer Candidate School, Private," the major said.

The private's eyes lit up with the compliment. A welcome change from the persistent admonishment she received from the colonel.

"Major, let the driver do her job. I want the captain at the aerial vehicle site before the general," Colonel Askeri said.

"Ma'am, we don't have enough time to transfer the captain before the general arrives," the major said as he anticipated the jolt from a hole in the trail that would swallow the right wheel of the armored vehicle. The suspension dampened none of the impact and jarred the occupants of the vehicle. The colonel's coffee thermos tumbled onto the floor of the vehicle.

"Dammit, driver, pay attention to the road!" Colonel Askeri said.

"Sorry, ma'am, the storm last night wreaked havoc on the trail," the driver said.

"I don't care about any excuses. Pay attention, or I'll have you replaced," Colonel Askeri said.

The private noticed another sizable washed out section of the trail and considered a drive through the hole to end the misery of chauffeur duty for the colonel.

"Major, get on the radio and have the captain report to the unmanned aerial vehicle site now!"

"Roger, ma'am, but the chief sent an encrypted message that the general will arrive at his location in five minutes. I know you don't want the general to talk with the non-officers, but the chief is a specialized expert in his field and the best unmanned aerial technician in the Army. You served with him on your first deployment to Iraq," the major said. He closed the text message window on the digital map after he sent a response to the warrant officer.

The colonel did not remember the chief, but she would never admit her lapse in memory to her subordinates. "Fine, let the chief brief the general but coordinate for the captain to report to the unmanned aerial vehicle site," Colonel Askeri said.

The major obliged with the colonel's order and coordinated for the captain's transfer from the infantry unit to the unmanned aerial vehicle site via FM radio. He also made a contingency plan to transfer a noncommissioned officer to the infantry battalion to assuage the ire of their unit's commander when he lost an asset because of the colonel's myopic decision.

"Ma'am, five minutes from the TOC," the private said in a timid voice.

Colonel Askeri checked her luxury watch and realized they had extra time without the need to increase speed. She would never admit her mistake to her subordinates. She removed her Kevlar helmet and gloves and opened a compact mirror to inspect her face and hair.

She hated the dirt, grime and discomfort of the field and longed for the days of the air-conditioned Pentagon instead of tents that baked in the desert sun. She wondered if the general will remember her from Germany when she had brought her friend to the general's hotel room when they were both captains.

"Ma'am, do you mind if I get out here and check on the maintenance operations?" the major asked.

"Fine, Major. You have not been any help today," Colonel Askeri said. She took a handful of skittles from a bag she kept in the vehicle.

The major ignored her comment. "Private, please let me out here, and good job this morning."

"Thank you, sir," the driver said.

The major noticed that the armored vehicle kicked up dirt when it drove away from him, an indication the colonel told the driver to increase their speed on the way to the TOC.

"Driver, do you know the sergeant major's location?" Colonel Askeri asked. She tossed the empty bag of skittles from the vehicle.

"I don't know, ma'am," the private said.

"Check the damn digital map for his vehicle," Colonel Askeri said in annoyance.

The private swiveled the olive drab display screen toward her. Besides a digital map, the on-board computer displayed every vehicle in the unit equipped with a global positioning device with a blue icon on the map. The icon identified the unit, location, direction of travel and speed among other pieces of information.

The private found the sergeant major's vehicle on the other side of the TOC with a few movements of her finger on the display.

"Found him, ma'am."

"Good, contact him on the radio," Colonel Askeri said.

"Yes, ma'am," She picked up the radio handset to contact the sergeant major. "Sentinel 7, Sentinel 7 this is Sentinel 6 Alpha, over," the private said on the radio.

The private waited a few moments before she sent another message on the radio. "Sentinel 7, Sentinel 7, this is Sentinel 6 Alpha, over. Nothing, ma'am, no response on the radio."

"Drive over to his vehicle," the colonel said.

"Sentinel 7, negative contact Sentinel 6 Alpha, out," the private said on the radio before she changed direction and drove toward the blue icon on the digital map display.

"Ma'am, I see his vehicle," the private said.

"Pull alongside him, driver."

The colonel saw the heavy armored door open and a few seconds later the sergeant major tumbled out of the vehicle and landed head first on the desert ground. Colonel Askeri cackled with glee.

"What a stupid idiot," the colonel said.

"How did he fall out of the vehicle?" the private asked.

"I think his gas mask got caught inside the cramped quarters of his vehicle," Colonel Askeri said.

The private parked the armored vehicle next to the sergeant major's armored vehicle and killed the diesel engine.

"Driver, how many times do I have to tell you to get the damn door for me?" Colonel Askeri yelled.

"Yes, ma'am. Sorry, ma'am," the private said. *I did not join the Army to chauffeur incompetent leaders around*, the private thought to herself.

The colonel donned her field gloves and adjusted her wrap-around ballistic sunglasses. "Private, check the digital map for the general's vehicle near our location and let me know when his vehicle arrives at the TOC," the colonel Askeri said.

"Yes, ma'am." The private looked forward to a brief respite from the colonel.

The colonel approached the sergeant major who dusted himself off and adjusted his body armor vest. "What the hell happened, Sergeant Major?" Colonel Askeri asked.

"My stupid gas mask got caught on the armored door," the sergeant major said with embarrassment. "Too bad you did not record it, Colonel, for my retirement ceremony. The soldiers would have enjoyed a good laugh at the expense of their sergeant major."

"Sergeant Major, how many times have I told you to render the proper military salute," she said.

"Ma'am, we don't salute in the field," he grumbled. The uncomfortable mandarin collar on the body armor pinched his neck when he looked at the commander of the unit.

"Sergeant Major, have you seen any snipers in this training area?"

"Ma'am, the opposing force has a robust sniper section for each of their infantry companies," the sergeant major said.

"Genuine bad guys, Sergeant Major, with live ammunition?" she asked. Her frustration with the sergeant major was apparent in her tone.

The sergeant major did not respond because he was not sure if she was serious about a salute in the field.

"Sergeant Major, down range in combat you will not salute me, but here in the 'box' you will render the proper military customs for an officer of my rank, understood?"

"Yes, ma'am," the sergeant major said. He snapped to attention and rendered the proper military courtesy while he imagined retirement.

"Sergeant Major, forget those thoughts of retirement. Your country needs you in this time of war, and you will deploy with this unit. After a successful combat tour, we can discuss your retirement plans," Colonel Askeri said after she returned his salute.

The sergeant major towered over the diminutive colonel and provided a brief column of shade for her petite frame in the oppressive afternoon sun. His dark sunglasses concealed the lack of respect he had for the colonel. He noticed she did not have on the same gear he and the other soldiers of the unit had to wear for field training by order of the training center commander. She did not have the cumbersome gas mask strapped to her side or wear the hot, uncomfortable body armor.

"Sergeant Major, why the hell are you here by yourself?" Colonel Askeri asked.

The sergeant major stammered, his thick southern accent churned up the air before his words rolled out to answer her question. "I checked on the soldiers in the observation posts, ma'am," he said. He pointed at the hills above the TOC and knew the colonel did not know how many of her soldiers occupied those posts.

More like you found a spot to take a nap, she thought as she noticed his vehicle parked in the shade. "Why did you not respond to the radio transmission? We attempted to contact you on the command net and company nets," Colonel Askeri said.

"I have an issue with the encryption fill on my radio, ma'am." The sergeant major would have preferred she spoke to him in a tone commensurate with his position as the senior noncommissioned officer in the unit with twenty-five years of service instead of a lazy soldier who shirked his duty.

"What happened to your driver?" Colonel Askeri asked.

"I dropped him off at como section for a new radio encryption fill."

"Good, I need you at the TOC before the general arrives to make sure the noncommissioned officers are ready for his visit."

"Yes, ma'am. The enlisted soldiers are familiar with the dog and pony shows officers like to schedule," the sergeant major said.

"Sergeant Major, the small details matter. This unit will be deployed soon, and we need to have the unit trained and certified. A lack of attention to detail will cause soldiers to lose their lives. I need your head in the game, Sergeant Major! Do you want dead soldiers on your conscience?"

The sergeant major's eyebrow arched in confusion at the stupid question. "Of course not, ma'am. The soldiers have situational awareness of the maneuver commander's mission for this phase of the operation. The security plan for the TOC is in place. The vehicles with crew-served weapons cover key terrain and are part of the overall defensive plan for the TOC. It is the same layout depicted in the last command and staff slide deck we briefed you on before our deployment to the training center. Slide 89 of the brief depicts the experimental footprint of the TOC and the comparison to the old TOC layout. My soldiers are ready for the general, ma'am."

"I know, Sergeant Major. I don't support my predecessor's new design for the brigade TOC, and I think it has many flaws but I went along with the design because I did not think your soldiers could adopt the changes I have in mind prior to our deployment to the training center," Colonel Askeri said.

"Well, ma'am, this exercise will validate the design of the new TOC layout. When the exercise is complete I would like to know more about the changes you have in mind for the unit," the sergeant major said. *I can't wait for the potpourri in the TOC*, he thought to himself.

"Sergeant Major, you have five minutes to return to the TOC and police up the area for the general's arrival," Colonel Askeri said.

"Yes, ma'am." The sergeant major saluted the colonel but did not wait for her to render a return salute as he sulked toward his vehicle. He removed his sunglasses and rubbed the sleep from his eyes before he started the engine on his armored vehicle.

CHAPTER 9

SHANKED FROM THE TEE

"ATTENTION, IN THE TOC we have indexed-exercise complete!" the battle captain announced. A thunderous applause filled the TOC. The soldiers had much to complete before the unit returned to home station, but the twenty-four-hour operations they endured for two weeks end today. Soldiers shredded exercise material, packed up the computer equipment and folded up sections of the TOC tents for travel.

"Has anyone seen the commander?" the operations officer asked in the TOC.

"Negative, we have not seen her since yesterday," the XO said as he backed up information from the exercise on his computer.

"Private, do you know the colonel's location?" the operations officer asked.

"She is on main post, sir. She took one of the civilian vans and told me to prep her vehicle for shipment to home station by rail," the private said.

The alarm clock buzzed at 4:30 AM. Colonel Askeri awoke to clean sheets and looked forward to a warm shower after eight hours of sleep—an enjoyable change from the last three weeks of little sleep on an uncomfortable air mattress in her trailer. Too bad the hotel in the local town next to the training center lacked a spa. She would have indulged after her round of golf while her unit toiled away in the hot desert sun for redeployment. Colonel Askeri called the local golf course after a few laps on the treadmill and breakfast.

"Hello, this is Colonel Askeri. I need a reservation this morning and the earlier the better," she said.

"Please hold, ma'am, while I connect you with the pro shop," a member of the golf course staff said. The colonel despised civilians because they lacked a sense of urgency, and she hated to wait for the smallest things.

"Hello, we can offer you a tee time today at 3:00," the pro shop attendant said.

"3:00 is not acceptable. Any chance for an earlier tee time? It is only for one person," Colonel Askeri said.

"We have no tee times this morning, but tomorrow morning I have a few early time slots."

"Tomorrow is not an option. I deploy to a combat zone soon and don't have the luxury of a round of golf tomorrow. May I speak with your head pro?" Colonel Askeri asked.

"Ma'am, he has a golf lesson, but I have a foursome scheduled in an hour with one cancellation in their group. May I pencil you in if their fourth player is a no show today?" the pro shop attendant asked.

"That works for me," Colonel Askeri said.

She removed her golf bag from the ballistic travel case and opened a bottle of polish for her white golf shoes. She recalled fond memories of the game at Fort Huachuca while she polished her golf shoes. She met her ex-husband, a green beret, at Fort Huachuca, and he had taught her the mechanics of the game. She discovered she had a natural talent for the game and enjoyed the challenge. She surpassed her husband's skill on the golf course before her promotion to captain, but he would never admit to it. The colonel enjoyed golf because economics, race, gender or rank did not decide the outcome of the game. Skill, mental focus and discipline brought victory. The rigors of Army life with a country at war unraveled her marriage, and golf could not keep them together.

"Hello, you must be Yvette," an older gentleman said as he extended his hand.

"Colonel Askeri," she said as she shook his hand.

"Glad you joined us for a round of golf. I'll introduce you to the other two golfers in our group. What brings you to this post, Colonel?" he asked.

She secured her golf bag on the golf cart before she answered him. "My unit had a rotation at the training center." The older gentleman introduced her to his two retired officer friends in the group.

"You found time for a round of golf while your soldiers train in the field?" he asked with a look of confusion.

"Our mission indexed yesterday, and my unit is in the redeployment phase of the operation."

The older gentleman shook his head and smiled at the other two golfers in the group. "I never found time for a round of golf until I retired," he said. The other two agreed, and both laughed at the thought of a round of golf on a training deployment.

"Did you ever command a unit?" Colonel Askeri asked with a tone of superiority.

"Yes, an armor battalion. We spent more time in the field than with our families, but when we had a lull in the field, I never played golf on those rotations. I did not bother to pack my clubs because they were not on the unit packing list. The digitization of the Army must free up most of your leadership responsibilities," he said with sarcasm.

The colonel ignored his insinuation. She delegated the work and, besides, her soldiers received twice the hours of sleep and twice the rations she did on the deployment. She wanted time for herself, and golf made it possible to rejuvenate and recharge.

"Did you ever deploy?" she asked.

"Nope, retired six months before the first gulf war, and I would not trade my career for a deployment with the Army mired in the current mess today," he said.

"I am surprised you did not schedule time for golf when you were on active duty during the Cold War. Some leaders know how to delegate, and others hold onto the reigns too tight," she said. She opened a new sleeve of golf balls.

"A fine line between leading from authority and leading by example regardless of the era. Don't you think, Colonel?" he said.

"I have three rotations down range, a brigade command, and when I retire I know I earned my pension," she said. She breathed in the smell of freshly cut grass as the golf cart sped toward the tee box.

"Let's play golf and leave the geopolitics to the professionals," he said. He stopped the cart on the first tee box.

"Hooah!" the colonel exclaimed. She placed her ball on the tee and assessed the first hole.

"At least she does not neglect physical training," one member of the group said to his buddies in a hushed voice while he admired her runner's physique.

The colonel's first drive sliced into the tree line of the golf course. She resisted the urge to unleash profanity because of the poor tee shot and instead pounded the golf club on the tee box.

"Take a mulligan for your second shot. We won't count the first drive because we warmed up this morning at the driving range before the round," a member of the group said.

The colonel placed another golf ball on the tee and assessed the fairway. The three golfers nodded to each other after they observed her take a practice swing.

"Since you're an officer, join us in our weekly ritual?" the former battalion commander asked.

"It depends on what you old timers do for a ritual," Colonel Askeri said. She addressed the golf ball for another practice swing.

"A little risk on the course keeps us young," he said as he adjusted his golf glove.

"What risks besides a broken hip do you guys dabble in on the course?" Colonel Askeri asked.

"A friendly wager between officers," he said. He removed his money clip from his pocket and counted the bills.

"I enjoy the game for the relaxation, and my swing requires work. Gambling might ruin the fun." She focused on the number six printed on her golf ball.

"We wager fifty dollars a hole, but if your game is not ready for that action you can learn from our skills on the course today, and maybe one day you could be at our level of performance," the former battalion commander said.

Colonel Askeri considered the fifty-dollar-a-hole wager and said, "I have TDY money to burn. Make it one hundred a hole and you have bet," she said.

Had the three golfers known the colonel had observed them on the driving range and evaluated their golf swings they might have avoided the bet. The former battalion commander thumbed through the folded bills in his money clip and looked at the other two golfers. They each nodded and agreed to the bet.

"Colonel, one hundred dollars a hole." He put the money clip in his golf bag, confident he would not need it after the round of golf.

Colonel Askeri crushed her second shot in the middle of the fairway, a good fifty yards past what they could drive. *Easy money,* she thought with a stoic look on her face and watched the ball land in the fairway.

She had them right where she wanted them.

CHAPTER 10

A BOX OF GRID SQUARES

THE ROAD BUCKLED, followed by a horrific explosion that sent dirt and debris everywhere. The colonel watched, horrified, when a Mine Resistant Ambush Protected armored vehicle with seven soldiers in the lead of the convoy flipped through the air and landed on its side. A fine mist of dirt cascaded on the fifteen-ton vehicle, embedded in an empty irrigation ditch parallel to the road. The explosives from the blast punched through the concrete road and created an immense crater big enough to devour a compact car. The insurgent ambush destroyed the lead vehicle of the convoy, and a second explosion destroyed the gun truck in the rear of the convoy.

"What happened?" the colonel yelled. Her mind struggled to make sense of the chaos. "I should not be on this convoy," she said. She had traveled above the threat of ambushes by helicopter in the war-ravaged country for the past six months. Her first unit convoy mission in theater began with an ambush.

"Ma'am, I need you to stay calm," the driver said. His voice became more animated as the adrenaline coursed through him. The M2 .50-caliber machine gun in the turret of the vehicle came alive and slung rounds at the enemy. The driver scanned the area in front of him for any movement from the destroyed armored vehicle.

"Get on the radio and report the improvised explosive device," the sergeant said from the turret in between bursts of fire with the M2.

"Ma'am, contact the TOC and let them know the situation," the specialist behind the wheel of the armored vehicle said.

The despondent colonel did not respond to the specialist.

"Ma'am, grab the radio handset and report the situation," the specialist said. He accelerated the armored vehicle past the ambush site.

The radio crackled. "Sentinel 6, Sentinel 6, this is Sentinel Base, over."

The colonel, afraid to move, did not react or take charge of the situation. The specialist reached for the handset on the encrypted radio, mounted between himself and the colonel in the front passenger seat.

"Sentinel Base, Sentinel Base, this is Sentinel 6 Alpha. We have one improvised explosive device with possible casualties, break."

"Ma'am, what is our grid? I think the blast damaged one of our antennas because our location has not updated on the network," the specialist said. He wiped sweat from his eyes to see the digital map display in between himself and the colonel. "Grid, ma'am, what is our grid?" the specialist yelled. "I need the grid to relay to the TOC, ma'am," the specialist said. He pounded his fist on the steering wheel, but the colonel did not respond.

"Sentinel 6 Alpha, say again over."

"Shit, Colonel, you need to get a hold of yourself. You are our commander," the specialist said in disgust.

The colonel looked at the digital map display for the grid location of their vehicle. "ET32391394," the colonel said in a whisper.

"Ma'am, you need to speak up. Here, you give our location to the TOC," the specialist said. He handed the radio handset to the colonel and checked the rearview mirror for other vehicles in the convoy but saw none.

The colonel buried her face in her hands and whimpered after she contacted Sentinel Base on the radio with their location.

"Specialist, drive the vehicle over to the high ground with the grove of trees!" the sergeant yelled from the turret.

"Roger, Sentinel 6, good copy on the grid, break, we have your position on the network, break. QRF is inbound in ten minutes, Sentinel Base out," a soldier from the Sentinel Base said on the radio.

"Ma'am, scan your sector for the threat and call it out to the sergeant," the specialist said.

"Did you hear me, ma'am?"

The colonel nodded.

The specialist stopped the vehicle and left the engine running while he contacted each vehicle in the convoy for a situational report.

"Roger, 3 killed in action and 4 wounded in action. Did you retrieve the wounded?" the specialist asked. He saw a new vehicle approach the ambushed convoy. "Sergeant, a technical is inbound toward the center of the convoy!" the specialist yelled. He pounded on the roof of the vehicle to alert the sergeant in the turret. The specialist picked up the handset and contacted the ambushed convoy. "Sentinel 4, Sentinel 4, this is Sentinel 6 Alpha, be advised you have a white pickup truck with about six dismounts, to include rocket propelled grenades inbound to your position."

"Roger, Sentinel 6 Alpha!"

The sergeant in the turret fired the M2 and sent a squall of lead rounds toward the white pickup truck. The rounds punched holes in the thin aluminum body of the truck and it rolled to a stop. White smoke billowed from the engine and a red stain covered the windshield. Small arms fire from the convoy finished the job.

"Oh, shit, more dismounts have converged on the ambushed convoy!" the sergeant yelled from the turret.

"Ma'am, get on the radio and give the TOC a situational report on the dismounts," the specialist said.

"I can't see them, and I don't know how many dismounts we face," the colonel said.

"Ma'am, stay in the game! I'll relay the information about the enemy to you, and you contact the TOC with a situational report," the specialist said.

"Sentinel base, Sentinel base this is Sentinel 6 with a situational report, over," the colonel said with a soft and incoherent voice.

"Say again last transmission, Sentinel 6, over."

The colonel relayed the information about the enemy soldiers to the TOC. A few bursts of fire from the M2 silenced the threat of the dismounts. The sergeant in the turret ducked into the vehicle for another can of ammo.

"How are my splendid foot soldiers?" the sergeant asked. He looked over each of the occupants of the vehicle with meticulous care. He removed a can of chewing tobacco from his cargo pocket, thumped the round case twice and assessed the despondent colonel.

"Sergeant, what are you doing? Get on the machine gun and kill the enemy!" the colonel said in a state of panic.

"Ma'am, the dismounts are dead, but I need you to chill and stay sharp," the sergeant said. He took a pinch of tobacco from the tin and placed it under his lower lip.

"Ok," the colonel said. Her state of panic subsided, but she did not take charge of the situation.

"Anyone injured?" the sergeant asked. He looked at the inside of the vehicle and each soldier again for signs of injury. "I have not heard shit from you, Private," the sergeant said. The private sat in the back right seat of the armored vehicle and pulled security with his M4 carbine weapon out the window.

"Are you good to go, Private?" the sergeant asked again.

"Good to go, Sergeant," the private said. He gave the sergeant a thumbs up.

"Good. Stay sharp," the sergeant hit him on his Kevlar helmet before he spit tobacco juice in an empty water bottle.

"You ok, Sergeant?" the specialist asked. He turned around to take a look at the sergeant in the back seat of the armored vehicle.

"Another great day," the sergeant said before he secured a can of ammo and climbed into the turret. A few moments later the sergeant dropped inside the vehicle.

"We are not out of the shit yet," the sergeant said. Anger and frustration attempted to fill the leadership void in the vehicle, but he took a deep breath and took responsibility for the soldiers in the vehicle. "Specialist, you will cover the private and me with the M2 while we move toward that fucked up building above the valley," the sergeant said. He pointed toward a dilapidated building.

"Roger, Sergeant," the specialist said as he looked at the war-ravaged building thirty meters away from their position.

The private checked his gear as his heart beat faster in anticipation of securing the objective.

"Colonel, you will monitor the radio, scan your sector between the edge of the building and the open area to the right and assist the gunner with ammo," the sergeant said as he loaded a magazine into his M4 carbine. "Do you understand your task, Colonel?"

"Roger," the colonel said. She removed her Beretta M9 pistol from the holster and placed it on the dash of the armored vehicle.

"Once we clear the building I will signal you to drive the vehicle toward the building. Move with the windows open in the armored vehicle and don't haul ass to avoid the rooster tails of dirt that might tip our position to the enemy. Once you reach the building, I want you to fold in the mirrors, take the litter for the wounded attached to the armored vehicle and cover the windshield with it. Colonel, you will take the extra ammo and the radio into the building. Specialist, once the colonel is inside take the M2 into the building. The private will provide security while you dismount the M2. Private, you will retrieve the tripod for the M2 when the specialist removes the M2 from the turret. Any questions?" the sergeant asked.

"Negative, Sergeant," the specialist said as he grabbed an extra can of ammo for the M2.

"Specialist, if we don't make it to the building I want you to drive to the alternate rally point with the colonel," the sergeant said.

"Sergeant, we will not leave you or the private in the building," the specialist said.

"Negative, Specialist, you will leave us and get the colonel to the rally point. That is an order, Specialist!"

"Roger, Sergeant," the specialist said with downcast eyes. He checked the rally point grid on the digital map and prayed the building did not conceal insurgents.

"Let's go, Private. We have work to do," the sergeant said as he exited the vehicle.

The specialist traversed the M2 to cover their approach to the dilapidated structure. The sergeant and private's muscles burned from the weight of their gear as they sprinted toward the building. They reached the side of the brick building out of breath. Their sweat mixed with the dust in the air and accumulated around their neck and face. The uncomfortable mandarin collar of the body armor absorbed the slurry and chaffed their neck.

"Ma'am, the sergeant and the private have made it to the building," the specialist said from the turret.

The colonel remained silent and stared at the open area the sergeant had told her to watch.

"Ma'am, take a sip of water. We don't need heat exhaustion added to the list of our problems today," the specialist said. His thumbs were ready to depress the butterfly trigger on the machine gun at any sign of the enemy.

"I brought no water. I thought this would be a quick trip. Besides, the load plan specifies a case of water in each vehicle," the colonel said.

The specialist begrudgingly lowered his hydration pack to the colonel. "Here, take some of my water, ma'am," he said. He traversed the M2 along the row of windows as the sergeant and private checked their weapons before they entered the building.

"You refill your own hydration pack with the case of water," the specialist said. He surveyed the remains of the obliterated wall around the mud brick building, alert to any threat. A shredded red curtain fluttering in the breeze caught his attention, and he traversed the M2 toward the last window frame devoid of any glass.

The sergeant wiped the sweat from his brow, angry with himself because he had left the infantry for a military intelligence unit. The decision in hindsight did not pan out with the retention officer's sales pitch. The promised college in the evenings, an air-conditioned office and covert missions in a European capital never happened for the sergeant. Instead, reality brought him thousands of miles away from civilization with three soldiers lacking training in small unit tactics.

"Private, remember what they taught you in pre-deployment training. Stay close and cover your sector," the sergeant said. He signaled to the specialist in the turret.

"Roger, Sergeant," the private said without a trace of anxiety in his voice. The private felt a sense of calm envelop him before he stepped into the breach of the unknown. He was a military intelligence analyst who had joined the Army to pay for college. He never dreamed he would have to clear buildings of enemy fighters down range and face the threat in close quarters. To him, the enemy lived on computer databases or power point slides, but today the enemy was real and threatened his life and his fellow soldiers. The private felt an iron grip on his shoulder—the signal to enter the building.

"They've entered the building, ma'am," the specialist said.

"Clear in my sector," the colonel said as she swatted at a fly, oblivious to the potential turn of events inside the structure.

The building provided excellent observation of the road and the ambush site—a possible over-watch position the enemy occupied to coordinate the ambush. A few tense moments later, the colonel saw the sergeant crouched low next to the building entrance. He signaled for the colonel and specialist to move the vehicle toward the building. The colonel was not familiar with the hand signals because she did not attend the training, but the specialist recognized the signal. He dropped into the vehicle and turned over the engine to execute the next part of the plan.

"Sentinel 4, Sentinel 4, this is Sentinel 6 Alpha, we have set up an observation post along the ridge line next to a small building at the following grid: WV53559572, how copy over."

"Roger, Sentinel 6 Alpha we have your location, Sentinel Base out."

"Hooah, we made it!" the colonel exclaimed as she holstered her M9 pistol. She did not bother to cover the specialist while he prepped the vehicle as the sergeant had requested. She exited the vehicle and walked toward the building. A strong hand pushed her into a kneeling position as she entered the building.

"What took you so long, ma'am?" the sergeant said.

"This is fun!" the colonel squealed as she looked around the barren one-room building with a dirt floor.

"It's not over yet, colonel. I want you to cover the specialist while he removes the M2 from the armored vehicle. Private, stand down, the colonel will cover the vehicle," the sergeant said.

"Not much of a house," the specialist said as he entered the dilapidated house with the M2 machine gun.

"We don't intend to flip it, so don't offer any ideas to redecorate. Specialist, your fighting position is the window to cover the approach to the door," the sergeant said.

"You mean the door frame," the specialist snickered. The remains of the door hung on one hinge with most of the door shattered in pieces on the dirt floor.

"You keep a sharp look out, Specialist," the sergeant said.

The sergeant set up the M2 to provide overwatch of the convoy vehicles in the ambush site. From this position, the sergeant could engage any insurgents that threatened the convoy. The private assisted the sergeant with the M2 and provided overwatch of the other half of the building not covered by the specialist's position.

"Ma'am, is the radio set up?" the sergeant asked. He scanned the open terrain beyond the ambush site.

"Radio is good to go, Sergeant," the colonel said. She crouched in a corner of the one-room house and removed binoculars from the container she retrieved from the vehicle.

"Colonel, let me have the binoculars," the sergeant said.

"Negative, Sergeant; you get on the radio with Sentinel Base and find out the status of the QRF. I will scan the area with binoculars," the colonel said with confidence.

"Roger, ma'am." *It is about time she took charge,* the sergeant thought to himself.

"Oh shit, Sergeant, I see another white pickup truck determined to engage the convoy," the colonel said as she adjusted the binoculars.

The sergeant reported the white truck to the convoy and updated the Brigade TOC. The sergeant saw a rocket plume ignite below their position.

"What weapon did they fire?" the colonel asked.

"It's an AT4-CS antitank weapon," the sergeant said as he prepared to engage the truck with the M2 machine gun.

"Come on, baby, hit the truck. Damn! It missed the fucking truck. How could they miss the truck?" she asked as she peered through the binoculars.

"I bet it is the first time they fired a live round," the specialist said in disgust.

"The convoy has coordinated fire on the white pickup truck," the sergeant said.

"Hooah!" the colonel yelled as she observed an Mk19 grenade launcher engage the truck along with small arms fire. The colonel scanned the ambushed convoy and the road network. She saw smoke from a pickup truck destroyed by a volley of grenades. Soldiers moved the wounded from the ambush site to a rally point for medical evacuation.

"Oh shit, Sergeant, three armored personnel carriers in 'V' formation are approaching the convoy. They are four clicks away from our position," the colonel said. She scanned the immediate vicinity of the ambush site for other armored vehicles.

"Let me see the binoculars," the sergeant said. "Shit, Colonel, a platoon of BMP-2 armored personnel carriers, each with eight dismounts, antitank missiles and a 73mm cannon in the turret," the sergeant said. He handed the binoculars to the colonel.

"Sergeant, contact Sentinel Base and report the three BMPs," the colonel said.

"Roger, ma'am. Sentinel Base, Sentinel Base, this is Sentinel 6 Alpha, SITREP follows, over."

"Roger, Sentinel 6 Alpha, send, over."

"Three BMPs in the open moving toward convoy ambush site, break on an azimuth of 274 break, location: MB43218449, at 1445 hours, how copy, over."

"Roger, Sentinel 6 Alpha, copy last transmissions, QRF is inbound."

Shit, this will get ugly quick if we don't have air support, the sergeant thought to himself.

"Sergeant, one of the BMPs changed course and is heading for our position," the colonel said with panic in her voice.

"Shit, contact Sentinel Base, ma'am, and let them know we are bugging out of our position. Specialist, prep the vehicle for movement, and Private, help me pack up our kit so we can get out of here!" the sergeant said as he prepared the M2 for transport to the vehicle.

"Sergeant, we need to stay and fight," the private said as he took his weapon off safe.

"I have no intention to sit here and slug it out with a Soviet armored vehicle behind these thin walls. Put your weapon on safe and carry the ammo to the vehicle, Private!" the sergeant said.

"Holy shit!" the colonel yelled. She reacted to the intense sound of *thump, thump, thump* followed by a *swoosh* sound over their position.

"Colonel, our QRF is here," the sergeant said as he looked up through the hole in the roof at the unmistakable shape of an Apache attack helicopter as it lined up to engage the BMP.

The colonel saw the BMP through her binoculars before it turned bright orange. The vehicle sides bulged outward and plumes of fire shot up toward the sky as the turret flipped through the air. The team looked to the sky, mesmerized by the Apache gunship as it dispersed flares and rolled in for another attack on the other BMPs. The colonel shouted a triumphant 'Hooah!' when the two other armored vehicles became molten slabs of twisted metal.

"Sentinel 6, Sentinel 6, this is Sentinel Base, over."

"Roger, Sentinel Base," the colonel said on the radio.

"Be advised the QRF has secured the location break, and the medical evacuation helicopter is inbound to the rally point, break. The combat recovery team will recover the damaged vehicles on site break," Sentinel Base said on the radio.

The colonel could not hear the last radio transmission because the

Apache fired its 30mm machine gun overhead of their position.

"Sentinel Base, Sentinel Base, say again last transmission, over," the colonel said.

"Roger, Sentinel 6, be advised the QRF commander has operational control. Sentinel elements will move to rally point Victor Tango Zulu for fuel and ammo and return to base, over."

"Roger, Sentinel Base, Sentinel 6 out. Sergeant, grab our gear and let's get the hell out of here," the colonel said as she exited the building first.

CHAPTER 11

TO BRAVE THE PREVAILING DARK

A THUNDEROUS ROAR echoed through the flimsy aluminum auditorium as hundreds of soldiers snapped to attention before Brigade S1 read the citations for heroism. Soldiers from the 5-20 Infantry Regiment quick reaction force and the 4077th Military Intelligence Brigade Commander were the center of attention for the awards ceremony. The commanding general of the forward operating base pinned bronze star medals with "V" devices for valor on four 5-20 Infantry soldiers. The sergeant and the two soldiers with the colonel at the ambush stood at attention in the audience.

"Sergeant, you should be on stage!" the specialist said.

"Specialist, shut the hell up while you're at attention in formation" the sergeant said in frustration.

"I have never seen her smile with such pride since she became our commander," the specialist said.

"Respect the ceremony," the sergeant said struggling to stay calm.

"A total disgrace. We know how she acted after the ambush. She did not lead, let alone execute the basic soldier tasks to extract us from that shit storm," the specialist said to the sergeant.

"Specialist, you open your trap one more time and I will hit you so hard the explosive ordinance disposal team will think a bomb exploded in here when I break your jaw," the sergeant said.

The specialist glanced at the sergeant and noticed his clenched jaw and facial expression showing his true thoughts about the awards ceremony. The sergeant's pride in his profession kept him silent while he honored the 5-20 Infantry Regiment soldiers. The commanding general on stage pinned the nation's third highest military decoration for valor on their colonel.

"Soldiers of the 4077th Military Intelligence Brigade, today we honor one of your own who exemplified courage and heroism under fire with the Silver Star Medal. Colonel Yvette Askeri remained calm under pressure and displayed heroic leadership to stymie the enemy attack. We lost three soldiers, and their loss weighs heavy on my heart, but without your commander's leadership, tactical skills and courage, we might have lost more soldiers to the cowards who rely on terror tactics. Military Intelligence, Always Out Front!" the commanding general shouted the unit motto with a deep command voice.

The soldiers of the 4077th Military Intelligence Brigade filled the auditorium with applause. The colonel soaked up the adulation from her soldiers. *A citation for valor as commander guarantees my promotion to brigadier general,* she thought to herself. She did not think once of the three soldiers with her that inauspicious day who stood at attention along with her assembled unit during the reading of the citation for valor in the auditorium.

"Ma'am, shall I drive your armored vehicle to the front of the auditorium for you?" her new driver asked. The driver fixated on the silver star medal pinned to her uniform after she spoke to the colonel.

"No, Private, I shall walk to the brigade building alone," the colonel said. She observed her soldiers filter out of the auditorium and cringed at the discarded awards ceremony pamphlets they left behind on their way to the exit.

A few of the officers and senior noncommissioned officers congratulated her before they left the auditorium. She removed the silver star from her uniform and traced the outline of the award with her fingers. She noticed the contrast between the smooth edges of the star and her stubby chewed fingernails. She sat for a moment in silence and imagined her promotion ceremony to brigadier general. The sound of a door opening and slamming shut interrupted her thoughts. She stood up, clipped the silver star on her uniform, and the lights in the auditorium went black.

"Turn on the lights!" she commanded.

The colonel received no response. Aluminum chairs clattered across the concrete floor.

"Who entered the auditorium? Answer me! This is Colonel Askeri," she said. Her eyes adjusted to the darkness and noticed movement to her left. The sound of more metal chairs tossed aside echoed through the auditorium. Her hands shook when she removed the 9mm service pistol from the holster. She loaded a magazine into the weapon and chambered a round. "Identify yourself." Her commanding voice echoed in the auditorium, but no one responded to her.

She depressed the button on her flashlight and illuminated the auditorium in a narrow beam of light. She saw a path of strewn chairs that led toward her. She spun around and shined the light in various directions but saw nothing. She gripped the pistol tighter; her eyes struggled to adjust between the halogen beam of the flashlight and the dark shadows that clawed at the light.

The hair on her neck stood up, and she thought she could hear her heartbeat echo off the walls. An intense fear resonated through every cell of her body—the intensity of the fear far greater than the convoy ambush. She tried to run, but she stood rooted to the floor, too afraid to look up into the rafters of the auditorium.

She perceived the presence above her and rehearsed in her mind the fluid movement to drop to one knee and aim the pistol above her. Her heart beat faster as the adrenaline coursed through her body. She took a deep breath, knelt, and aimed her pistol toward the ceiling. The light from the pistol illuminated a figure that descended from the rafters.

She succumbed to the inevitable because she could not fire a shot. The figure's labored breathing preceded the feel of thick leather gloves that clutched her wrist and pistol. An immobilizing pain shot up her arm. She dropped her pistol and felt the flashlight swatted away from her other hand. Darkness claimed the room when the flashlight turned off from the impact of the floor.

"Ma'am, ma'am, you okay?" a sergeant from her unit asked as he nudged her shoulder. Her eyes opened wide with fear and she lashed out at the circle of soldiers that stood above her. "Easy ma'am. We are on your side," the sergeant said as he avoided her kicks and fists.

"What happened, ma'am?" another soldier asked.

"Someone attacked me," she said in an angry and embarrassed voice when she realized her soldiers had found her unconscious.

"Who attacked you, ma'am?" the sergeant asked as he helped her to her feet.

"Here, take a drink," one of the other soldiers said after they removed the cap from the water bottle with Arabic writing splashed on the side.

She took a sip. The warm plastic taste of the water calmed her. Her tension returned when she heard her pistol being cleared of ammunition as it echoed through the auditorium.

"Your side arm, ma'am," a soldier said as he handed her the pistol and magazine.

"Did you see anything?" she asked as she holstered her pistol.

The sergeant overturned a chair and offered her a seat. "Unfortunately, no. We arrived to clean up the auditorium about five minutes ago and saw the overturned chairs with you on the floor when we turned on the lights."

"You're positive you saw nothing else?" the colonel asked. She shook as the fear took hold of her again.

"No, ma'am. Do you recall anything?" the sergeant asked.

"Only the labored sound of his breathing. He might have suffered from asthma or he was a chronic smoker, and he wore thick leather gloves. I could see nothing else because of the darkness, but he attacked me from the rafters," the colonel said.

"Ma'am, two soldiers will escort you to your quarters, and you better let security know what happened," the sergeant said. The sergeant shined a flashlight into the empty rafters. "Ma'am, we found this next to you. Do you recognize it?" he asked.

The colonel's hands trembled as she reached for the object.

She traced her finger over the wax seal, a coat of arms with a goat head pressed into the red wax. She held the package with both hands and felt the weight of the item. The hand-printed address label in ornate penmanship with crimson ink looked out of place in the dusty and austere auditorium. The colonel scowled when she noticed her name without rank on the address label. A gold-leaf etching of a coat of arms with a goat head was in place of the return address label.

"Do you recognize it?" the sergeant asked.

"We should call the explosive ordinance disposal team and have them check it out. It could be dangerous," one of the other soldiers said.

"Sergeant, the package is not a threat. Take me to the TOC."

"Roger, ma'am." The sergeant helped the colonel stand up and offered his arm for support, but she ignored his gesture.

The package made her feel uneasy as she held it close to her. A menacing presence emanated from the ornate package, but her curiosity about what it contained suppressed her fear and overruled her intuition to discard the package.

CHAPTER 12

HARPOONED AND LAMPOONED

JERRY TOOK A SEAT in a worn, uncomfortable chair, two sizes too small for the average American's girth today, but he had room to spare. The set of chairs originated from the birth of the republic.

Jerry watched with disgust as the water buffalo thrashed around in his leather chair, asleep again behind his desk at work. He yawned, stretched and thought, *what a perk to sleep while in charge of the people's work*. He managed an average of five hours or less of sleep, and this buffoon with a damp shoulder from drool took a nap at work every day.

The thrashing subsided and shallow, labored breathing displaced the silence of his boss's grand office. Plenty of time to take a picture of the comb-over plastered to the side of his head. Jerry reached for his cell phone in his designer messenger bag on the plush carpet. He paused and marveled at the silver frames arrayed in formation behind his boss's desk before he retrieved his cell phone.

Hard to believe great power and influence emanated from this office despite his boss's appearance and intellect. The elegant frames preserved photos of many heads of state and other famous people taken on exclusive golf courses around the world. His boss's nicotine-stained smile beamed in each picture. The framed pictures reminded Jerry of the network of opportunities for his career and motivated him to endure the misery of working for Senator Jack Seavan.

"Senator, Senator, wake up," Jerry said from across the antique desk, choosing not to take a picture of his boss while he slept.

He hated this part of the job the most. This humiliation should not be the reward for a four-year degree from Columbia. The senator twitched and continued to snore but was undisturbed by his command.

Jerry picked up the golf club that rested on a custom-made oak base with the crest of Columbia at the edge of the desk. Jerry jabbed the club into the leviathan and imagined he held a harpoon in his hand. The senator's eyes opened wide as he scanned the room for the source of discomfort and locked onto Jerry.

"Jerry, don't touch my club!" the senator said. He wiped the drool from his face with the sleeve of his dress shirt.

Jerry ignored his boss, the club ready for another jab, but he thought otherwise because of the senator's infamous temper.

"Why did you wake me, and who allowed you in this office this time of day?" the senator asked as his head descended toward his desk.

"You have a meeting in an hour with the majority leader," Jerry said.

"Well, wake me in an hour."

"Senator, we need to coordinate travel arrangements for the summer recess before your meeting," Jerry said.

The mention of travel invigorated the senator, and the sleep induced grogginess vanished from the torpid public servant. When the senator stood up from behind his desk, his wrinkled dress shirt unfurled around his sides and the suspenders struggled to contain the mass of his midsection. Travel meant new opportunities for golf, his only passion in life. The senator waddled from around the desk toward Jerry. The stench of cigars greeted Jerry before the senator swiped the golf club from his hand.

"Did I ever tell you the story about the National Championship in college and how I won with this golf club, Jerry?" the senator asked. He turned away from Jerry and held the club high in the air as he recalled that glorious victory.

Jerry exhaled, disturbed by the memory of when the senator had told him about the golf match the first time in the locker room of the Congressional Country Club.

"Yes, Senator." His shoulders slumped in the chair.

The senator dropped a handful of golf balls with the presidential seal on the plush blue carpet and continued to recount the highlights of the match.

Jerry interrupted the senator's story. "Senator, do you have travel plans for this recess?" Jerry asked.

The senator sized up the putt and licked his lips. "Did you want to travel with me, Jerry?"

Jerry felt uncomfortable with the question, shifted in his chair and looked toward the silver picture frames behind the senator's desk.

"Another time, Senator," Jerry said. He hoped his response did not anger the senator.

"Too bad, we have much work to improve your game. Tell Steve I will call him with my travel plans later today. Speaking of Steve, my scheduler, tell me the latest gossip about him," the senator said. He dropped more golf balls on the plush carpet and sank every one of them on the makeshift green.

"I know nothing about Steve, Senator," Jerry said.

"My staff speaks candidly in your presence because most don't notice you, but you must hear some juicy tidbits. You can tell me. What do you know about him and my deputy chief of staff?" the senator asked.

"Senator, I do not have time to listen to the gossip, and they talk little around me since I joined your personal staff," Jerry said. He looked at his designer messenger bag the senator had presented him as a gift on his first day of work. He did not want to return from the senator's office without his travel plans and disappoint Steve.

"You are new; give it time. Remember, information, any information, is valuable currency in these halls, Jerry," the senator said.

Jerry noticed the senator's mood change as he kicked golf balls from his path when he walked toward a picture on the opposite wall. Jerry resisted the urge to thank the senator for his time and leave the office without the information. Instead, he stayed in the room, determined to obtain the information. He approached the senator, took the golf club from him and placed it in the wood cradle on the desk.

The senator looked over his shoulder at him and breathed in the smell of Jerry's cologne.

"Do you know I am the only member of Congress with a PGA tour card?" the senator asked as he gazed at the picture on the wall.

Jerry suppressed a smile when he discovered new information about the senator.

"I did not know you had a tour card, Senator," Jerry said as he walked toward the senator and the picture. "What is a PGA tour card?" he asked. His eyes betrayed his interest in the subject.

"It means you earned a spot on the tour. Who knows where I might have ended up if I hadn't injured myself?" the senator said.

"That is you in the picture next to the man with the golf flag on the course?" Jerry asked. Jerry placed his hand on the senator's slumped shoulders. Jerry could detect a smile as it struggled to surface from the sadness etched on the senator's creased face.

"Yes, that is Lee Trevino, and he has the golf pin or flag stick in his hand on the green. Jerry, I thought I taught you the proper golf terminology so you don't embarrass me on the golf course."

Jerry detested golf and loathed the game when he played a round with the senator, but he did not want to jeopardize any network opportunities.

"Sorry, Senator, I did not forget the proper golf terminology. Was he your golf coach?" Jerry asked to show interest and a sympathy for a subject he could not care less about.

The senator's eyes narrowed, etching the lines deeper on his forehead before he responded to Jerry. "No, he was a professional golfer, smart butt," the senator said. The senator noted his young staff member's ignorance on his favorite sport. "The young have no respect or interest in the past," the senator mumbled. The senator turned his attention toward Jerry, curious if Jerry's ignorance was genuine or he did not care to learn about the subject because of indifference.

The senator could read people well and discern truth from bullshit, a cunning trait to have on Capitol Hill and his only other talent besides golf. It was a skill learned from his father, a state senator from Virginia.

"Senator, I don't follow golf," Jerry said. He removed his hand from the senator's shoulder but reconsidered the error in his statement. He placed his hand on the senator's shoulder again and said, "I do enjoy the game but have not had the time to learn about it on my own, but I think I will change my priorities."

The senator ignored Jerry's insincere remark. "Lee Trevino is one of the best golfers to have played the game. This picture captured the moment when Lee Trevino congratulated me for sinking a putt to win the qualifying tournament for the tour in 1970," the senator said.

Jerry watched the senator take a cheap plastic comb out of his pocket and comb what remained of his disheveled hair over his bald spot. *How does the senator wield such power and influence in the capital, despite the urbane good looks and intelligence of the junior senators?* Jerry wondered. Jerry had witnessed the senator on numerous occasions sound out words when he read white papers from his staff or other congressional sources. The senator embarrassed himself in private without the aid of teleprompters and prepared speeches because of his low intelligence. It baffled Jerry how this dolt could win elections. For a moment Jerry felt sorry for the senator, the chubby kid not blessed with intellect, height or looks. His sympathy was short lived after he recalled the work schedule for the past six months and the senator's tirades. The senator's inherited wealth from his mother's tobacco fortune and the numerous deals designed to steal from his constituents made it difficult to feel sorry for the senator. The more time Jerry spent in Congress, the more he realized most elected officials had no real talents, charisma or skills of value beyond the Beltway.

The senator did what any silver spoon dolt would do in his position: leverage a family inheritance to buy his way into office. Jerry watched the senator limp to his desk and collapse in his oversized leather chair, out of breath.

Why can't this clown use email and social media like everyone else on the Hill. It would save me numerous trips to his office, Jerry thought to himself.

The senator rummaged through piles of papers and folders stacked precariously on his desk until he found a red folder. He fanned himself with the folder and took in the sight of Jerry by the picture on the wall.

Jerry felt the intrusive stare from the senator and walked toward his messenger bag on the floor. "Senator, don't forget your meeting," Jerry said.

The senator waited for him to reach the office door before he spoke. "You forgot the information for Steve."

Jerry let go of the door knob and turned toward the senator. "What information for Steve?" Jerry asked. He slung his messenger bag over his other shoulder, annoyed at the games the senator played.

"This red folder," the senator said. The senator held the folder close to his chest.

"I don't recognize the folder, Senator," Jerry said and turned toward the door to leave the office.

"It is my travel itinerary for Steve," the senator said with a mischievous grin.

The senator stood and reached for his blue suit jacket that had enough material to cover a circus tent on the back of his leather chair. The senator struggled with his suit jacket until Jerry approached to guide the senator's arms through the sleeves of the off-the-rack suit. Jerry adjusted the bow tie for the senator and stepped aside before the stench of body odor and cigars made him nauseous.

The senator stood in front of the full-length mirror by his desk and admired his reflection. He was oblivious to the effects of the short hem that exposed his dingy white socks around his ankles and scuffed black leather shoes. The unofficial nickname for the senator was "High Water" among the capitol aids and staff.

Satisfied with his reflection, the senator picked up the red folder from his desk. Crystals in the shape of golf balls on his cuff links scattered the light from the window and created little rainbows on the senator's desk. The senator's pudgy digits thumbed through the contents of the folder as he licked his lips and looked at Jerry's tie. He extended the folder toward Jerry and said, "My itinerary for the summer recess."

Jerry smiled and reached for the folder, but the senator moved it away from his outstretched hand. The red folder now rested below the senator's leather belt that struggled with the suspenders to restrain the mass of the senator's gut.

"We have a few minutes before my meeting, Jerry," the senator said as he unbuttoned his jacket and pulled Jerry toward him by his tie.

CHAPTER 13

SILKY SMOOTH

A RANCID ODOR found its way through the thicket of hairs in the senator's nose.

"Frank, damn tourists got lost in the capitol. I can smell them. I will call you after I close my door. Look, Frank, I don't care about your deadline with the speaker or the conservative coalition you serve. I will give you my corrections to the Defense of Sharia Law Act on my time line," the senator said. He slammed the phone on the cradle. The senator covered his mouth with his soiled handkerchief and stood to close his office door.

"Sit down, Jack Seavan," a deep baritone voice commanded from behind the senator. Fear displaced the rage the senator displayed toward the person who startled him and disrespected him in his office. The senator, immobilized by some unseen force, could not turn around and face the unannounced visitor.

"How dare you intrude upon my privacy," the senator said. He looked at the golf club on his desk.

"Jack, I told you to sit down," the person said in a menacing tone. Two powerful gloved hands on the senator's shoulders pushed him with little effort into his chair.

The senator's nails dug into the mahogany arm rests of the chair as he fought to stand up and face the intruder. The pressure from his shoulders dissipated, and he saw movement by his desk.

Stacks of papers scattered as a package slid across his desk. The package stopped short of the cradled putter. The senator, released from his fear, spun his chair around, ready to berate a member of the Senate mail delivery service for their lack of respect entitled to a member of the US Senate, but he was alone in the room.

The senator's hands trembled as he reached for the package. He noticed it did not have the proper stamps and bar codes of the Senate mail service.

His nicotine-stained fingers traced the crimson ink of his name, devoid of the proper title for a member of the nation's political elite. This slight of etiquette infuriated him. His name looked less impressive without the title of "Honorable" written before his name. The package intrigued him despite the breach of etiquette. He kept the package instead of his initial thought to toss it in the Senate incinerator.

The detail of calligraphy, the deep crimson ink, and the gold-leaf coat of arms in the return address balanced class with darkness. The senator reached for his letter opener with the seal of the Commonwealth of Virginia on the handle and sliced through the folded ends of the carefully wrapped package.

The energy of the letter opener blade dissipated as it snagged on a wax seal. The senator let go of the letter opener and pulled the red wax seal the size of a silver dollar from the package with his Vienna-sausage-shaped fingers. He noticed an ominous goat head in the indentation of the wax and placed it on his desk. A chilling draft embraced the senator the moment he stabbed the goat seal with his letter opener and flicked the wax across the room.

He turned his attention toward the package the size of a gift box for clothing. The quality of the paper felt luxurious as he unwrapped the package. The paper had a glossy black finish that resembled polished onyx with no creases. The senator removed the outer wrapping paper and tossed it on the floor to reveal a box made of rare ebony wood. The smooth polished finish of the black box contrasted with a red silk ribbon tied in an ornate bow. The senator's gut told him to discard the box and its contents, but he did not listen to his intuition.

He removed the ribbon from the box. The ribbon felt cool and smooth to the touch. He rubbed it across his cheek and thought of Jerry's red hair. He put the ribbon in his jacket pocket.

The senator's pudgy fingers shook as he lifted the lid. He felt intense fear and gasped for air until he let go of the lid. The senator stared at the black box and became lost in thoughts from his childhood. The senator leaned forward and mustered the courage to open the lid and discover the contents of the box. He peered inside the open box with trepidation and reached in with both hands when the phone rang. Startled, the senator removed his hands from the opened box and answered the phone.

"Senator Jack Seavan. Yes, I will hold for the president," he said.

CHAPTER 14

VIOLENCE AS A SECOND LANGUAGE

TITO CRUZ RAISED HIS LEFT ARM with a tattoo of the Dominican Republic flag draped over his bicep. His outstretched fingers could have palmed a basketball, but he grew up with baseball.

"About time Princess DR showed up for practice," a southern-drawl voice laced with sarcasm said as Tito approached the plate.

Tito's cleats clawed at the loose dirt as he shifted his weight to settle into his stance. He glanced at the man crouched behind home plate. A shaggy beard protruded from the catcher's face mask.

Tito dropped his hand and tightened his fingers around the maple handle. Beads of sweat rolled toward the edge of his brim. One by one, they jumped like paratroopers toward the ground.

"Craig, I thought the GM demoted you to the minors this season," Tito said. His heavy accent pronounced "Craig" like "Creeg."

The catcher pounded his leather mitt and gave the hand signal for the pitch.

"Let's see how long you remain on the roster before the owner trades you," the catcher said.

Swoosh! The sound of Tito's bat sliced through the air, followed by the familiar thud of the ball as it impacted Craig's mitt. Craig lifted his face mask and spit a wad of tobacco juice across home plate. "Strike one, DR," Craig said.

Tito grunted, kicked dirt on home plate and stepped outside of the batter's box to adjust his jersey with the number thirteen that clung to his powerful shoulders. The oppressive humidity rolled in early from the bay this year.

"Oh come on, DR, hurry the hell up so we can finish practice," Craig said.

Tito entered the batter's box and ignored Craig's cries of discomfort. His mind drifted to a happier time in college while he scanned the outfield. He modified his grip above the knob of the bat how his hitting coach at the University of Texas taught him.

"You reek of alcohol, DR, and I bet you strike out!" Craig said.

Craig's comment, made with a southern drawl, lured Tito to the present. The orange star with a white letter "H" on the pitcher's hat appeared fuzzy as Tito narrowed his focus on the pitcher's release. The spinning white orb hurled toward him with great velocity. An average mortal would miss the ball before he had a chance to blink, but Tito was not average. With his heightened eyesight, he could see the red stitching on the ball flash the type of pitch. His agile reflexes bought extra time to make minuscule corrections on his swing plane.

Thwack! The precision of Tito's bat sliced through the saturated air and interrupted the trajectory of the white ball. A deep laugh bellowed from within Tito's chest as the ball sailed out of the stadium.

"I have yet to see you hit a dinger. It is only a matter of time before the owner sends you to the bush leagues, Craig," Tito said.

Craig pounded his mitt and crouched behind home plate. "Go to hell, DR. We enjoy the drills more when you miss practice," Craig said.

Tito dropped his bat on his shoulder, stepped out of the batter's box and pointed his bat toward the bleachers along first base. "Look in the stands, Craig. Most of those fans bought my jersey number. Do you have any fans at the park today, Craig? I see no one with your number," Tito said.

Craig didn't bother to look in the stands. Fans did not buy his jersey or ask for his autograph. When he received the call to play alongside his childhood hero, he felt fortune smiled twice on him. He discovered after his first season in the majors what most fans did not know about their favorite player. The World Series champion was petulant and despised by most of his teammates.

The Dominican Republic flag tattoo on Tito's bicep rippled as his muscles tightened around the handle of the maple lumber, and he sunk into his hips for another pitch. "The game is not for everyone, Craig. Any little league team would be proud to call you coach," Tito said.

Craig snarled at the tattoo flag on Tito's arm, confused about why the league did not allow a stars and bars tattoo.

"Wasted trade," Craig said before the pitcher released the ball.

Tito got a piece of the pitch, but it went foul into the third base bleachers. Tito watched as his fans jostled for the ball.

Craig pounded his catcher's mitt. "You have brought grief to this club, DR, and you can have those illegal island dwellers you call fans!" Craig said.

"My name is Tito. Call me DR one more time, and you will eat your face mask, Craig."

Craig gave the sign for the next pitch. "We call you DR because you're drunk and reckless," Craig said.

The pitcher wound up and released a scorcher of a fastball at Tito's head. Tito stumbled as he moved out of the trajectory of the pitch. "Too much heat for you, DR!" Craig said. The catcher spit tobacco juice on Tito's white cleats.

Tito raised his bat above his head, medieval-executioner style, and Craig was oblivious to the imminent pain. Tito pointed his bat at the pitcher and snapped it in two over his tree trunk of a leg after he knocked Craig unconscious. Fans in the stands scrambled toward the field to record the melee on their smart phones. The pitcher backed away from the mound.

"DR, the pitch got away, I swear," the pitcher said.

When the pitcher called Tito by his nickname, it fueled his rage.

Tito's build resembled an NFL lineman, but he moved with the speed of a track star. Tito closed the distance toward the pitcher before other members of the infield could intercept him.

The lanky pitcher stood his ground when a member of his own team charged the mound with the momentum and mass of a Spanish bull.

"Chill, man; you're crazy," the pitcher said.

The instincts learned as a homeless kid on the streets of Santo Domingo took over, and Tito pummeled the pitcher. The size thirteen shoe with bone shattering cleats missed their mark when the second baseman attempted to tackle Tito. Tito, unfazed, left the pitcher to writhe in pain in the infield and gnashed his teeth at the second baseman. Many of his teammates wanted to beat the crap out of Tito, but they hesitated to rush the enraged gladiator on the field.

"Tito, don't move!"

Tito sensed movement on his periphery and did not recognize the voice. His ears locked on to the hypnotic sound of a shotgun being armed.

"Put your hands over your head and kneel with your legs crossed!" a voice commanded.

Tito scanned to his left and right and saw uniformed security envelop his position with stun guns at the ready. The smell of ozone displaced the humid air in his nostrils. The rage dissipated with each exhale of his lungs as the effects of the adrenaline diminished in center field.

"Tito, last chance. Put your hands over your head and kneel on the ground," a uniformed member of the phalanx shouted.

Tito considered rushing the wall of officers arrayed before him but thought otherwise after he noticed the red aiming dots of the stun guns pointed at him. He complied with their command. The nylon uniforms rushed forward in unison and knocked him to the ground. He thrashed in defiance as the flex cuffs gnawed at his wrists and numerous knees pinned him to the ground.

CHAPTER 15

YOU THE MATATÁN

Tito's cell phone interrupted the tranquility of the morning. The sound of the waves and the gentle breeze that coaxed a few notes from a wind chime on the balcony could not persuade them to stay in bed.

"Shit, what time is it?" a sultry voice laced with anxiety asked.

Tito pushed her away and took the remaining sheets on the bed when he reached for his phone on the night stand. Her porcelain skin absorbed the morning sun that streamed in from the windows. The sound of the ocean attempted to quell the chaotic morning to its previous peaceful state. Tito knocked over an empty bottle of tequila on the nightstand and fumbled for his smart phone after he noticed a gold-framed picture of his wife and kids.

"It's 9:40," he said as he silenced the smart phone on the way toward the bathroom.

"The office is already open for business," the woman said.

"Stay for breakfast. I'll have the chef prepare your favorite breakfast on the balcony," Tito said.

He admired her naked body on the bed.

"No, I can't; I have work." She put on her earnings from the nightstand as Tito traced a finger along her spine.

"It won't work this time. I have to get to the office, Tito," she said again.

Tito enjoyed as she scampered around the room for her clothes. The ocean breeze revealed her crumpled up dress and one stiletto heel behind the curtains.

"Don't you have to get to the ball park today?" she asked. She bounded to the bathroom on her toes with a bundle of clothes and shoes.

"Damn, I forgot; it's Monday, the start of a new week. The three-week suspension flew by so fast," he said. He checked his cell phone for any messages. Tito saw a text from his agent about the 1:30 meeting with the manager and owner of the team.

Strange that the owner would be in Florida for a meeting during spring training, Tito thought to himself.

"Tell your boss you had a client who wanted to see the house early today. My house will sell in this market, and the fat commission will smooth over any issues between you and your boss," Tito said as he opened the shower door to join her.

"You don't have to sell the house." She pushed him away and shut the shower door.

"I sure as hell don't want to sell it, but I know my wife plans to file for divorce, and I don't want this place claimed by her team of lawyers as part of the settlement," Tito said.

"Tito, check my cell phone on the night stand for any messages from work and shut the bathroom door, please," she said. Her red lips puckered to blow him a kiss.

She looked good in the morning, unlike most of the playthings he brought home from the night club. Her naked body, though, could not distract him from his concern about the odd meeting at the stadium today.

The sleek black Bentley moved through the uncomfortable Jupiter air like a gator in a canal. The air conditioner worked overtime to keep the driver and occupant protected from the misery of the Florida humidity outside.

"Would you like to exit the vehicle at the loading dock behind the stadium, sir?" the driver asked. The chauffeur looked at Tito in the rearview mirror when he did not hear a response.

Tito had his eyes closed behind his dark sunglasses and his head rested on the embossed headrest with the Houston Astros logo. Rap music streamed through the luxury headphones that cupped his ears. His driver drove behind the stadium anyway. Tito's lack of conversation made him uncomfortable. *Smart move, driver,* Tito thought to himself as he sensed a change of direction. He opened his eyes to see a crowd of fans outside the stadium.

"Look at those pathetic middle-aged men parading their kids as bait for my signature," Tito said as he removed his headphones.

"I figured a low profile today is best since the incident on the field last month," the driver said.

Tito said nothing to the driver and answered his cell phone.

"Hola." He checked the time on his diamond-encrusted watch to make sure he was not late for the meeting.

"Hi, Mr. Veracruz. Did you make it to practice today?" a perplexed voice asked.

"Yep, I am in the ball park parking lot. I might stop and sign autographs for the fans. Do you think you can delay the meeting for an hour?" he said with sarcasm. He saw his driver's concerned expression in the rearview mirror.

"Tito, I don't think that is a good idea," Ethan said as he glanced at the other people in the room.

Ethan had been his agent from the day he graduated college and was one of the few people Tito trusted in life.

"Why, Ethan? The PR guys from the team said I need to reconnect more with the fans," Tito said.

"Today is not the best time to connect with fans, Tito. Everyone is here, including the owner," Ethan said. Ethan attempted to read the owner's level of impatience, but he revealed no emotion.

"I was kidding, Ethan; I did not want to ruin my afternoon with pathetic fans who leach autographs to sell. Any idea why the owner flew here for a meeting with me?" Tito asked.

"I don't think he left his restaurant empire in Houston to only see you, Tito," Ethan said.

"Anything I should know before the meeting today?" Tito asked. He checked his Twitter feed for any news about the team.

"Yes, my wife enjoyed the tickets to the show you gave us, and she said when you are in town to stop by and she will cook your favorite meal for you," Ethan said.

Tito was aware his agent avoided the question and in a subtle way had told Tito the meeting might not go well today.

"You cool, Mr. Veracruz?" Ethan asked before he took his seat at the table in the owner's suite. Tito hated when the old Jewish guy attempted to sound half his age.

"I have been with you since your adopted parents brought you home from the Dominican, Tito, and I have always brought you the cheddar, right?"

"Yes, you the matatán," Tito said. He rolled his eyes at his agent's choice of the word cheddar.

"What does matatán mean, Tito? Ethan asked.

"In my country, it means someone you respect. Someone who does big boss things," Tito said.

Tito noticed the owner's white Rolls Royce in the parking lot.

"I am going to add that word to my vocabulary."

"No, don't, Ethan," Tito said.

"Tito, I'll let everyone know you will be on time for the meeting," Ethan said and ended the call.

Ethan was a friend of Tito's stepfather. It took Tito a while to understand Ethan's humor—as dry as a west Texas infield in the summer—but his negotiation skills were worth the premium Tito paid to manage his finances and career prospects.

Tito's raw talent earned him a considerable sum in salary, but his agent's skills with numbers made him the highest paid athlete in the league. If you included endorsement deals, he earned more revenue than athletes in other professional sports.

"Everything okay, boss?" the driver asked with a concerned look.

The driver did not want to lose this job. Tito did not keep many people on his payroll for very long, but he remained loyal and took care of those he trusted with many perks besides generous pay.

"Anda el diablo," Tito said in a serious tone as he scanned the parking lot for any fans determined to poach autographs.

"I got the devil part, but I didn't catch the other part, sir," the driver said as he placed the car in park.

"'The devil lurks,' an expression from my country," Tito said. He finished the contents of his flask and waited for the driver to open the door.

The driver removed his chauffeur's cap and scratched his head before he asked in a nervous tone, "Anything I can do, boss?"

"Nope. Make sure you arrive here at 3:30 this afternoon with my golf bag. It might be a short day at the office," Tito said. He noticed a figure leaned against the wall by the entrance dressed in a western-style trench coat.

Why would anyone wear a trench coat in this oppressive humidity? Tito wondered. A Spanish Córdoba hat concealed the figure's face.

"Do you need your bag from the trunk, boss?" the driver asked.

"Yes, I'll need my bag," Tito said after he noticed the odd figure. Tito continued to observe the figure and noted he did not move while his driver retrieved the bag from the trunk. Tito towered over the little Puerto Rican who held the car door open for him. The driver's rolled up white sleeves revealed arms stained with tattoos.

"Sir, your bag," the driver said as he handed it to Tito.

Tito ignored his driver, took the bag and focused on the figure.

"Later, boss; see you at 3:30," the driver said.

"Don't be late and make sure you have my clubs," Tito said.

Tito missed the privacy and security of the MLB stadium, but at spring training the environment allowed the fans greater access to the players.

"Oye, mi mano," Tito said as he walked toward the service entrance of the stadium.

The figure did not respond to Tito.

"Hey, my brother, are you waiting for someone?" Tito asked. He repositioned the batting practice bag slung over his shoulder.

The figure did not resemble the average fan who stalked players for autographs. His build and height resembled a professional athlete. Tito wondered if he could go toe-to-toe with the figure. At six-foot three and 250 pounds, most people did not intimidate Tito, but this figure stood six-foot five and 50 pounds heavier than Tito.

"Identify yourself!" Tito said with a thick Spanish accent.

The figure moved to shift his weight but continued to lean against the wall. Tito's focus went from baseball to the streets of Santo Domingo. Tito removed one of his baseball bats from the bag slung over his shoulder.

Tito tensed four feet away when the figure turned to face him. The figure pulled the wide brim of his hat over his eyes to block the sun and shoved his leather-gloved hands into the side pockets of his trench coat. The adrenaline surged through Tito and reminded him of the many fights on the Dominican streets.

Tito dropped his bag, tightened his grip on the bat and approached the figure with aggression in his eyes. "I will fuck up your hat on your head if you don't answer me," Tito said.

The figure did not move or respond to Tito. He stood motionless with his head down and hands in his coat pockets. Tito scanned the building for any security cameras before he was in range to swing the bat.

The figure lifted his head. Furnace-red eyes peered out from beneath the brim of the black Spanish Córdoba hat. Tito could not discern any other features about the figure, only the red eyes that bore into him.

The figure lunged toward him.

Tito turned his waist and swung for the figure's head.

The figure's baleful red eyes narrowed when Tito swung the bat. The figure's gloved hand intercepted the bat mid-swing with no sign of discomfort. The figure tightened its grip around the barrel and shattered the bat. A sharp pain shot through Tito's arm, causing him to drop the splintered remains of the bat.

The street-smart kid became the prey. Tito could not look away from the eyes that glowed with the intensity of a steel foundry. His limbic system pumped adrenaline into his bloodstream, but he could not move. The leather hand around his throat tightened as the figure lifted him from the ground with one hand. He shut his eyes; his entire body went limp like an overcoat on a coat rack.

Tito gave up while suspended in the air. He had no fight left in him. He succumbed to defeat and prepared for the worst. The figure sensed capitulation and let go of his neck. Tito felt the solid ground beneath his feet. He tried to run and yell at the figure, but he stood motionless with no control of his physical body.

Tito saw the creature remove a package from his coat and thrust it toward him. He clutched the package like a ball caught in the outfield as the force knocked him to the ground. He cowered on the ground as the figure stepped over him. Tito saw the figure lumber toward the shade of the parking garage. The coal-black duster billowed out from around the figure as the breeze increased from the storm on the horizon.

CHAPTER 16

PANNED OUT PROSPECTS

AN ASIAN MAN in a bespoke blue suit observed the storm clouds gather from the head of a mahogany conference room table in the owner's suite.

"Ethan, did Tito arrive at the stadium?" the Asian man asked with an annoyed tone.

"Yes, sir, when I called him he answered from his car in the parking lot and I have no new text messages from him," Ethan said.

"Good, I don't have the patience or desire to wait on anyone to include my best player. Ethan, open the window to the field so I can hear the sound of batting practice," the owner of the Houston Astros said.

Ethan loathed the way Jim, the owner of the team, ordered him around when he was not on the team's payroll. Ethan retrieved the remote for the window on the table and pressed the button. The motorized mechanism lowered the window in silence and exposed the stadium suite to the sounds of practice on the field.

"Jim, what do you think will be worse, the meeting with Tito today or the afternoon storm on the horizon?" the manager of the team asked.

Jim swiveled his leather executive chair toward Eric and leaned forward. Eric, I like Tito. He brought us three World Series titles and a slew of playoff runs, and I see no reason not to keep him. Jim opened a leather portfolio on the table with Tito's performance numbers. Check out his stats, best in the National League and a negligible decline from last year. His jersey sales exceed the next five players combined in the league," Jim said.

"People flock to the stadium any day of the week when we are in town," Ethan said.

Eric tugged on his beard as he thought of the tasks to accomplish before the start of the season. "Jim, you don't interact with him on a daily basis and notice the intangibles that do not appear on a spreadsheet. These intangibles waste my time and impact the morale of the team," Eric said.

An obese middle-aged man out of breath stumbled into the suite and disrupted the conversation. He clutched a cracked leather briefcase in his left hand.

"It is about time you showed up for the meeting, Dominic. Did you oversleep from your afternoon nap after the buffet feast?" Eric asked.

Dominic removed his Jacket. Sweat stains under his arm pits and shoulder blades became visible when he draped the jacket with enough fabric for a sailboat over an empty chair at the table. "I don't see all members of this meeting in attendance. His agent is here to cover for him because he is drunk and can't attend the meeting," Dominic said. Dominic jutted his double chin and scowled at Ethan.

Ethan opened a can of root beer and took a sip. "Dominic, why don't you relax with a cold soda?" Ethan asked.

Dominic glanced at the sugary smorgasbord of various juices, sodas and other snacks on the other side of the room, but he chose not to exert the energy to get his own soda. Instead he turned his attention toward his briefcase and removed various documents.

"We know your position with Tito, Dominic, since you caught him with your sister-in-law last year at the Christmas party," Jim said, amused.

"Any last thoughts on the subject, Eric?" Jim asked.

Eric poured himself a glass of water from a pitcher with the Houston Astros logo. "My position has not changed. Attendance at the stadium will decline and television ratings will suffer when the fans discover the true nature of Tito. We could have missed the playoffs last year because of Tito," Eric said.

"You can't pin everything on Tito; it's a team sport. The high-priced pitching prospects who you endorsed were a bust last year," Ethan said.

"Ethan, we agree his performance metrics are MVP quality, but you forget Tito's antics away from the field: the fighting, substance abuse allegations, and dissension in the locker room.

He no longer mentors the young crop of rookies and belittles anyone when their numbers decline through the season," Eric said.

"He lashed out at team mates with violence and could have killed the catcher," Dominic said.

"Violence, yea right, the pitcher threw at him in the batter's box and the catcher said a racial slur before the pitch. Isolated incidents, with no other physical altercations on the field or in the locker room," Ethan said.

"He has been on suspension, hence the reason no other acts of savage violence have occurred," Dominic said.

"Stop the exaggerated drama, Dominic," Ethan said.

Eric stood up from the table and walked over to the window to observe his team on the field. "Jim, this is the subjective element you don't see in the numbers. A leader of the team would not club his catcher with a Louisville slugger or charge the mound against his own pitcher," Eric said.

Dominic removed his briefcase from the table and placed it on the floor next to him. "We were lucky no one received an injury that ended their career, or worse, because of Tito's overt aggression toward him team," Dominic said.

Eric paced the room and vented more frustration with Tito.

"Tito is the source of my grief. His personal problems take me away from my place on the field with the team. Sir, with respect, get rid of Tito before the season. Shop him around to other teams before we lose any more trade value from the brawl on the field," Eric said.

"Sir, Eric has a point. If Tito lashes out at a player on another team or a fan, we will have serious legal consequences," Dominic said.

"I have heard enough. Dominic, call security and have them send Matt and Jeff to the executive suite. The flag in center field fluttered in the breeze. Ethan, did you convey our concerns and the possibility of a trade to your client?" Jim asked.

"Ethan rubbed his eyes before he spoke. I did, sir, in various conversations. I have mentioned your concerns and the team's concerns, but I have not per your instructions mentioned to him what might occur at this meeting," Ethan said.

A member of the security team entered the room and informed the group that Tito was in the elevator with his batting practice bag.

"What? Why would he have his bag with him? The bag could contain guns or he intends to hit us with a bat. It is only a matter of time before he turns on us," Dominic said with a frantic voice.

"Dominic, relax and don't provoke Tito. I'll take the lead from here,"

Jim said.

Tito entered the suite and scrutinized the room. He appeared nervous and acknowledged no one when he proceeded toward the other end of the table, away from the group. Tito dropped his bag on the floor, slumped in the chair and faced the open window.

Everyone had the same thought. This guy looks shaken; he is not his usual stoic self.

Does he know? Both the owner and manager looked at Ethan to discern any cues between him and Tito for any sign the agent tipped his hand to his star client.

Ethan got up from his chair and walked toward Tito. "You okay, Tito? May I offer you a soda or water?" Ethan asked.

"I am good," Tito said.

Jim observed Tito's behavior and did not speak.

Tito swiveled his chair to face the group and traced the inlaid Houston Astros logo along the edge of the table before he spoke to the owner. "Jim, I apologize for my delay today. I ran into an excited fan on the way up to meet you," Tito said.

Tito's calm demeanor and apology stunned the group, including Ethan.

Jim stood up from his chair. "Tito, I am glad you acknowledged the fan. This franchise owes you a debt of gratitude for your sportsmanship, work ethic, and determination to win championships, but I have had to make a difficult decision for our team today," Jim said.

Tito continued to slouch in the leather chair and gazed at the lightning in the distance.

"Tito, effective today, you are suspended from the team, and we will not renew your contract," Jim said.

A silence hung in the air. Everyone waited for the explosive Tito temper but he remained calm. He showed no indication of anger or any emotion.

"Tito, did you hear what the owner told you?" Ethan asked.

"Yes, I understand. Thank you for the opportunity to play in the Major Leagues, Jim. You believed in me, and I had a great time with this organization. You're the matatán," Tito said.

Tito stood up and reached for his bag.

Everyone tensed, except for the owner who took a step toward Tito.

"I respect your decision, sir," Tito said with the bag slung over his shoulder.

Looks of astonishment crossed the table as the group did not believe Tito's professional attitude. Previous meetings erupted in profanity-laced tirades at whoever angered Tito.

"Oh shit, he's going for a gun!" Dominic screamed as he tripped over his briefcase in his haste to exit the suite.

Tito, surprised at Dom's reaction, dropped his bag on the table. Security moved to flank Tito, but Jim motioned for them to stop.

"You take care, and if you need help with anything, please let me know. Thank you for your professionalism and your tip about the leak in our organization," Jim said. Jim extended his hand toward Tito.

Tito shook the owner's hand and smirked at Dominic's struggle with gravity to get up from the floor because of his immense girth and atrophied muscles.

"We confirmed what you told us," Jim said.

"Glad I could help, sir," Tito said. Tito took a seat when Jim walked toward the door with security.

Dominic pulled himself up from the floor and opened a folder, out of breath. "I have documents for you to sign before you leave our organization, Tito," Dominic said.

Tito's nostrils flared, and his eyes locked onto the fat man across the table.

"Screw you, *pariguayo!*" Tito said.

"What the hell did he call me?" Dominic snorted in disgust.

"I called you a fool," Tito said.

Jim stopped at the door and turned toward Dominic. "Security, escort Dominic out of the building," Jim said.

"What, what did I do?" Dominic asked with a look of panic-laced guilt.

"You compromised our organization with the sale of sensitive data about our farm system and, effective immediately, you are no longer part of this organization," Jim said.

"This is a conspiracy. I do not understand why you would make these false accusations," Dominic pleaded. Tears welled up in his eyes as security escorted Dominic away from the suite begging for a second chance.

"What the hell happened, Jim? We inform Tito of a trade and you fire Dom on the same day?" Eric asked.

"I kept the information about Dominic to myself because I did not know if others in my organization were part of the plot. Tito, take the next few days to gather up your things and say goodbye to the players and staff," Jim said.

Thank you, sir," Tito said.

"Eric, you and I need to discuss the mess Dom might have created for our organization over dinner tonight," Jim said before he left the room.

"Who told the owner about Dominic?" Ethan asked.

"I told Jim about Dominic and his plan to sell information about our team," Tito said.

"How did you find out about Dom?" Eric asked after he sent a text to his wife about dinner with the owner.

Tito smiled as he recalled Dom's sister-in-law. "You remember Dom's sister-in-law?" Tito asked as he propped his feet on the table.

"Say no more. I don't want to know," Eric said. Eric shook his head in disbelief and left the room. Only Tito and Ethan remained in the suite.

"Are you okay, Tito?" Ethan asked. "Everyone thought you would go ballistic after the owner told you he would not extend your contract."

"I need time to myself. Let everything sink in," Tito said.

"Sure thing, no problem," Ethan said before he got up from the table to leave the room.

Ethan turned around to face Tito before he exited the suite.

"Why didn't you inform me of Dominic's scheme?" Ethan asked, concerned his client might have other information he did not want to disclose to him.

"Jim told me to tell no one. He needed to be certain other traitors did not exist in the organization," Tito said.

Don't worry about the trade. I'll take care of the details and contact the Chicago Cubs first," Ethan said.

"I know you will," Tito said.

Ethan shook his head as he shut the door to the suite. *I bring him the most lucrative contract in baseball for ten years, resolve issues with the team, and he refuses to show any emotion toward me*, Ethan thought.

Tito could hear the crack of the bats from his former teammates on the field. He knew this would be the last time he would be in the owner's suite at the Houston Astros spring training facility. He considered a visit to the field to say goodbye to his teammates, but instead threw the remote on the table out the window of the suite.

Tito unzipped his batting practice bag and removed the package he received from the figure. His heart rate increased as his mind replayed the incident. He noticed the contrast of the ornate penmanship of the red script on the glossy black wrapping paper and ran his finger over the gold-leaf coat of arms. He removed the wax seal that secured the paper and felt a sense of dread when he recognized the goat indentation in the wax.

One of the few memories he had of his mother was her belief in the island superstitions of spells cast by witches. She told him stories about "bakas" or evil spirits reincarnated in the form of goats and summoned by witches. Tito did not believe in such superstitions. His curiosity about the contents of the package guided his hands instead of an evil presence. He removed the red silk ribbon and lifted the lid. He peered inside the suede-lined ebony box and saw a lustrous red silk bag. The sky darkened with the approach of the storm outside the stadium when he reached into the box to retrieve the item.

Tito reached into the red silk bag. The moment his fingers touched the cracked leather, he felt a cold presence in the room. He removed his hand from the leather object and the emotions dissipated.

He scrutinized the red silk bag on the table for a few minutes before he mustered the courage to remove the object. His instinct told him to toss the bag out the open window of the suite, but he ignored his gut. He removed the item wrapped in the same silk fabric as the ribbon.

A crack of thunder echoed near the stadium and startled him as he placed the object from the silk bag on the table. An icon of a goat head burned into the cracked leather cover, like a cattle brand, mystified him.

A red glow seeped from the edges of the leather cover. Curious about the source of the red glow, he traced the outline of the edge of the cracked leather cover and opened it to reveal a tablet device.

Ornate Spanish calligraphy in deep crimson materialized on the screen. It read: "Congratulations, we chose you to play a round of golf at the most exclusive golf club in the world. All expenses covered for four days to include transportation to Goat Trails Golf Club."

Goat Trails Golf Club? What an odd name, Tito thought. He did not recall the name of the golf course in any of the blogs or magazines he followed about golf.

He swiped his finger across the tablet to access any apps on the device, but the screen did not transition away from the text. He instead searched for Goat Trails Golf Club on his own smart phone and found no evidence of the course on the internet.

The red text of the invite vanished and a goat head with the same design on the leather cover appeared, but this image had more detail. The red eyes of the goat followed his movements. The image on the screen changed again to depict a tunnel. At the end of the tunnel he saw an image of the earth rotate on its axis. He felt weightless and disconnected from the suite as the earth rotated on the tablet screen. The rotation of the earth stopped and the image centered on North America. His ego bristled with anticipation of the exclusive opportunity. A digital thumbprint icon appeared on the display.

"Tito Cruz, please place your thumb on the tablet for authentication," a woman's voice said from the tablet.

Tito followed the instructions and the icon on the screen vanished in a cloud of digital smoke. The sound of Sergei Rachmaninoff's "Isle of the Dead" played through the tablet speakers as an image of an obelisk with esoteric symbols materialized on the screen.

"Congratulations. We look forward to your visit, Tito Cruz. You will receive further instructions once you sign the non-disclosure agreement, but most importantly you must not discuss this trip with anyone, or we will revoke your chance to play golf. You have twenty-four hours to review and sign the document," the voice from the tablet said.

Tito's stomach churned from the odd nature of the invite and the anonymity of the entire process, but he signed the document despite his gut instinct. Instructions on the screen informed him of the date, time and location he was to meet for transportation to the golf course. A second message on the screen advised him to pack one small carry-on bag and his golf clubs.

Hail pelted the stadium bleachers and the sound of rain outside caused him to look up from the tablet. An afternoon thunderstorm unleashed a torrential downpour on the stadium. The grounds crew struggled to secure a tarp over the infield because of the strong gusts of wind.

Tito looked at the tablet again, but the images, text and red glow vanished. He depressed the power button, but the tablet remained dark. Tito closed the cracked leather cover and slid the tablet into his bag.

A gold chain with a crucifix dangled from his watch when he removed his hand from his batting practice bag. He held the cross in his palm and remembered when the missionary couple from the states gave it to him as a kid. He thought he had lost the necklace.

An incoming text message interrupted his thoughts. It stated that Dominic had died in a freak traffic accident when a shipping container came loose from a truck and crushed him in his car at a stoplight. Tito deleted the text and put the necklace in his pocket.

CHAPTER 17

A CHANGE IN THE GULF STREAM

THE COLONEL NOTICED THE DESERT LANDSCAPE beneath the private jet on its final approach with disappointment. Dilapidated hangars and abandoned buildings became visible as the plane descended toward the runway.

"Stewardess, what is our location?" The colonel munched on a piece of celery in her Bloody Mary. "It looks like we did not leave the combat zone," she said.

"We traveled thirteen hours nonstop, and we are far from where we picked you up yesterday," the stewardess said.

"You have not told me of our location," the colonel said with impatience.

"Colonel, you slept for most of the flight. Would you like to freshen up before we land?" the stewardess asked.

"No, dammit; answer my question! I want to know our location, stewardess, and if you don't tell me I will go ask the pilots," the colonel said.

The stewardess took a seat in a leather chair across from the colonel with an insolent look before she smiled. "Colonel, please remain in your seat until we land, and do not bother the pilots. Once we land, a member of our staff will answer your questions," the stewardess said.

The colonel felt uneasy in the stewardess's presence because of her model looks and refined manners, but her instincts about the stewardess also made her feel uncomfortable. Most people didn't intimidate the colonel, but the stewardess made the colonel feel inferior despite her profession as a stewardess.

"Fine. I thought we would be over blue water on our way to Hawaii or the Italian Alps, but I see dismal sand outside the window," the colonel said.

"You will enjoy the course accommodations. When the cabin door opens, please proceed toward the red carpet and meet the other guests," the stewardess said.

"What other guests?" the colonel asked.

The stewardess ignored her question and walked toward the galley.

The windows in the cabin went opaque the moment the plane landed on the runway. The colonel depressed the button on the window to make it transparent, but it did not respond. "Could this be a terrorist plot to kidnap me?" she wondered. She checked her cell phone and discovered she had no service.

Her thoughts became muddled as she thought of the "what if" terrorist scenarios. She breathed in shallow breaths as she glanced around the cabin for a weapon. She swiped a marble obelisk sculpture from an end table and hid it next to her.

Why did I accept this invitation? No one knows where I am and I don't know my location, she thought to herself as she struggled to think of a plan.

The plane stopped taxiing on the runway. She tried the window again, but it remained opaque.

The pilots have control of the windows from the cockpit, she thought. The cabin door opened, and she gripped the marble sculpture.

"Colonel, we have landed. Please follow me," the stewardess said.

The colonel walked toward the entrance of the plane with the stewardess and saw the closed cockpit door. She took a deep breath before she stepped outside of the airplane.

"Colonel Askeri, we hope you enjoyed your flight, but I don't think you intend to take any souvenirs with you," the stewardess said. The colonel placed the sculpture in the stewardess's hand.

"It fell over when we landed, and I did not want it to break," the colonel said.

"Watch your step on the stairs and have fun this weekend," the stewardess said. The cabin door closed behind the colonel.

The colonel stepped forward onto the portable stairs that connected to the fuselage of the plane and she could not believe the sight in front of her. A cavernous military hangar twice the size of a football stadium extended well beyond the nose of the plane. An American flag draped from the support beams on the opposite end of the hangar appeared small and blurred with her perfect vision. The hangar did not have the standard bright halogen lights common in other military hangars. Instead, the lights resembled oil lanterns from the nineteenth century. The low light made it difficult to see very far in front of you. The colonel took her time on the steep stairs with her worn tennis shoes.

"Hello, Colonel; it is an honor to meet you. My name is Cyrus," a gentleman dressed in a tan bespoke British suit said. Cyrus offered his hand to the colonel to help her with the last step.

"I can manage myself," the colonel said, startled by his presence. She pushed aside his outstretched hand and stepped onto a red carpet that extended beyond the plane.

"As you wish, Colonel. The other members of your golfing party will be pleased you arrived on time," Cyrus said.

"Who are these other golfers? I did not see a golf course on the approach. Can someone tell me our location?" the colonel asked in rapid-fire succession.

Cyrus ignored her questions and allowed her to catch her breath before he led her away from the aircraft on the red carpet. The colonel stopped and noticed three people sitting at a table. Waiters dressed in formal attire stood to the side of the dining table and attended to the guests' requests for more food or drinks.

"Turn on some lights in this place. It is too dark in here," the colonel ordered.

"The dim lights help with jet lag," Cyrus said.

"Cyrus, tell me more about the other golfers before I meet them," the colonel said.

"You will play a round of golf with Dr. Sean Matson, a plastic surgeon from San Diego, Senator Jack Seavan from Virginia, and Tito Cruz, a Major League Baseball player with the Houston Astros," Cyrus said.

"Senator Seavan, of the Armed Forces Committee? Why did you choose him to play a round of golf with me? Besides his oversight of the military, we have little in common.

"You have more in common than you know," Cyrus said. His smile revealed a perfect set of white teeth, iridescent in the dim glow of the hangar. "Please follow me, and I shall introduce you to the other guests," Cyrus said. Cyrus offered his right arm, bent at the elbow and with his forearm parallel to the floor, but the colonel ignored the archaic gesture of chivalry.

Tito Cruz and Dr. Sean Matson both stood up when Cyrus and the colonel approached the table. The senator remained seated and gorged himself on *foie gras* appetizers.

"Hello, Colonel. Surprised someone of your background received an invitation," the senator said as he licked his fingers.

"My background, what do you mean by my background?" the colonel asked.

"I could understand a general or an admiral invited to play at this exclusive course, but a colonel? I assume a last minute change because someone more important canceled. It is a disappointment we waited for a common army colonel for over an hour who is not a member of the Special Operations Community or a pilot," the senator said. He beckoned a waiter for more food.

"Pay no attention to him. Consider yourself lucky you did not have to endure his company for the past hour. He has complained about the lack of cell phone service, the food selection and the substandard conditions for a United States senator," Tito said. The doctor offered a chair for the colonel. The senator let out a loud belch and continued his assault on the plate of food.

"Cyrus, where the hell are we, and what time do we play golf?" Dr. Matson asked.

"Gentlemen, allow the lady to indulge in food and drink before I answer your questions," Cyrus said.

"Cyrus, the food can wait. I want to know our location," the colonel said. Cyrus checked his vintage watch before he informed the golfers of their location.

The golfers arrived at an abandoned Cold-War-era secret Air Force base. During the Cold War, the base tested captured enemy aircraft and exotic experimental aircraft for the US military. The base closed after the Cold War, but the airfield and basic aviation services remained operational for military and civilian use in Arizona.

"We landed in Arizona? I thought those mountains we flew over today looked familiar. I remember them when we traveled to play the

Diamondbacks," Tito said.

"Good observation, Mr. Cruz. We landed in Arizona, but the golf course location is in a remote part of the state you have never seen from the air or the ground," Cyrus said. A waiter arrived with a plate of fresh seafood for the colonel and a glass of wine.

"The most exclusive golf course in the world resides in the barren desert of Arizona," the colonel said, disappointed. She took a sip of wine and responded with a 'Hooah!' in approval of the taste.

"First time you tried an expensive wine, Colonel?" the senator asked.

"Senator, it would be impressive if any of you have tasted a 35K-dollar bottle of Château Cheval Blanc from the Bordeaux region of France," the doctor said.

"That bottle costs 35K?" the senator asked in disbelief.

Tito poured the colonel another glass of wine from the vintage bottle and one for himself and said, "If it is worth that much, better pour a glass because it will not last long between the colonel and me," Tito said.

"Your transportation for the final leg of the journey will be here in ten minutes," Cyrus said.

"Final leg of the journey? We did not arrive at our destination?" the colonel asked.

"Cyrus, get on with it and spare us the details," the senator interrupted. The senator gestured with his fork in the air at Cyrus.

Cyrus resisted the temptation to berate the senator's poor table manners.

"The golf course does not have road access or an airstrip and is about one hour away from the hangar in very rugged terrain," Cyrus said.

"I don't like the sound of this remote location," the colonel said

"You have nothing to fear, Colonel. Enjoy the food and conversation," Cyrus said. Cyrus excused himself from the group.

"What is your job in the Army?" Tito asked the colonel.

"Intelligence work," the colonel said.

"Wow. Very cool. So you're a real life James Bond or Jason Bourne?" Tito asked.

Before the colonel could respond, the senator almost choked on a piece of lobster while he laughed at the image of the colonel as an assassin spy.

"Don't let her spin any tales about her Hollywood adventures. Believe me, her job lacks any glamour or Hollywood action. I would know; I've traveled to combat zones, observed US military operations, read numerous classified reports and received intelligence briefings in theater," the senator said with a smirk.

"Your understanding of the military consists of budget reductions and destroyed careers of officers you parade on Capitol Hill before bogus war crime inquiries. You care more about terrorists' rights instead of our own soldiers," the colonel said.

"Colonel, enjoy the wine and food. You can tell the doctor and me about your top secret missions later," Tito said.

"It will give her more time to embellish her drab military life," the senator said.

"Relax, Senator. Give her a break. She arrived from a combat zone without the praetorian guards you travel with," the doctor said.

"A toast to the colonel," Tito said. The doctor and Tito both raised their glasses to the colonel, but the senator ignored the toast.

The colonel, disgusted with the senator, excused herself from the table after the toast.

"Too bad she is not attractive, but I like how she takes none of the senator's crap," the doctor said.

"I don't follow politics, but I would not vote for him if I lived in Virginia," Tito said.

Cyrus emerged from the shadows and smiled at the gluttonous senator.

"Box this food for me to go, Cyrus," the senator said. The senator snapped his fingers and pointed at his plate of king crab legs and dessert.

Tito saw Cyrus clench his fist before he spoke to a waiter to attend to the senator's request.

"Do you guys hear a low rumble in the distance?" the doctor asked.

"It is a thunderstorm in the distance. We can't see the daylight cooped up in this building like cattle," the senator said.

"I hear the noise again. Everyone, quiet," the doctor said.

Soon they heard the deep, low pitched sound that resembled a low rumble. The noise increased in intensity with each minute. They could not pinpoint the exact direction of the sound.

"The sound you hear is the aircraft for the last leg of the journey," Cyrus said.

"I don't recognize the aircraft in the distance," the colonel said.

"Hey, Senator, do you recognize the aircraft, since you make frequent trips on the taxpayers' tab to your vacation home in the Hamptons?" the colonel asked.

"Envious of my travel options, colonel?" the senator asked. The senator rose from the table and wiped crumbs and other debris from his feeding frenzy.

Two attendants shuttled the guests' luggage on a trolley toward the massive hangar doors.

"You will see your transportation soon enough," Cyrus said.

The sound abated until the hangar shook and vibrated in a violent manner as the aircraft hovered above the building. The noise and vibration stopped. The hangar walls relaxed and settled on the foundation. The sound of aircraft turbines subsided and cued the hangar doors to slide open and reveal a futuristic aircraft painted flat black with a red goat symbol on the fuselage.

The aircraft resembled a cross between an airplane and a helicopter. The unique combination of two rotors on top of the fuselage and a pusher propeller at the rear of the aircraft enabled it to gain altitude vertically like a helicopter and cruise like an airplane. The ground crew attendants placed chock blocks under the wheels, and a fuel truck arrived to fill the aircraft's parched fuel tanks. Two pilots with black flight suits and helmets exited the aircraft.

"Are we on the set of a movie about special operations?" Tito asked.

The doctor removed his cell phone from his jacket pocket and snapped pictures of the futuristic lines of the aircraft.

"Hey, Colonel, does the Army use one of those to hunt insurgents?" Tito asked.

"You should ask the senator, Tito; he is responsible for why the Army does not have a similar aircraft in their inventory," the colonel said.

The doctor and Tito turned toward the senator.

"Is that true, Senator? The military wanted to purchase this aircraft?" the doctor asked.

"I am not familiar with any aircraft the Army attempted to purchase," the senator said with a vapid look.

"If you read the procurement reports, you would have recognized the similarities between this aircraft and the Army prototype, but you accepted bribes from the competition to squash the program," the colonel said with a look of disgust.

"The colonel is correct, Senator. This is the civilian version of the program canceled with the influence of the senator," Cyrus said.

"Why does it continue to fly if my committee canceled it?" the senator asked.

"Your committee might have canceled the military version, but we convinced the company to produce a commercial variant of the aircraft," Cyrus said. Cyrus donned a pair of black gloves an auto enthusiast would wear for track time and dark sunglasses before he stepped from the shadows of the hangar into the afternoon sun.

"Better the private sector waste money on it instead of the military," the senator said.

"After this flight, you might change your mind about the military version, Senator," Cyrus said.

The senator laughed and smirked at the colonel. "Unlikely; I will cut more of the Army's budget when we are in session," the senator said.

"Follow the yellow line on the tarmac and board the aircraft through the open door on the fuselage," Cyrus said.

The ground crew gave the thumbs up to Cyrus when the occupants and their luggage were on board the aircraft.

Cyrus leaned into the cabin and said, "Enjoy the adventure."

"Cyrus, you are not going to the course with us?" Tito asked.

"I only travel at night," Cyrus said. Cyrus nodded to one of the ground crew and slammed the door shut on the aircraft.

"Seems odd he had gloves on to walk us to the aircraft," Tito said to the colonel.

"It is their safety protocol. The ground crew wore black military-style uniforms with helmets and gloves," the colonel said.

CHAPTER 18

FIRST TIME FLYING SOBER

THE PILOT SCROLLED THROUGH A SERIES OF PREFLIGHT CHECKS on the cockpit display, and the copilot monitored the engine revolutions to prepare for takeoff. The occupants of the aircraft admired the plush accommodations of the interior. Each captain's chair contained a fifteen-inch display screen tucked in the armrest that folded out on the side of the chair for movies, music or to monitor the flight progress.

"The quality of the materials reminds me of my Bentley," Tito said. Tito reclined his chair into a makeshift bed and prepared for a nap.

"Your Bentley lacks the power to do this," the pilot said on the intercom. The vertical blades clawed toward the heavens and released the aircraft called "The Raider" from the pull of gravity. The extra insulation kept the engine noise to a minimum, and the guests did not have to wear headsets to talk to each other. Windows on both sides of the aircraft offered each guest their own view of the desert landscape, but the windows lacked the dark limousine tint of the cockpit windows.

"Welcome to Goat Trails Golf Club Executive Services. My name is Annabelle, and my copilot is Olivia. If you have questions, please press the intercom button on your chair or text us from the display screen. The flight will last an hour, so relax and enjoy the flight," the pilot said.

"Does this bird have a bar with mixed drinks for the flight?" Tito asked.

"The aircraft lacks a galley, bathroom or stewardesses on board, but the scenery will more than make up for the lack of drinks," Olivia said.

"My first time flying sober," Tito said.

"Senator, please don't smoke cigars or cigarettes on the aircraft," Olivia admonished from the cockpit.

"How did they know I enjoy air travel with a good cigar?" the senator asked, dumbfounded.

"They have cameras in the passenger compartment and saw you about to light one up without the consideration to ask us if we mind or if we would care to join you," the colonel said.

"My mistake, Colonel; sometimes I don't notice my new golfing buddies," the senator said.

"Annabelle, this is Colonel Askeri. The flight profile on my display indicates our airspeed is 300 miles per hour heading for restricted airspace. Do I have a faulty display?" the colonel asked.

"Colonel, our onboard diagnostics show your screen checks with no issues," Olivia said.

"How can you identify restricted airspace on your display?" the senator asked. "My map is blank."

"Bring up the navigation display; the red area is the restricted air space, Senator," the colonel said.

"I don't think they intended to change course," the doctor said.

Wow, did you feel that sudden drop in altitude?" the colonel asked.

"You will not believe what is outside our windows, Colonel," the doctor said. The doctor enjoyed the display of precision flying outside his window.

Wow, why do we have to fly so low to the ground? the colonel thought. *We might crash into one of the Joshua trees.* "Captain, why have you not deviated from our current heading?"

"Colonel, ask the pilot why I have no connectivity on my phone," the senator said.

"Senator, the restricted airspace is the cause of your lack of cell phone coverage," the colonel said.

"Restricted airspace? We entered restricted airspace? I order this aircraft to change direction toward the nearest airfield to comply with US aviation laws, the Patriot Act and national security," the senator stammered.

Both pilots laughed at the senator and played a game of rock, paper, scissors to decide who would respond to the irate senator and colonel.

"Looks like you lose, Olivia. You tell them," Annabelle said. Annabelle increased power to the engines and slalomed through the Joshua trees.

"Colonel, Senator, we have special clearance to fly this part of the restricted airspace to reach the golf course," Olivia said. Both pilots enjoyed the colonel and senator's expressions on the closed circuit camera feed in the passenger compartment.

"It does not excuse your reckless flying," the colonel said.

"Annabelle flew Cobra attack helicopters for the Marines to include a stint as a test pilot. She is more than qualified to fly above a few cacti in the desert," Olivia said.

The colonel chewed on her fingernails, annoyed her rank and position could not influence the situation. She detested the civilian world for its lack of respect for military protocol and procedures. Annabelle might as well have never served since she did not retire from the Marines.

"I will submit a formal inquiry with the FAA and both of you pilots will lose your license to fly," the senator said.

"That is enough, Colonel and Senator; leave the pilots alone," the doctor said. "Annabelle, have you or Olivia played the golf course?" the doctor asked.

"Yes, we have both played before our current jobs with the company," Annabelle said.

"Can you tell us more about the course?" the doctor asked after he stowed his display screen in the armrest.

Shouts of joy from the colonel interrupted the conversation. "It reminds me of a roller coaster," she said.

"I hate roller coasters," the senator said as he reached for his air sickness bag.

"Quick, wake up Tito; he can't miss this," the doctor said. Only the doctor and the colonel enjoyed the steep climb in altitude.

"Ten minutes from our destination and I recommend you look out your window," Olivia said.

The colonel and doctor could not believe the scenery outside the aircraft windows.

"Tito, wake up and check out the scenery," the colonel said.

Tito continued to snore with his headphones on, oblivious to the doctor or anyone else.

"Senator, tap Tito on the shoulder, and wake him up," the colonel insisted.

"Do it yourself, Colonel; I am busy," the senator said. His head and neck resembled a vulture while he pecked notes on his cell phone about the restricted airspace.

"Fine, I'll do it myself," the colonel said,

"Colonel, stay in your seat," Annabelle said over the intercom.

"Senator, put the phone away and enjoy the view," the colonel said. The senator ignored her and the unique desert landscape outside the aircraft.

On one side of the aircraft, open desert expanded toward the horizon. On the other side of the aircraft, a colossal rock formation jutted up from the barren landscape. The rock formation resembled a massive medieval castle with sheer rock faces worn smooth from the seasonal monsoon rains.

"Captain, why do we spiral up the rock formation? We took plenty of pictures. Let's fly past it and get to the golf course," the colonel said.

"Patience, Colonel; we have to reach the top of the rock formation," Annabelle said.

"The top of the formation? Who would build a golf course on the mesa?" the colonel asked.

"You will see," Annabelle said.

"Did we arrive at the golf course?" Tito asked.

"You're awake. Look out your window," the colonel said with excitement.

"We have not arrived at the golf course?" Tito asked. "Wake me when we land."

"Ah, come on, Tito; you will miss the impressive view," the colonel said.

"What is impressive about sand and cacti?" Tito removed his headphones and looked out the window. "Wow, why didn't you guys wake me? Nature knows how to create masterpieces," Tito said.

"I told you it was impressive," the colonel said.

The aircraft continued up and around the massive rock formation until it reached the top of the mesa. The colonel noticed they had not left restricted airspace, but the latitude and longitude coordinates no longer appeared on her display. She attempted to recall the last coordinate she saw, but she could not remember the digits.

The aircraft transitioned to a hover and descended toward the open chasm like an elevator. The rock formation could fit four NFL stadiums side by side with room to spare.

"The rock formation is hollow?" the baseball player asked.

"Yep, best part of the trip," Annabelle said on the intercom. She focused on a windsock perched on a ledge and made subtle corrections as the aircraft descended toward the bottom of the rock formation.

"A hollow rock formation sounds like the perfect hideout for a James Bond villain," the doctor said.

"Glad you stayed awake, Tito?" the colonel asked.

"We are on the devil's elevator to the center of the earth, or worse, hell. I have a bad feeling about this," Tito said.

Lush vegetation encircled the inside of the rock formation and sprouted from natural terraces carved into the rock wall. The aircraft came to a rest on an outcropping of rock inside of the formation.

"Welcome to Goat Trails Golf Club. Once the blades stop, you can exit the aircraft," Olivia said.

Annabelle went through a post-flight checklist while the guests disembarked the aircraft.

The world inside the rock formation did not compare to the desert landscape they had flown over earlier. An oasis of such pristine splendor rivaled the garden of Eden on the inside of the rock formation.

Tito plucked a blade of grass from the ground. *This is very soft, lush grass, perfect for an outfield,* he thought.

From the heliport ledge, the guests could see a vibrant valley floor with streams that meandered under a canopy of trees.

"How high do you think we are?" the senator asked.

"At least a thousand feet from the ground," Tito said. He backed away from the ledge and walked toward the aircraft as the other members of the group approached.

"Afraid of heights, Tito?" the senator teased.

"It would be tragic if you slipped and fell because of the lack of a safety rail, Senator," Tito said.

Tito climbed into the open door of the aircraft and saw his headphones on the chair where he had left them. One pilot turned toward him with an open visor on her helmet. Tito froze; his mind attempted to make sense of what he saw behind the pilot's visor. Olivia, startled by his presence in the aircraft, reached up with a gloved hand and shut the visor to conceal her face. Tito made the sign of the cross, a gesture he had not done in years.

"I saw nothing—honest," Tito said. He moved toward the exit of the aircraft with caution.

"Did you change your mind about the trip?" she asked.

"No, I left my headphones," he said. His outstretched hand trembled with the headphones.

"Sure you did, Tito. Do you want our phone numbers?" Annabelle asked with sarcasm.

"I think it's best you join the group, and I would not mention anything you saw here to your new friends," Olivia said.

"See what?" Tito asked, his voice meek and hollow with no bravado or confidence.

Tito backed out of the aircraft with caution. Both pilots ignored Tito and laughed while they finished a series of preflight checks.

The door slammed shut when Tito exited the aircraft. He took one last look through the cabin window, but it went opaque before he could see inside the aircraft.

He turned toward the other three guests who gathered along the ledge and saw three black Bentley SUVs drive up the graveled road toward the group. His street instincts told him to run, but his curiosity about what other secrets lurked among the bucolic scenery overruled his instinct.

"Hey, our ride is here!" he shouted to the others. The other three guests saw the two vehicles stop equal distance from each other at the exact time, and the driver side doors opened simultaneously on both vehicles as if choreographed. A pair of tall well-dressed men who could have passed for a presidential security detachment complete with dark sunglasses and communication ear pieces exited the vehicles. The first driver opened the passenger door of the lead vehicle. The third vehicle did not stop but drove toward the aircraft.

"They don't appear armed, but their movement suggests former military," the colonel said.

"Great. Surrounded by more military," the senator grumbled.

"You might learn about selfless service the more time you spend with the military," the colonel said.

The senator ignored her comment and pointed at the person who exited the passenger side of the lead vehicle.

"He does not appear to be former military," the senator said.

Tito observed the third vehicle where two similarly dressed men unloaded their luggage and golf bags from the aircraft.

An older gentleman with gray hair that matched his impeccably tailored charcoal gray suit ambled toward the group.

"Hello, distinguished guests. I am Mr. Smilodon, the Director of Goat Trails Golf Club," he said.

The colonel studied the man's face to ascertain his age. The wrinkles suggested an older gentleman, but his eyes shone with a bright green intensity instead of the sunken orbs of someone in their twilight. He had a full head of hair and moved without pain, stiffness or struggled movements from poor posture. She noticed the crisp white collar of his dress shirt with sophisticated ruby cuff links that matched his silk tie and pocket square. She was most impressed with his black leather shoes polished to a mirror finish without a spec of dirt.

Mr. Smilodon shook hands with the guests. When he smiled, the guests noticed his brilliant white teeth and oversized canines. Not one person could maintain eye contact with him. Each person felt uncomfortable or guilty in his presence despite his warm personality.

"Before we leave for the lodge, please help yourself to the facilities," he said. His outstretched hand with manicured nails gestured toward a Bhutanese-style building across from the vehicles.

"Colonel, did you see the building when we landed?" the doctor asked.

"I notice every detail of my environment," she said.

"Well, I did not notice the building, and if I had your James Bond training the world would look different indeed," the doctor said.

"Mr. Smilodon might have conjured it out of the thin air," Tito said.

The colonel looked at the building and thought to herself, *how could I have missed it when we landed?*

"Can we hurry and get to our accommodations? The travel has exhausted me," the senator said.

"Senator, you and the doctor will ride with me in the first vehicle. Colonel, you and Tito will follow in the second vehicle," Mr. Smilodon said.

"Nothing has changed, Tito. The two African Americans travel in the second vehicle, and the white guys take the lead vehicle."

Tito buckled his seat belt and adjusted his headrest before he responded, "I am Dominican, Colonel."

"You okay, Tito? You've seem aloof since we landed," she said.

He considered describing what he witnessed in the aircraft to the colonel but changed his mind. "I am ok," he said.

The black aircraft lifted into the air as the convoy of luxury vehicles meandered through a gravel road from the heliport to the valley floor.

"Hey, Doctor, switch places with me?" I want to take pictures of the valley, not this rock wall.," the senator said.

"Senator, keep your seat belt buckled. You can take pictures on the way home, or I can text you some of mine," the doctor said.

"Thanks a lot, Doc. I thought you came from better stock than our other two guests, but you're no different either," the senator said.

The senator lied; he loathed any successful person in the private sector. He considered them tax cheats who obtained their wealth through tax schemes and other corrupt business angles to steal from the common man and deny the government its fair share. He also detested the doctor for his urbane presence and good looks.

Mr. Smilodon observed the senator in the rearview mirror and spoke to the driver in a language unrecognizable to the senator or the doctor. The senator lit a cigar and rested it in a crystal ashtray while he scrolled through his text messages.

"Smilodon, why doesn't my cell phone work here? I have had no signal since we left the drafty hangar," the senator said.

"The mineral content of the rock formation negates the ability for wireless devices to work. It wreaks havoc with any digital device, and line of sight with a satellite can be a challenge on the valley floor," Mr. Smilodon said.

The senator looked dumbfounded but was too proud to ask for a further explanation.

Mr. Smilodon sensed his confusion and said, "Remember your recent trip to South America to inspect the condition of the mines owned by a US corporation?"

"Yes," the senator said. *How did Mr. Smilodon discover my trip?* the senator thought.

"The forest canopy blocked your phone's line of sight and prevented the signal from the satellite to reach your phone. A similar situation occurs here at the lodge."

"How did you find out about my trip to South America, Smilodon?" The senator's scowl deepened the lines between his eyes.

"A member of my staff called your office to inquire about your schedule."

"With whom did he speak?" the senator asked. The senator detested the public or anyone who inquired into his business.

"He said his name was Jerry, and he answered our questions." Mr. Smilodon could see the senator's pudgy face turn red from the anger he felt.

"My travel arrangements are none of your business or anyone's business, Smilodon. The stupid public does not need access to the daily activities of the Senate," the senator said.

"Senator, we meant no harm. We understand your busy schedule, hence the reason to find a window of opportunity to offer you the invitation." Mr. Smilodon positioned the sun visor to block the sun through the side window.

The senator clenched his fist while he listened to Mr. Smilodon. "I need my cell phone to work so I can stay up to date on events inside the Beltway, Smilodon," the senator said.

"The clutter of the connected world does not breach the impenetrable walls of Goat Trails Golf Club. Enjoy the tranquility, Senator," Mr. Smilodon said.

The doctor enjoyed the senator's frustration and added his own jab to the conversation. "So much for the plan to send you the pictures I took from the heliport, Senator," the doctor said.

"Screw you, Doc! I hope you don't wake up from your nap. How long have you served as the director of the lodge, Mr. Smilodon?" the senator asked.

"Sometimes it feels like an eternity, but I enjoy the job," Mr. Smilodon said.

"How did you obtain your job at the golf club?" the senator asked.

"I also received an invitation to play a round of golf. The course invigorated my spirit and the first class accommodations felt like home. So, I inquired about a job."

"You built a career in the hospitality business?" the doctor asked.

Mr. Smilodon paused for a few minutes as if in deep thought before he responded. "The hospitality business chose me," Mr. Smilodon said. He removed a well-worn red skull cap from his jacket pocket.

"Are you Jewish, Smilodon?" the senator asked after he noticed the object in his hand.

The caretaker's eyes narrowed before he responded in a proud tone.

"No, *Sanctae Romanae Ecclesiae cardinalis.*"

"What did he say?" the senator asked.

"His Eminence said, 'A cardinal of the Holy Roman Church.'"

"Excellent, Doctor; very few understand Latin in this age. In accordance with canonical law, I retired when I turned seventy-five years old, and this opportunity has filled the void since," Mr. Smilodon said.

"Your Eminence, how do you stay so young?" the doctor asked.

"Please, I have no use for titles anymore—a lesson I learned well from my employment at Goat Trails Golf Club. 'Mr. Smilodon' will suffice. Mark Twain once said 'golf is a good walk spoiled,' but I disagree. Life at the lodge keeps me young and insulated from the vices of the world," Mr. Smilodon said.

"The secret to a long life includes being marooned in a remote location and playing a lot of golf?" the doctor asked sarcastically.

"Unfortunately, I did not negotiate a salary to cover the cost of a daily commute via helicopter. The club offers other perks to make up for the loss of freedom," Mr. Smilodon said. Mr. Smilodon held the skull cap for a few minutes and recalled the memories of a different era. The driver spoke in a strange language not recognized by the occupants and Mr. Smilodon put away his skull cap.

"Thank you, driver," Mr. Smilodon said.

"I neglected to inform you about an attaché case we have for each of you located in the seat pocket in front of you." Mr. Smilodon paused and spoke in an ancient language to the driver. Both laughed. Mr. Smilodon continued, "The contents contain an itinerary for the next four days and additional information we compiled about each of you. Think of it as our dossier on each of you," he said with amusement.

The senator plunged his pudgy hands into the seat pocket for the item. The attention to detail, the quality of paper and the luxury pen engraved with the date of the golfers' visit next to a goat head logo displayed true first class treatment.

Mr. Smilodon smiled when he noticed the senator's familiar scowl appear after he read his dossier.

"Smilodon, I need to speak with you in private when we reach the lodge," the senator said.

"Senator, we are among friends; you can speak openly in the vehicle," Mr. Smilodon said.

"I would prefer to speak with you in private, Smilodon."

"Is it about the dossier?" Mr. Smilodon asked with amusement.

"Yes, Smilodon."

"As you wish, Senator."

The doctor removed his bespoke pen from the attaché case, slipped it into his sport coat pocket and did not bother to read the contents of his folder. "Mr. Smilodon, I look forward to the next four days," the doctor said.

CHAPTER 19

THE LODGE

The road from the heliport led to a vibrant forest on the canyon floor. The well-maintained trail provided a peaceful view of the idyllic scenery. Lush green fairways, emerald greens, and raked sand traps with a Zen-rock-garden appearance spread out across the canyon floor. Topaz blue ponds fed by natural streams dotted the golf course. Hundreds of goats grazed on the outcroppings around the course.

"Driver, do you have any information you can share about the six-foot-tall black obelisks scattered around the valley?" the colonel asked. The driver seemed agitated when the colonel inquired about the stone statues.

"Relics from an ancient civilization," the driver said.

The vehicles passed a group of goats gathered close to the road. The driver of the vehicle with the colonel and Tito licked his lips when he saw the goats.

"How long have the goats lived on the property?" the colonel asked.

"I don't have an answer. I took them for granted. The name of the course is in honor of them though," the driver said.

The gravel road disappeared under a driveway of cobblestones that led up to the lodge. The great building resembled a ski lodge with Bhutanese-style architecture. The exterior walls of the building stood thirty-one feet from the ground without windows or any ornamentation. The facade shimmered from the intensity of a setting sun. Above the massive stone walls, the architecture opened with a ring of Moorish-shaped windows and balconies that overlooked parts of the golf course. Above the balconies, a band of stucco walls twenty-two feet in height separated the balconies from a Mediterranean-style roof. Thick wood beams extended past the eaves of the roof and provided load-bearing support and space for decorative carvings.

"Welcome to Goat Trails Golf Club," the driver said. He parked the Bentley underneath a car port in front of a massive wood door stained cherry red. The entrance to the lodge was big enough for an SUV to pass through with extra clearance.

"Hooah, home for the next four days!" the colonel exclaimed. She admired the fountain in front of the entrance, comprised of jagged boulders and carved stone goats with meticulous detail at various levels on the rocks. The fountain sculpture resembled a miniature mountain.

Bellhops dressed in tailored suits with tails trimmed in red and top hats greeted each guest.

Tito made the sign of the cross when he saw the goat head logo seared into the red carpet that extended from the driveway to the building entrance.

The senator noticed the colonel shivering from the cool air and asked, "The little soldier can't take the cool air?"

"Bet you could not survive one hour in the cold, Senator, despite the layer of blubber you have to keep you warm," the colonel said in response.

"The senator's gut could feed a mountain lion for a week," the doctor said. Tito and the colonel both laughed at the doctor's comment despite the senator's look of disapproval.

The group turned their attention toward Mr. Smilodon, whom waited for them at the lodge entrance.

"Please follow me, to escape the clutches of the cool air," Mr. Smilodon said.

Two attendants on cue tipped their hats toward Mr. Smilodon and, with the precision of white-gloved marines at the White House, opened the doors to the lodge. Simulated medieval torches flanked the lodge entrance and kept the shadows at bay.

A massive fireplace made of stone with a hearth big enough to accommodate the four guests side by side occupied the center of the room. The warmth from the fireplace rushed forward like a Roman formation to repel the cool air that infiltrated the lodge from the open entrance.

The immense fireplace provided permanence to the room. To the right of the fireplace a grand staircase carved from stone twisted toward the second floor rooms. The interior of the lodge resembled a ski lodge nestled on top of a mountain. It exuded warmth, but shadows hugged the corners of the room and competed with the light from the windows on the second floor.

The four guests followed Mr. Smilodon into the lobby and stopped in front of an oval-shaped glass table with beveled edges perched on carved stone legs with a centerpiece of blood-red flowers arranged in a crystal vase. A chandelier hung above the table. Its wrought iron branches extended outward, each end caped with a simulated torch with LEDs instead of flames. Soot blackened the ceiling from an earlier time when oil lamps lit the room.

The crackle of the fire and the clicking of Mr. Smilodon's shoes on the marble floor provided the only sounds in the room. The atmosphere of the room conveyed a sense of two opposing forces struggling to dominate the space in the lobby: one force exhausting as it pulled you toward the ground; the other rejuvenating as it lifted you toward the sky.

Two women dressed in stylish red uniforms stood behind the check-in desk and smiled at Mr. Smilodon and the guests.

"Please go check in with the staff. You will have an hour to relax in your rooms, but meet me by the fireplace at six," Mr. Smilodon said.

The senator waited for the other three guests to walk away before he spoke to the director of the lodge in a serious tone. "Smilodon, we have to talk."

"What troubles you Senator?" Mr. Smilodon asked.

"I read my dossier, as you call it, and found it full of lies and half-truths. I want to speak with the owner about this libel," the senator said.

"Senator Seavan, the owner is not interested in this inane discussion about your dossier because you know the information in the dossier is not fiction but the truth," Mr. Smilodon said.

The senator despised Mr. Smilodon's deliberate mispronunciation of his name with a hissing noise. "You don't treat a senator this way without repercussions, Mr. Smilodon. It would not surprise me if a few of my inquiries into the business practices of this lodge lead to audits and legal proceedings on behalf of the federal government," the senator said.

Mr. Smilodon shook his head at the arrogant ignorance of the senator before he seized the senator around the shoulders and drew him in close so others could not hear his words. Mr. Smilodon's arm draped heavy, like an iron bar wrapped in flesh on the senator's shoulders as he tried to escape Mr. Smilodon's grasp.

"We know about your professional life: the embezzlement of campaign funds, offshore accounts for foreign governments to deposit cash in exchange for favors and other unsavory things detrimental to the country you claim to selflessly serve. We know about the web of deceit you have constructed, anchored by murder and blackmail. You are not the apex predator you believe yourself to be, Senator," Mr. Smilodon said.

Mr. Smilodon released the senator from his hold but remained in the senator's personal space.

The senator became enraged and shouted at Mr. Smilodon, "You don't threaten a senator of the United States without serious consequences!"

The other three guests, startled by the senator's outburst, saw him six feet away from Mr. Smilodon. His arms flailed as he pointed his corpulent finger at Mr. Smilodon.

"I will not tolerate insubordination, Smilodon. I want to speak with the owner of the lodge!"

"Senator, we also know about your personal life, so let's enjoy the four days and keep the owner out of this. We only mention these things in the dossier because we strive to keep our location a secret. We each have our own secrets. Think of this as privileged information shared between two colleagues to establish trust between two influential forces of nature," Mr. Smilodon said.

The director of the lodge moved closer to the senator and made him feel uncomfortable.

The senator's power, influence and connections did not bend reality to his will at the lodge. The moment he accepted the invitation, he became a worm on a hook, suspended over the boat and unaware of what lurked in the abyss below him. The senator accepted the circumstances for now.

"Mr. Smilodon, pardon my behavior. The more time I spend away from the people's work the more anxiety I have," the senator said.

Mr. Smilodon did not speak or offer any sympathy or understanding toward the senator.

"I appreciate the invitation to play at this exclusive golf course and want both of our secrets to stay in the dark," the senator said. The senator's shoulders slumped, and he no longer appeared confident.

"Well said, Senator; no need for you to check in. We have reserved the

presidential suite for you," Mr. Smilodon said.

The senator straightened his posture and puffed out his chest when the director of the lodge acknowledged his ego.

It is about time they extend the proper respect I deserve, he thought to himself. "Smilodon, the presidential suite is perfect for my accommodations," the senator said with a broad smile.

"The least we can do for a senator. Your suite is at the end of the hall at the top of the stairs, room number four. Your thumbprint is the room key. The group meets in an hour by the fireplace for dinner and, Senator, be on time," Mr. Smilodon said.

The director left the senator and ambled toward the other three guests.

The senator did not appreciate how Mr. Smilodon made him feel insignificant, but he detested how the old man remained in control. The senator climbed the stairs and ignored the other three guests.

"Colonel, do you notice anything odd about the fireplace?" Tito asked. He had scrutinized the fireplace while he waited in line at the check-in desk.

"Besides the massive dimensions? No, why do you ask?" the colonel said.

"Look around at the cleanliness of the place, but the fireplace has a layer of dust and the staff appear to avoid the fireplace," Tito said.

"I never identified you as the type of person who concerned himself with the cleanliness of a place. I thought you had a staff to attend to such details at your homes. I would not concern myself with the dirt around the fireplace when the majestic course beckons. You're next to check in," the colonel said.

"Your're right, Colonel, Golf is why we accepted the invitation," Tito said.

The lodge felt comfortable, but an element lingered beneath the opulent accommodations he could not place yet, Tito thought as he approached the woman behind the check-in desk.

CHAPTER 20

SILVER SCREEN

THE SENATOR PLACED HIS THUMB on the sensor with the goat head logo. The eyes of the logo changed from red to green, and the door opened for him. A few steps into the presidential suite and the motion sensor activated the lights in the foyer.

"Hello, Senator, my name is Gavage. I am your butler," a wizened gentleman said in a well-tailored butler uniform.

"Does this place come with a mini bar?" the senator asked.

"The accommodations of the presidential suite are not mini in scale, sir."

The heavy door of the suite was counterbalanced, to avoid slamming shut, and closed with precision behind the senator. The senator followed Gavage into the presidential suite and tapped on a crystal sculpture of a goat on an antique end table.

"You guys go a bit overboard with the goat motifs, don't you, Gavage?" the senator said.

"Senator, the goat is a cherished symbol at the lodge and we honor its presence among the tranquility, but I digress. Please allow me to show you the accommodations of the presidential suite," Gavage said.

The senator breathed in the smell of lavender while he peered through the French doors at the balcony suite above the fourth hole of the golf course.

"Fine, Gavage, if you insist on providing a tour. I'll sip some cognac and smoke a cigar on the balcony this evening," the senator said.

"We decorated your suite in the style of Louis XIII based on your style of taste in this decor," Gavage said.

The senator was intrigued by the paintings of French nobility embellished in gold-leaf frames complete with their own light to optimize the artist's choice of colors.

"You decorated this suite to match my tastes? I am impressed, Gavage," the senator said.

"Many of the pieces look like what I have at my home. How did you know I prefer this style of decor?" the senator asked.

"Senator, we take pride in the details of life, and from this view you can watch the sunsets," Gavage said. The butler ignored the senator's question and opened the thick gold drapes.

The senator noticed the authenticity of the decor, which was unlike the reproductions in his house. He scowled and ignored the impressive view from the window. The 100-inch curved television on the wall surpassed his own television at home.

"Senator, your suite has a full-size kitchen with a bar and your own private wine cellar," Gavage said.

The senator took a seat on a white piano bench and opened the cover to reveal the smooth white and black keys. His pudgy digits fumbled across the keys as he attempted to remember how to play a few of the notes he learned as a child.

"You play the piano, Senator?" Gavage asked with astonishment.

"No, I never had the right teacher!" the senator said. He slammed the lid shut and recalled the disappointment in his mom's eyes when he could not play a complete song after six months of lessons.

"You will enjoy this part of the suite. Please follow me," Gavage said. The butler led the senator through a hallway past the kitchen and stopped in front of a vintage-movie-style ticket booth. The enticing aroma of popcorn lingered in the air.

"Hell, yes, an indoor movie theater. Where do I get the popcorn?" the senator asked. The senator's girth plopped on one of the thirteen leather chairs, and he noticed the framed movie posters of *Cloud Atlas, Groundhog Day, Lucy* and *Apocalypto* on the walls of the theater room.

"Make yourself comfortable. Here is the tablet to control the lights, temperature, volume and movie selection, Senator."

"Gavage, fetch me some beer and a big bowl of popcorn. I'll watch a few war documentaries before dinner," the senator said.

CHAPTER 21

IT'S A KATSUNUMA VINTAGE

The guests enjoyed the tranquility of the warm fire, each lost in their own thoughts as they waited for Mr. Smilodon. At exactly 6:00 PM local time Mr. Smilodon met the golfers. His dress shoes clicked across the marble floor and alerted the guests to his presence.

"The group looks refreshed after your journey today. Please follow me to the private dining room. We have a special feast prepared for you tonight," Mr. Smilodon said. The mirror finish of his black dress shoes reflected the flames from the fire.

Mr. Smilodon led the group through a restaurant decorated in a more contemporary style with warm colors, open spaces and comfortable chairs. A fireplace like the grand fireplace in the lobby, but without the colossal dimensions, clashed with the contemporary décor of the restaurant.

"Hooah! It would be cozy to have dinner by the fire. Mr. Smilodon, light the fireplace for our meal tonight," the colonel said.

"You would not enjoy dinner with third-degree burns." Mr. Smilodon's comment about third-degree burns dumbfounded the guests. "The private dining room entrance is through the fireplace," Mr. Smilodon said. Mr. Smilodon removed the fire guard in front of the eight-foot-tall hearth. "Please follow me," he said as he touched a stone. The stones scraped against each other, and the hearth opened to reveal a spiral staircase carved from stone.

Simulated torches illuminated each step in a yellowish glow.

The medieval dungeon motif gave way to a modern, climate-controlled, well-lit room about 2,000 square feet in size at the base of the staircase.

Three-foot-tall stainless steel racks cradled rare vintage wines along one wall that extended deep into an unlit tunnel. The opposite side of the room contained a cooler chiseled from the rock foundation, stocked with beer that rivaled any beer connoisseur's collection or microbrewery.

"Where is the dining room?" the senator asked. The senator waddled over to the wine rack and picked up a bottle. "The only way I will make it up those stairs is with a bottle from your collection, Smilodon," the senator said.

"Excellent choice, Senator. You have chosen the bottle for the main course," Mr. Smilodon said.

Mr. Smilodon unlocked the stainless steel door to the beer cooler and held the door open for the guests. "This way, Senator; the dining room is through the beer cooler," Mr. Smilodon said.

"This bottle can't be that good. It's from Japan, and I don't like Saki," the senator said.

"The bottle you chose is from Katsunuma, Japan. They produce small vintages at the winery with most of the production reserved for domestic consumption, but a few bottles find their way across the ocean. The bottle you selected is a very rare vintage," Mr. Smilodon said.

"This bottle is a rare vintage?" The senator scrutinized the bottle in the dim light. "This one bottle will not be enough for everyone tonight," the senator said.

"You may drink until your thirst for wine is quenched tonight, senator," Mr. Smildon said.

"What is in the tunnel besides wine, Mr. Smilodon?" Tito asked. The guests strained to see in the darkness beyond the lighted portion of the room.

"The underground catacombs," Mr. Smilodon said. He noticed Tito made the sign of the cross and said a prayer in Spanish in a hushed voice.

"We found no evidence of a crypt in the tunnel, Tito," Mr. Smilodon said. He understood Tito's prayer for protection in Spanish and a glint of anger was evident in Mr. Smilodon's eyes.

The doctor paused before he entered the beer cooler and admired the ancient stone work and touched the smooth surface of the tunnel.

"Mr. Smilodon, whoever excavated this tunnel must have had immense engineering knowledge to bore through solid rock with such precision," the doctor said.

"We can explore the catacombs another time, Doctor. Please follow the colonel through the cooler to the dining room. I thought you would be more interested in the beer selection instead of the ancient catacombs, Doctor," Mr. Smilodon said.

CHAPTER 22

CHEF'S TABLE

THE PRIVATE DINING ROOM could accommodate ten guests at the only table in the room. The table accommodated four people on each side with place settings set for the four guests. The dim lighting made it difficult to notice details of the room beyond the table.

"Please take your seats," Mr. Smilodon said. He stood at the head of the table bathed in the soft glow of simulated candlelight from the crystal chandelier above the table.

"Impressive table setting," Tito said. His hand disrupted the delicately spaced silverware next to him.

"The dark shadows around the table go with the ambience of eating in ancient catacombs," the doctor said. A waiter appeared from the shadows and repositioned the silverware Tito had disrupted.

"Glad you approve, Doctor," Mr. Smilodon said. Tito felt uncomfortable with the formalities of the culinary Stonehenge arrayed before him and discreetly asked the colonel, "What fork do I use first?"

"Follow my lead," the colonel said and pointed at the salad fork. "The dining room is creepy; I can't see beyond the person next to me," the colonel said.

"Concerned with terrorists?" the senator asked. The senator played with an empty wine glass and looked bored. A waiter behind Tito took a step out of the shadows and reached for the napkin on Tito's plate, unfolded it and proceeded to place it on Tito's lap.

"Whoa, easy with the hands. I got the napkin," Tito said as he seized the waiter's wrist before he could place the napkin on his lap.

"As you wish, sir," the waiter said. Tito noticed tufts of black hair protruding from the waiter's pressed sleeves with ruby cuff links.

"Tonight we will indulge your culinary senses with a meal prepared by our own world-renowned chef, but before the meal I will summarize the history of the lodge. After the meal, we will explore the amenities of the lodge and the golf course." Mr. Smilodon said. He motioned for the sommelier hidden in the shadows to pour the wine from the bottle the senator had selected.

"A toast for past, present and future rounds of golf at Goat Trails Golf Club and to our own chef for his culinary masterpiece," Mr. Smilodon said. The guests clinked the fine crystal glasses and noticed a man dressed in spotless chef attire enter the room.

The senator straightened his posture in confidence because he no longer had the fattest gut or shortest stature at the lodge.

"Chef, please announce the menu for tonight," Mr. Smilodon said as he handed his empty plate to a server, who also removed his place setting.

"With pleasure, Mr. Smilodon. Tonight, you shall feast on carrot Wellington with a flaky crust wrapped around a hearty filling of carrots and sunchokes, followed by chestnut soup with seared *foie gras*, farro and pomegranate. Sides of roasted broccoli with aioli and smoked salmon salad with soft boiled eggs and capers. The main course for tonight comprises rosemary lamb chops with tomato coulis and goat cheese," the rotund chef who resembled one of the Three Tenors said.

"Sounds succulent," Mr. Smilodon said. The chef bowed to the guests as a round of applause echoed in the room.

"Your Eminence, if I am no longer needed, may I leave for my brigade to prepare tonight's feast," the chef said.

"Yes, we look forward to your cuisine. We added a few upgrades to the dining room I think you will enjoy," Mr. Smilodon said to the hungry guests.

One side of the dining room opened theater-style curtains to reveal a modern kitchen, with the chef and his brigade the center of attention behind a glass wall for the guests to observe the preparation of the meal.

"Mr. Smilodon, why do the other chefs have dark glasses on in the kitchen?" Tito asked.

"A fad from the kitchens of Europe. I don't understand it myself. The chef allows them to wear the glasses, provided the taste and presentation of the food does not suffer," Mr. Smilodon said.

The smell of fresh bread wafted into the room and preceded two waiters who carried three baskets covered in white linen to keep the bread warm. The senator thrust his corpulent hand into the warm basket of bread and ignored the small silver tongs on a plate next to each basket.

Tito saw the senator's poor table manners and selected a piece of bread from a different basket. The senator slathered a glob of garlic butter onto his bread and bit into it. He spit out the morsel of food that offended his taste buds into his hand and flung it beneath the table. He wiped his hands with the edge of the tablecloth and asked, "Do you have any butter without garlic?" A waiter appeared and replaced the garlic butter on the table with a non-garlic option for the senator.

The colonel, disgusted at the scene she saw, wondered how he could reach a high level in the government with atrocious table manners. He must have learned table etiquette from his attendance at formal dinners inside the Beltway, she thought.

The doctor, also disturbed at the senator's table manners, leaned in toward the colonel and whispered, "I wonder how many poor heads of state from other countries have had the misfortune of sitting next to this buffoon?"

"His table manners alone could unravel years of carefully orchestrated diplomacy and weaken national security more than any scandal or military budget cuts," she retorted.

"I'll drink to that," the doctor said.

"Why the whispered comments?" the senator asked. His face resembled a rat gnawing on a piece of bread with his mouth open at the table.

"I'll tell you later," the doctor said as he savored the fresh baked rolls and ignored the boorish beast at the table.

CHAPTER 23

ONE MEAL A DAY

THE NOVELTY OF THE CHEF'S TABLE soon waned, and the golfers engaged in small talk with each other, except the senator who did not bother to talk with the other guests.

"Smilodon, when will the first course be ready?" the senator asked.

"Patience, Senator; fine cuisine takes time to prepare. This is not a fast food restaurant," Mr. Smilodon said. Mr. Smilodon listened to the colonel's stories of wartime heroics and soon became bored with the tall tales of valor and fabricated stories of espionage.

"Everyone, I would like to give you some background on the history of the lodge," Mr. Smilodon said. The other guests ceased their conversations and turned toward Mr. Smilodon.

"The lodge resides at the center of an ancient civilization much older than the Native American cultures of this region. The early inhabitants stumbled upon this oasis by accident. A hunting party found an entrance in the rock formation to escape a torrential storm. The group ventured deeper into the cave and their curiosity pushed away the slimy tentacles of fear. A lush, vibrant land protected by impenetrable walls of rock rewarded them for their courage to continue through the darkness.

"We believe the discovery of a natural spring hastened the relocation of the tribe. The location's natural protection and abundance of fresh water impressed the tribal leaders. They established permanent residence inside the walls of the rock formation and abandoned their nomadic lifestyle. Stories of strange encounters with beings and creatures mixed with their folklore as the civilization thrived," Mr. Smilodon said. He paused to assess the guests' expressions.

Mr. Smilodon continued to describe the prosperity of the inhabitants after they built aqueducts. The engineering marvels of the ancient world transported underground water hundreds of miles in every direction. The natural spring transformed the desert valley into a fertile farming community that sustained millions.

However, disaster struck at the pinnacle of the civilization and removed evidence of their advanced culture. The desert sands reclaimed the rich farmland that once radiated from the center of the current location of the lodge.

Some of the ancient civilization's wisdom and knowledge lived on through the Native American cultures in the Americas, but most of it was lost with the demise of the civilization.

With a skeptical look the doctor asked, "Any idea how the civilization perished?"

"Excellent question, Doctor. We can discuss that after we feast!" Mr. Smilodon said. Glorious smells of freshly made soup drifted from the kitchen. The waiters placed the warm bowls of soup before the guests.

"Mr. Smilodon, you're not eating soup with us? It smells delicious," Tito said. He breathed in the smell of the soup. The combination of spices and freshly picked ingredients offered a unique fusion of taste.

"Please don't interpret my lack of eating with you as an insult, but I only eat breakfast," Mr. Smilodon said. Mr. Smilodon was satisfied the chef had prepared another culinary masterpiece as he took delight in the guests' enjoyment of their soup.

"Smilodon, your story sounds impossible," the senator said. He soaked a piece of bread in his soup and continued. "I do not recall any lesson on this ancient civilization in school. How convenient no records exist to support your story," the senator said. He wiped the excess soup that dripped from his lips on his sleeve.

"The senator does have a point, Mr. Smilodon. The story adds to the mystique of the lodge," the colonel said. She also thought the story far-fetched and unbelievable.

"Historical accounts of the ancient Hohokam civilization that once occupied this land exist, but the reason for their civilization's abrupt collapse also remains a mystery. Mr. Smilodon's story might have some validity. However, I would like to know who built this golf course. You're not suggesting the ancients from this civilization invented golf, are you, Mr. Smilodon? That would be blasphemy to suggest the Scots did not invent the game," the doctor said in his best Scottish accent.

Laughter from Mr. Smilodon and the guests filled the room. The group continued to discuss the merits of Mr. Smilodon's story, but Mr. Smilodon steered the conversation away from the ancient civilization and toward how golf came into existence at the lodge.

During World War II the rock formation became part of the Manhattan project because of the remote location and abundance of fresh water below the surface. Construction began on facilities to support the project, but too many anomalies interfered with the timeline for completion. Generators failed, equipment broke, workers became ill, foundations poured for buildings cracked and other structural defects plagued the job site. The government tolerated these delays in the schedule because of challenges with other aspects of the program.

However, the government ceased operations when a tunnel built for access to the valley collapsed. The incident killed nineteen men and buried the special equipment to bore through the rock. The government lost patience and shifted the secret operations to other locations.

"See, I told you this place has ghosts," Tito said. Tito made the sign of the cross and did not notice the ire it invoked in Mr. Smilodon.

"Leave your superstitions on the island. Have you witnessed anything to suggest ghosts roam the grounds or any other strange anomalies?" the senator asked sarcastically.

Tito kept quiet about what he had seen in the aircraft. "You're right, Senator. Please continue, Mr. Smilodon," Tito said. He thought of his mother, her superstitions and the possibility she was right.

Mr. Smilodon continued with the story about the origin of the golf course at the lodge. Before the end of World War II a member of the Office of Strategic Services (OSS) reached an agreement with the US government to purchase the valley for one million dollars to include the mineral rights. Only select civilian and military aircraft would have access to the airspace above the rock formation. The OSS operative intended the location as his retirement home away from civilization, but the government had one condition.

The valley would be used to house German scientists and other important Nazis until they received their new identities during operation

Paper Clip. The OSS operative reluctantly agreed to the conditions but requested funds to build the lodge and golf course.

The government never did house German scientists at this facility, but the OSS operative had spent the money in anticipation of the guests from Germany. The secret nature of the golf course and the invitations for a select few to play a round began in the early 1950s at the behest of the OSS operative.

"What is the OSS?" Tito asked.

"My apologies, Tito; I should have explained more about the organization," Mr. Smilodon said.

The colonel interrupted Mr. Smilodon before he could explain the organization to Tito. "The OSS is the predecessor to the Central Intelligence Agency," she said proudly.

Tito nodded in understanding.

"Does the OSS operative have a name?" the senator asked in a skeptical tone.

"His name has been lost to history," Mr. Smilodon said.

The senator rolled his eyes at the explanation. "How convenient his name is also lost to history. It seems like everything is lost to history at this place," the senator said sarcastically.

"He chose to influence events in anonymity. Only a few people knew his name and how he helped defeat the Nazis. He also did not want any monuments or buildings named in his honor," Mr. Smilodon said.

"Who owns the lodge and the land today?" the doctor asked.

"The descendants of the OSS operative own the land through a trust. The trust also provides for the upkeep and maintenance of the property to include the wages for the staff. Another anecdote of interest about this location is that the land might be similar to a sovereign nation separate from the jurisdiction of the federal government and exempt from taxes," Mr. Smilodon said.

"Here we go. The real reason for this lodge to exist is for another tax loophole. Do you know how much we lose in tax revenue every year to tax cheats and loopholes?" the senator asked in anger. He smashed his fist on the table and caused soup to splash onto the white linen table cloth.

"You rake in trillions and squander more money lost to tax loopholes," the doctor said.

"I can't believe the federal government would agree to this agreement.

Hell, this trust should compensate the treasury with interest for the golf course and the lodge since this OSS operative, whoever he is, used federal money to build this place," the senator said in frustration.

"The original agreement between the government and the OSS operative remains in effect for perpetuity," the old man said. Mr. Smilodon enjoyed the senator's loss of composure. Similar outbursts from other government officials who were invited to the lodge had occurred when he told the OSS story.

"I don't believe it! This requires a congressional hearing to sort out in Washington. I will discover the identity of this OSS tax cheat and drag his descendants before Congress," the senator said.

"Who cares about your inquiries, Senator? Let Mr. Smilodon finish the story," Tito said.

The OSS operative fought against the tyranny of the Nazis by infiltrating the inner sanctum of Hitler's cabal. The Allies might have lost the war without his valuable intelligence. Truman and members of the military establishment felt a great deal of gratitude for his heroics and would have offered him anything. The government honored his request to remain in anonymity without any recognition for his heroics besides this lodge.

"Speaking of buildings honoring prominent members of society. Did you break ground on the Senator Seavan Library for Progressive Policy at Columbia?" Mr. Smilodon asked.

Everyone at the table laughed except the senator, who looked at his plate in disgust. "None of you are invited to the ribbon cutting ceremony next month except for you, Mr. Smilodon."

"Thank you, Senator, but the hallowed grounds of academia no longer interest me. But enough talk of the past. The main course is served!" Mr. Smilodon said.

Four waiters brought each guest their food. The heavy drapes drew closed and provided the kitchen staff with privacy for cleaning the kitchen. Mr. Smilodon continued with stories about the OSS operative during the war and the impact he had on defeating the Nazis. Most listened with casual interests. The food, however, provided the most enjoyment.

"This meal is the finest cuisine I have ever tasted. It far exceeds the Michelin-starred restaurants I have visited in the world. The quality of the ingredients and the creativity of the flavors exceeded my expectations.

Another toast to the chef! The only thing I would change about the meal is the choice of a specific dinner guest," the doctor said. The doctor raised his glass in approval of the meal and smirked at the senator who rested his elbows on the table and picked food from his nicotine-stained teeth.

Mr. Smilodon raised his glass at the last remark and said, "A toast to the chef, and may you live long enough to sample his dessert."

"To the chef!" the three golfers said in unison. The senator did not bother to raise his glass.

CHAPTER 24

3D BLISS

THE SOUND OF FANS circulating air increased in volume as the dinner table with dirty dishes and empty bread baskets descended into the floor.

"Hooah! That is how you do dishes," the colonel said in approval.

A series of miniature projectors concealed in the ceiling no larger than a pack of cigarettes created a 3D wire diagram of the lodge and the eighteen-hole golf course in the space where the dining room table once stood. Depth, colors and textures enhanced the 3D wire diagram and created a three-dimensional-scale model in virtual reality.

"Mr. Smilodon, I have never seen such incredible technology in my twenty-five years in the military. Have you shared this technology with the military? It would make an excellent mission rehearsal tool," the colonel said.

"Glad you approve of our cutting-edge virtual reality technology with no 3D glasses, Colonel." He moved the terrain model with his hand to zoom in above the lodge. "I don't concern myself with geopolitics; I manage a golf course."

The colonel crossed her arms and thought to herself, *once again the best toys originate with the private sector and the Army lags in innovation because of budget cuts.*

"Tomorrow is a day of leisure, and you will have access to the spa indicated here in blue," Mr. Smilodon said. He zoomed in on the spa. A representation of the spa entrance appeared in the room.

"Wow. If you wanted to, you could expand the building into a full-size representation of the spa?" the doctor asked.

"Yes, provided the room's dimension exceed the model. Otherwise, the program adjusts the scale to accommodate the size of the room."

"Major Tony Stark technology," Tito said.

"We will not spend too much time on the other amenities of the lodge tonight since your interest is golf," Mr. Smilodon said.

The golfers nodded in agreement. The additional amenities of the lodge included an indoor Olympic-size swimming pool, a gym that exceeded the standards of professional sports teams and miles of trails on the grounds. A new equestrian center with polo fields is under construction and scheduled for completion next year.

"Mr. Smilodon, what do the red 'X' icons indicate?" Tito asked.

"Those mark entrances to the subterranean catacombs below the valley. We ask you to avoid the areas because of the dangerous conditions," Mr. Smilodon said.

"Do you offer rock climbing or spelunking?" the doctor asked.

"Hooah! I have never explored a cave. I would prefer that adventure instead of polo," the colonel said.

"A good idea. I'll inform my staff to look at the possibilities for future expansion."

"Senator, you could donate embezzled money and have a hole in the ground named after you," the doctor said.

"Careful, Doctor, the desert has many holes for the disloyal."

"I look forward to a ride on one of your black helicopters to take me to my hole in the desert," the doctor said.

The senator tensed at the disrespect he felt from the doctor.

"I have no desire to descend into a cave with supernatural entities," Tito said.

"For a professional athlete, you are a chicken," the colonel teased.

"Don't underestimate the supernatural," Tito retorted. He made the sign of the cross and noticed Mr. Smilodon wince.

"Screw this supernatural nonsense," the senator said.

"Senator, consider our state-of-the-art movie theater if the outdoors is not your style of leisure. The most important point: Please return to the lodge before sundown. We restrict access to the golf course after dusk," Mr. Smilodon said.

"Are the areas around the lodge and other buildings off limits tonight?" the senator asked.

"Yes, I recommend you stay in the lighted areas of the lodge for your own safety. The terrain is dangerous at night," Mr. Smilodon said.

"You're keeping us cooped up in the lodge at night to avoid the boogie man that roams the grounds," the senator said with sarcasm.

"No nightlife exists beyond these walls, only wildlife, so I don't mind the indoors," Tito said.

"Don't forget—the Sasquatch play golf at night," the colonel said with a laugh.

"Tito is correct about the wildlife. We have reports of mountain lions on the grounds, but I digress. Let's talk about golf." Mr. Smilodon changed the orientation of the model so the golfers had a perspective from the first tee box.

The simulation enabled the golfers to observe obstacles and the layout of the fairway or the greens first hand. It resembled a first-person view as you walked the course. They could determine if a tree to the right of a tee box impeded a second shot or how a sand trap might affect the approach to the green. The detail of the simulation impressed the golfers, and they understood how this technology could enhance the play of the game but also uproot tradition.

"Mr. Smilodon, the precision of the model lacks only a couple things," the doctor said with amusement.

"And what did we neglect to include?" Mr. Smilodon asked with curiosity.

"The smell of freshly cut grass and the sound of golf shoes on a rain-soaked green," the doctor said. The three golfers laughed, and the senator cracked a smile.

The golfers had access to the latest golfing technology, but they agreed this kit teetered on science fiction. The 3D model rotated and re-created a pebble cart path that led to the entrance of the golf course. A massive stone sculpture of a goat towered over them. This goat statue did not resemble the images on their invitation or various parts of the lodge. Instead the sculpture captured a look of fear in the goat's eyes as if it sensed a predator in the midst. The model also depicted the pro shop, driving range and a red barn.

"Smilodon, zoom in on the barn," the senator said in a tone he used with his staff.

The barn came into view with incredible detail. A thirteen-foot black obelisk stood a few feet away from the barn entrance in a fire pit with orange flames that lapped at the base.

Tito and the colonel both noticed the iron bars that covered the blacked out windows. The barn was an odd departure from the architectural design of the other buildings on the grounds. Steel bars with etched symbols on them similar to the symbols on the obelisk covered the four windows.

"Do you keep the golf carts in the red barn, Smilodon?" the senator asked.

"This course honors the traditional aspects of the game, and we don't offer golf carts to our guests."

The senator groaned and folded his arms, his thick blubbery lower lip turned up. "You expect me to carry my own clubs for eighteen holes? You better have someone carry them for me," the senator said.

"A caddie will carry your clubs and assist with divot repair, raking sand traps, attending the flag on the green and other elements of etiquette on the course," Mr. Smilodon said.

"I hope you honor the tradition of the beer babe in a beverage and snack cart on this course," Tito said.

Everyone laughed except the colonel who rolled her eyes at the remark.

Four members of the staff entered the room and passed out tablets in leather-bound covers complete with the goat head logo like the tablets they had received as invitations.

"These tablets will be your score card for the round of golf, and for this walk-through of the golf course, you may enter notes on the tablet to reference tomorrow," Mr. Smilodon said.

The staff helped the golfers with a series of menus to configure the biometric thumb reader and input physical information about their height and weight.

The colonel interrupted and asked, "Why do we have to enter this data about our physical traits and scan our thumbs?"

"No one mentioned the stakes of the game?" The four golfers looked at each other and wondered if they had missed information in their invitations.

"The winner of the round receives a lifetime membership to this golf course," Mr. Smilodon said.

"Shit. Guess the stakes increased big time," Tito said.

"So much for a relaxed round of golf," the senator said. The senator's competitive alpha traits took over as he sized up his adversaries. "Is it free or do we pay annual dues?" the senator asked in a serious tone.

Mr. Smilodon smiled. "The membership does not have annual fees, Senator. The information entered helps us monitor your performance on the golf course for comparison with other golfers. We also want to reduce the element of cheating because of the stakes of the game. The biometric scanner adds a layer of security, so only you can access your scorecard and other data about the course. Does this explanation sit well with you, Colonel?" Mr. Smilodon asked with impatience.

"You should have mentioned in the invitation that we are playing for a membership to the club," the colonel said.

Mr. Smilodon laughed and said, "We disclosed the opportunity for a lifetime membership with earlier groups, but it changed their demeanor and ruined dinner." Everyone in the room laughed, including the senator.

Each golfer asked specific questions commensurate with their experience and level of play. The senator surprised everyone by his insightful questions of the course. The doctor deduced by his level of knowledge about golf that he may have an advantage over the other golfers. The senator was articulate, poised and very competitive when he discussed golf. He offered suggestions to the other golfers for the best way to approach a shot. The senator's assessment of each hole and insights of the game he shared with the group impressed Mr. Smilodon.

The doctor did not trust the senator or his insights he offered to the group. He thought the senator wanted to rattle their confidence and make them second-guess their own knowledge. Mr. Smilodon offered them dessert and the opportunity to ask more questions about the game or retire for the evening after the virtual tour of the golf course. The four golfers took him up on the offer of dessert and continued discussions about golf.

Mr. Smilodon checked his watch and noticed sunrise was in thirty minutes. "Enjoy your day of leisure today. Tomorrow morning please meet at the red barn at 4:00 AM. If you are late, you will be disqualified from the round," Mr. Smilodon said.

"Mr. Smilodon, before you leave can you explain why we are the only guests at the lodge?" the colonel asked.

"The red 'X's on the map could mark the grave sites of the other guests," Tito said. The others were not sure if his comment was a joke or he was serious.

Mr. Smilodon leaned toward the four golfers and said in a hushed voice, "I will tell you why you are the only guests at the lodge, but you must keep what I will share with you a secret, understood?"

The golfers nodded in agreement and with trepidation. Mr. Smilodon glanced around the room in a serious manner. "The red 'X's on the map are graves from the sacrifices. We have four graves left to fill before the curse is expunged from these grounds," Mr. Smilodon said.

The four golfers looked at each of in disbelief and fear.

Mr. Smilodon and the waiters in the room laughed with amusement.

"The explanation is a joke. Safety is the most important reason for the off-limits areas of the lodge because of the construction this past year. We also limited the guests to four at a time until completion of the project. Your expression made my evening tonight," Mr. Smilodon said.

"Where are the construction equipment or the work crews, Mr. Smilodon," Tito said. He was skeptical of the explanation offered by Mr. Smilodon.

"On hold until after the golf match to avoid disrupting the tranquility of the lodge," Mr. Smilodon said.

He glanced at Tito with a hostile expression, but his smile returned before the others noticed. "I have enjoyed your company and will see you the day of the tournament in front of the red barn," Mr. Smilodon said as he excused himself from the group.

CHAPTER 25

A MUSTY METALLIC SMELL

"DON'T YOU EVER SLEEP, Colonel?" the senator asked. The orange embers from his lit cigarette revealed his location in the ink-black darkness that covered the valley floor.

The colonel struggled to see the time on her watch because of the faint illumination from the digits. "Late as usual, Senator," the colonel said. "I only need four hours of sleep. Anything more weakens the ambition," she said.

"Where is everyone? It's too early to be outside in the miserable dark," the senator said with impatience.

"Senator, watch where you are walking," the doctor said.

"You could have alerted me to your presence. I can't see in the dark," the senator said.

"When did you show up this morning, Doctor?" the senator asked.

"We arrived a few minutes after the colonel," the doctor said.

"Tito is also here this morning?" the senator asked.

"Yep, Senator, and you're the last person to show up as usual," Tito said.

"Any sign of Smilodon?" the senator asked. Orange embers bounced across the cobblestone path when he flicked his lit cigarette.

"Senator, we have not seen Mr. Smilodon. We have been alone in the creepy silence to go along with the darkness. The only sign of life is from the barn," the colonel said.

The senator turned and faced the barn. A dim orange glow of light seeped out of the four covered windows with steel bars. The orange glow from within the barn matched the orange flames that burned at the base of the obelisk.

"Did anyone bother to knock on the barn door?" the senator asked.

Tito stood up and stretched. "A sinister presence lurks inside the barn. Go knock on the door, Senator, since you believe in science," he said.

The streets of the Dominican Republic honed his sense of danger and his instincts told him to leave the lodge. His anxiety increased with each minute as he considered his options. How could he escape the canyon? They had flown in by helicopter, and if he found his way out of the canyon, his next challenge was to traverse the desert on foot without water, provisions or proper clothes.

"Are you afraid of the dark, Tito?" the senator asked.

"Senator, why are you here? Go knock on the barn door," Tito said.

"Mr. Smilodon said to meet him outside of the barn at 4:00 AM. He did not instruct us to knock on the barn door," the colonel said.

"Fine. If you want to stay in the cold darkness, go ahead, but I will wait in the barn for Smilodon," the senator said. The senator took cautious steps toward the barn entrance with his hands in his pockets.

A loud shriek similar to the noises of a zoo pierced the early morning hours.

"Any idea what the hell caused that noise?" the doctor asked.

"I think it came from the barn," the colonel said.

"I told you guys the barn has more than ordinary maintenance equipment for the golf course. Evil lives in that ghastly barn," Tito said.

The macabre noise continued for the next few minutes, followed by the sound of heavy chains dragged across a concrete floor. The senator turned around and increased his pace toward the group after he heard the eerie sounds from the barn.

"I thought you went to knock on the barn door, Senator?" Tito asked.

"You don't hear those noises from the barn? You can go knock on the door, but I will wait for Smilodon right here," the senator said.

Tito made noises like a chicken to antagonize the senator. "I thought you did not believe in the supernatural, Senator," he said.

"Damn, Senator, is that you?" the doctor asked.

"What the hell do you mean, Doctor?" the senator asked.

"An odd musty, metallic smell. I did not notice it until you came closer to us," the doctor said.

"It's not me. The stench is from the barn," the senator said. The metallic odor lingered in their nasal passages.

The doctor took out his handkerchief and covered his nose. "What time is it, Colonel?"

"It's fifteen after four, Doctor."

"I'll be at the gym," the doctor said.

"If you leave for the gym, Doctor, you will miss the introduction to your caddie and a chance to play golf, but if you have other matters to attend pack your things and I will summon transportation for you to go home," Mr. Smilodon said.

Mr. Smilodon's voice and the sound of his shoes on the cobblestone path startled the golfers.

"Good morning, Mr. Smilodon. The gym can wait. Golf is a better choice. I'm eager to play golf is all," the doctor said.

"My apologies, everyone, for my late arrival but breakfast for the caddies took longer than usual this morning," Mr. Smilodon said.

"I hope the second course does not include us," the doctor said. Everyone laughed except Tito.

The senator lit a cigarette to calm his nerves, but he lashed out at Mr. Smilodon with questions after a long exhale of smoke from his cigarette. "What the hell is in the barn, Smilodon? You kept us in the cold long enough, and why don't you have any lights for this part of the lodge. Plenty of light surrounds the other buildings and walkways, but it is pitch black here. You have violated numerous health and safety codes and who knows what other code violations are in the barn."

Mr. Smilodon removed an object from his leather trench coat and ignored the senator's rant. The noise from the barn abated and curiosity displaced the tension in the air.

Mr. Smilodon depressed the button on his radio and static crackled in the air before he spoke.

"Caddies ready to meet their golfers?" Smilodon asked. "I would not smoke anymore today, Senator."

"Why, Smilodon, is it bad for my heath?"

"Smoking in the barn is detrimental to your health. We prohibit tobacco products around the caddies," Mr. Smilodon said.

"This must be a gag to rattle us before the game. They have a laptop with recorded noises and speakers to broadcast the sounds," the colonel said.

Tito held the crucifix around his neck and asked, "How do you explain the smells from the barn?"

Mr. Smilodon's radio crackled with a reply of "Roger. Caddies ready.

"Excellent. Unlock the door."

Mr. Smilodon placed the radio in his coat pocket and, with his other hand, he retrieved a stun gun in the shape of a truncheon from his coat pocket. "Follow me," he said. Purple electricity arced along the edge of the stun gun as he led the group toward the barn entrance. The sound of metal against metal displaced the silence of the early morning void as the barn door opened for Mr. Smilodon.

Dim orange light spilled into the darkness of the canyon floor.

"Avoid any sudden movements and stay close behind me," Mr. Smilodon said. The stun gun crackled to life again with purple arcs of electricity.

CHAPTER 26

A LOST LANGUAGE

A COMBINATION OF DOG KENNEL and slaughterhouse smells overwhelmed the golfers as they entered the barn. Mr. Smilodon did not seem bothered by the stench. The soft orange flicker of real torches illuminated the interior of the barn, but the light could not chase away the shadows that clung to every corner and concealed the details of the room.

The interior resembled the behind-the-scenes areas at a zoo not witnessed by the visitors. The barn was subdivided into well-organized and clean sections for food preparation, veterinarian care and storage. A concrete floor covered the expanse of the barn with a drain the size of a city manhole cover. A Celtic knot design of steel bars covered the drain in the center of the room. The ventilation system provided the only sound in the barn.

"Smilodon, turn on the lights. The torches don't provide enough light to see," the senator said. Mr. Smilodon sensed the senator was scared from the tone of his words.

"Your eyes will adjust. The soft glow of torch light calms the caddies," Mr. Smilodon said. The heavy steel doors slid closed. A loud *thunk* echoed through the barn as the tumblers of the locks fell into place.

"This is a setup; I want out of here! Turn on the lights and open the door!"

"Tito, it is too late. You have committed to this path," Mr. Smilodon said with a calm voice.

"You can't detain me here! Open the door!" Tito said with a panicked voice.

Mr. Smilodon approached Tito without malice. "Tito, take a deep breath and breathe. You are not in danger," Mr. Smilodon said.

"Out of my way; I have had enough of this freak show! Demons are in here, and I want nothing to do with this place!" Tito said. He attempted to push Mr. Smilodon out of his way, but Mr. Smilodon took hold of Tito's arm and positioned it in a joint lock. "Let me go!" Tito yelled in pain. His free hand flailed around to strike Mr. Smilodon.

Mr. Smilodon maneuvered behind Tito, released the joint lock and clamped his hand around Tito's thick, muscular neck and lifted him from the ground. Two figures dressed in black SWAT team attire approached Tito from the shadows. Their faces were concealed by black helmets, and each held five-foot-long staffs that crackled with arcs of electricity. Mr. Smilodon waved them away with his free hand. The arcs of electricity stopped and the guards positioned themselves as sentries by the entrance.

"Shit, should we help him?" the colonel asked the senator in low voice.

"No, he disrespected Smilodon, and don't draw any attention to me," the senator said.

"What could we possibly do to assist Tito, Colonel? Look how easily Mr. Smilodon overpowered a professional athlete," the doctor said. The doctor scanned the room for anyone or anything concealed in the shadows that clung to the inside of the barn.

The colonel felt anger but also confusion about the situation and looked away from Tito in fear.

"Are you finished, Tito? Do you want leave the lodge? If the fear is too much for you, go ahead and quit the chance to earn a lifetime membership to this club. Say the words, 'I quit and I want to go home,' and we will make it happen," Mr. Smilodon said in a calm voice.

Memories of his youth flooded Tito's mind. He had never lost a fight because of his size, and strength trumped any aggressor when he fought for his own survival on the streets of Santo Domingo. Tito breathed in short, shallow breaths, exhausted and immobilized, while he considered the offer. He shook his head, "No, I do not quit, Mr. Smilodon."

"Excellent; your spirit endures," Mr. Smilodon said.

Mr. Smilodon, without any indication of fatigue, lowered Tito until his feet touched the ground. Mr. Smilodon sensed Tito about to fall after he released his grip and caught him before he crumpled to the floor.

"Easy, Tito. You don't have anything to fear," Mr. Smilodon said after he smacked Tito in between the shoulder blades. The hit did not injure or cause pain. Instead, Tito felt energized. The fear and fatigue dissipated through his feet into the floor.

"Do any of you want to leave the lodge? Do you want to return to your familiar routines? Go ahead and tell me you want to go home," Mr. Smilodon asked of the other golfers.

The question hung in the air as the others considered the implications. The curiosity of what other secrets lurked within the canyon walls convinced each one to stay and compete for a membership.

"Good. I like people who compete until the end," Mr. Smilodon said. His incisors resembled fangs as he smiled at the four golfers.

The golfers followed Mr. Smilodon with caution across an image of the lodge's icon painted on the floor. Mr. Smilodon stopped and turned to face the four golfers.

Thirteen cages, each six feet in height, arrayed on the far end of the wall behind Mr. Smilodon came into view when the golfers crossed the icon of the lodge on the floor. Creatures with ominous red eyes swayed in their cages.

Mr. Smilodon spoke in a strange language, and on cue four creatures approached the golfers from the shadows.

Fear immobilized the four golfers the moment they saw the creatures behind Mr. Smilodon. The golfers attempted to reconcile their concept of reality with the sinister creatures only ten feet away. The smell no longer caused discomfort as their eyes absorbed the gruesome images of the creatures. Tito regretted his decision to remain in the barn.

Mr. Smilodon reached his hand toward one of the creatures. His signet ring reflected the torch light as he spoke to the creature in a bizarre language.

"What language did you speak to that thing, Mr. Smilodon?" the colonel asked in a meek voice. "I don't recognize it," the colonel moved behind Tito after she asked the question.

"A lost language no longer spoken outside of these grounds, but in time you might learn to speak the ancient language. Senator, out of respect for your position in society, you should meet your caddie first," Mr. Smilodon said.

"No, I am good, Smilodon; I can wait. Ladies first. Let the colonel introduce herself to the caddie," the senator said. The senator trembled at the sight of the creatures. Mr. Smilodon called caddies.

"Senator, act with courage and meet your caddie. They pose no immediate threat to you unless you allow fear to permeate your spirit in their presence. They thrive on fear and are known to react violently when they sense it," Mr. Smilodon said. Mr. Smilodon felt invigorated from the fear and confusion he sensed from the four golfers.

The creature stood about five feet in height and lumbered toward Mr. Smilodon with movements like an orangutan on two legs. Massive bundles of coiled muscles comprised the creature's legs. The leg muscles could propel the creature into the air or provide short bursts of speed for short-distance sprints.

The creature's arms were twice the length of a human's with much greater muscle density. The creatures dragged their arms behind them with palms up. The hands and feet were armed with razor-sharp nails on the ten fingers and ten toes. The head resembled a canine's but with large pointed ears on top of the head instead of on the side like a wolf or dog.

The creature's deep crimson eyes had a vapid look, a hollow appearance as if the creature was in a trance. The creature's movement suggested it would be more comfortable on four legs instead of two because of the bundle of muscles on its shoulders.

The overdeveloped muscles caused the creature to hunch over instead of walk with an upright posture. Thick and curly matted caramel-colored hair covered the senator's caddie from head to toe. Mr. Smilodon smiled, and his outstretched hands beckoned the other three creatures to stand next to him.

"Golfers, may I present your caddies? The black-haired caddie is 'Azmur.' The brown with white splotches is 'Pooka,' and the charcoal -colored one is 'Shampe.' Senator, your caddie's name is 'Wendingo,'" Mr. Smilodon said with an animated voice.

The other caddies in the cages growled and banged their heads on their cages. Mr. Smilodon spoke with authority in the ancient language, and the noise from the cages stopped.

"These creatures are our caddies? They smell terrible and look horrid," the senator said. The senator covered his nose from the putrid stench in the air.

"These caddies look familiar, Mr. Smilodon," Tito said. Tito held his crucifix with one hand around his neck.

"Well, what do they remind you of, Tito?" Mr. Smildon asked. Mr. Smilodon scratched Wendingo behind his ears as he waited for Tito's response.

Tito said in Spanish, "God protect us from the infamous *chupacabra*!"

"Correct, Tito, these caddies are chupacabra, and we are the only golf course in the world that offers chupacabra as caddies for your round of golf," Mr. Smilodon said with pride.

"This is a Hollywood production. We must be on a hidden camera television show," the doctor said.

"This is such crap; the doctor is right. I bet they are actors dressed up in an elaborate costume. Look, I'll prove it," the senator said.

"Senator, don't. These are not actors," Tito said.

The senator moved toward Wendingo and grabbed him by the arm. Wendingo unleashed a loud shriek that echoed through the barn. The other chupacabras in their cages went crazy and responded with growls and shook their cages. Mr. Smilodon remained calm and spoke in the ancient language to silence the mayhem.

"I don't think this is a costume. This thing feels solid and strong. I can't hold on to its arm," the senator said.

Wendingo stood motionless while the senator pulled on his arm. Wendingo turned toward the senator. His furnace-red eyes focused on the senator's throat. His snout quivered and revealed two blood-stained fangs.

"Senator, if you have not found the zipper to the costume, I would suggest you walk away from Wendingo."

"Shut the hell up, Tito," the senator looked at Wendingo. The caddie opened his mouth to reveal rows of sharp fangs and yellow stained teeth, a detail the senator did not expect from an actor in a costume.

Wendingo's fork-shaped tongue dangled from the side of his snout before it curled into his mouth. A low growl rumbled before Wendingo unleashed a frightful howl. The senator let go of Wendingo's arm and fell backwards onto the concrete floor. His pudgy legs kicked like a frog to get away from the creature. Wendingo approached the senator as the senator scrambled to his feet.

"Senator, don't run away from your caddie. Stand your ground or Wendingo will rip out your spinal column," Mr. Smilodon said.

"Look at him shake," whispered the colonel to Tito.

"I bet he craps his pants," Tito said. Wendingo's red eyes locked onto the senator's pudgy face."

"What the hell is he going to do?" the senator asked.

"Stay calm, no sudden movements," Mr. Smilodon said.

Wendingo poked the senator with a knuckle, his razor-sharp nail curled underneath like a closed switchblade.

"Smilodon, get this smelly thing away from me."

"His name is Wendingo. Tell him good morning, Senator, and don't show any fear," Mr. Smilodon said.

Wendingo's nostrils flared as he smelled the senator.

"When he no longer pokes or smells you, scratch him behind the ears," Mr. Smilodon said.

"Hell no, he has razor-sharp teeth," the senator said. The senator's blubbery lip quivered as he struggled to remain calm.

"Senator, this is important. Show courage and a little compassion for your caddie," Mr. Smilodon said.

Reluctantly, the senator scratched behind Wendingo's ears. "His fur is disgusting. It feels like a dry sponge in a kitchen sink," the senator said.

Mr. Smilodon laughed. "He likes you, Senator."

Wendingo extended his long, hairy arms to hug the senator.

"Aw, he wants a hug, Senator. Go ahead and give him a hug," the colonel said. The other three golfers hoped Wendingo would shred the senator to pieces.

The senator could sense Wendingo's strength, but the overall demeanor of the chupacabra did not reflect his fearsome appearance.

"Nicely done, Senator," Mr. Smilodon said with approval. The senator's caddie sat in the lotus position with his legs crossed and arms folded in his lap next to the senator.

"Golfers, notice Wendingo's behavior. It indicates the caddie has established an initial bond with his golfer," Mr. Smilodon said.

The senator suppressed his first instinct to kick Wendingo as he sat next to him, but he restrained himself because of Wendingo's razor-sharp nails.

The other three caddies moved toward their golfers. "Doctor, this is Azmur. Colonel, meet Pooka, and Tito, meet Shampe. No sudden movements; let the caddies approach you," Mr. Smilodon said.

The more time the golfers spent with their caddies, the more relaxed they became with each other. The caddies' overall demeanor resembled a combination of a golden retriever and two-year-old eager to please the golfers with an abundance of curiosity.

"Why does he keep staring at me? Why is his behavior different from the other caddies, Mr. Smilodon?" Tito asked nervously.

"Sometimes the bond is not established, Tito. A different caddie for you might be required. Give it a few more minutes, but no sudden movements. Let him approach you."

"Yeah, I got it, Mr. Smilodon, but his red eyes have not moved. Do they have quick reflexes, Mr. Smilodon?"

Shampe deftly snatched the crucifix that dangled from Tito's neck and howled in agony before Mr. Smilodon could answer Tito's question.

Shampe jumped into the rafters of the barn, growled and dangled the crucifix for the other caddies to see. With the agility of an acrobat, Shampe bounded from the rafters onto the row of cages with the other chupacabra. Shampe ran along the row of cages as the locked up chupacabra growled and shook their cages with distress from the crucifix.

Mr. Smilodon yelled a command in the ancient language with a formidable voice, and the noise from the agitated chupacabra in their cages ceased.

The caged chupacabras began to sway from side to side in their cages as if in a trance and made no further noises. Shampe lumbered toward Mr. Smilodon with his head lowered and kneeled before Mr. Smilodon in submission.

Mr. Smilodon spoke to Shampe in the ancient language and the chupacabra stood up and trudged toward Tito with the crucifix in his furry clenched fist.

"Take the crucifix from Shampe and tell him in a stern voice, 'No, never again!'" Mr. Smilodon said.

"It happened so fast he could have killed me. I did not see him move until he bolted across the room," Tito said.

"You need to tell Shampe you don't approve of his behavior. Otherwise he will never respect you or respond to your commands," Mr. Smilodon said.

Tito, shaken from the ordeal, said in a stern tone. "No! Never again!"

Shampe sat in the lotus position next to Tito and raised his arm toward Tito with the crucifix in his hand.

"Tito, you're bleeding," the colonel said.

Tito took the crucifix from Shampe and saw blood on his shirt.

Mr. Smilodon ambled toward Tito to look. "It's a small nick. You will be fine. My humblest apologies. Some of the caddies recoil in fear or act out in anger when they see religious icons or symbols. We should have mentioned this to you outside of the barn, but we did not think any of you venerated these trinkets of superstition."

Mr. Smilodon removed two items from a storage bin. "Here, take this ointment and bandages, and go clean yourself up in the bathroom. You will live, Tito. The bathroom is the last door by the entrance," Mr. Smilodon said.

Mr. Smilodon motioned for one of the sentries to follow Tito to the bathroom.

CHAPTER 27

BUTCHER SHOP BLUES

"Don't stop. You have no need to look in that room," the guard said.

The smell of ozone and the crackle of electricity arcs from the staff kept Tito from going into the room. The guard's heavy footsteps caught up to him and blocked most of what he saw in the room.

"What goes on in that room?" Tito asked with trepidation.

"Nothing!" the guard said and slammed the door. "The bathroom is at the end of the hallway! Go clean yourself up and make it quick."

The guard followed Tito into the bathroom and leaned his staff against the wall next to a sink. The guard studied Tito's face. "I thought I recognized you. You're a professional baseball player," he said with excitement.

Tito wanted to immobilize the guard with the staff and flee the lodge, but the threat of the desert on foot convinced him to clean his wound instead. "Yeah, I play some ball. So, what the hell did I see in the other room?"

"What do you think you saw?" the guard asked. He removed his gloves and Tito saw thick tufts of black hair in between his fingers as he washed his hands.

"It's not what I think. I saw a dozen or more goats suspended from the ceiling," Tito said.

"And why is that strange? It's no different than a butcher shop," the guard said.

"A butcher's shop in hell. The goats were deflated and pressed flat. I want to know what happened to those goats," Tito said.

"Talking to you can get me in a world of trouble, but I took the chance because you play for the Houston Astros," the guard said.

"I did play for the Astros," Tito said. He remembered his team and the incident at the ballpark. *It seemed like a lifetime ago,* he thought as he smoothed the edges of the bandage over his wound.

"I also thought about hitting you in the face with my staff because you lost the World Series three years ago in four games," the guard said.

"You want to kick my ass because of a World Series game?" Tito asked. He saw the staff against the wall and rehearsed in his mind what he would do if the guard followed through with his threat.

"I considered it. I lost a lot of money that day," the guard said. He donned his black gloves after he dried his hands and reached for his staff.

"It is a team sport; I don't deserve all the credit for the loss." Tito remembered the day well, the capstone event symbolized his out-of-control life. He struck out at each bat because of the drugs and made multiple errors on the field. "Why did you change your mind about beating the crap out of me?" Tito asked.

"Who said I did? I am only kidding. You brought us three championships in the last five years. I made a boatload of money from those games," the guard said. He smacked Tito on the shoulder as a gesture of respect and nearly knocked him to the ground because of his unnatural strength.

"So you're a gambler," Tito said. His shoulder ached from the guard's friendly punch, and he was nervous about what the guard could do if he intended to hurt Tito.

"Yep, one of the reasons how I found this place. Disconnected from the twenty-four-hour sports cycle is akin to therapy. Today is your lucky day. I'll tell you about the goats. Besides you will find out anyway," the guard said.

Tito turned toward the guard, prepared to fight if necessary.

"The room you saw contains the carcasses before they are transported to the burn pit."

"Burn pit? It does not explain what happened to them," Tito said.

"Hold on. You and the other golfers arrived before feeding time this morning."

The explanation made sense to Tito. The caddies sucked the blood from their prey. "My older brothers told me stories about the goat sucker as a kid," Tito said.

"I have said too much. We need to return to the group," the guard said. He opened the door to the bathroom and stepped into the hallway.

"Any tips on the golf game?" Tito asked.

The guard came closer Tito and whispered, "Yeah, don't win the game."

Shampe's nostrils flared and he extended his arms to hug Tito when he saw him. Despite the stench and the risk of lacerations from Shampe's claws, Tito hugged Shampe. The other caddies and the caged chupacabra howled with approval.

"You good to go?" the colonel asked Tito.

"Yes, considering the circumstances."

"Shampe needs to wear these goggles to protect his eyes from the sunlight," the colonel said.

"Protect his eyes from the light?" Tito asked, confused by the statement.

"The colonel is correct. If the caddies remove their goggles in the daylight, they will lash out in agony as they lose their vision. Here, let me show you how to put the goggles on your caddie," Mr. Smilodon said. He motioned for Shampe to approach him.

"Do they always have to wear eye protection?" Tito asked.

"As they age, their eyes adjust to the light," Mr. Smilodon said. He tightened the strap around Shampe's head and checked the position of the dark goggles.

"So why don't we have those guys caddie for us?" the senator asked.

"They caddie for the members of the club. Enough questions. Let's go watch the sunrise and have breakfast with your caddies," Mr. Smilodon said.

"Do we leave the caddies here in the barn?" the colonel asked.

"From this moment forward, your caddie goes everywhere with you until the end of the golf match."

"How do we control them if they misbehave?" the senator asked.

"Be forceful in your commands like we taught you this morning."

"Let's leave them here while we have breakfast since they have already been fed," the senator said.

"Tradition at the lodge calls for the caddies to dine with the players before the match," Mr. Smilodon said.

A heavy black curtain descended from the ceiling and separated the group from the chupacabra in the cages. The four caddies howled as the dawn displaced the evening darkness. The fresh morning air invigorated the golfers and was a welcome change from the stench of the barn.

CHAPTER 28

ALPHA AND THE CADDIE

CURIOSITY WITH A TWINGE OF DESTRUCTION overwhelmed the caddies the moment they left the confines of the barn.

"Get over here, Wendingo!" Wendingo, oblivious to the senator's commands, dove head first into the freshly landscaped flowerbeds piled high with manure and mulch.

"Five minutes from the barn, and the senator has already lost control of his caddie," the colonel said.

"Keep laughing. It's only a matter of time before Pooka gives you hell, Colonel. Damn it, Wendingo, get over here and don't touch those flowers," the senator said.

Wendingo ignored the senator and continued his assault on the moist flower beds soaked with the morning dew. He pulled up the freshly planted flowers and launched them at the other golfers.

Mr. Smilodon told Wendingo to stop the destruction in the ancient language. Wendingo paused at the mention of his name before he threw the freshly pulled flower at the senator when Mr. Smilodon turned away.

"Stupid caddie; Smilodon told you to stop!" the senator shouted. The senator dodged the tossed flower. Satisfied, Wendingo climbed out of the flower bed. The senator was furious. His face was red with embarrassment because he lacked the ability to control his caddie.

"Smilodon, I hope my caddie's behavior does not reflect on my membership consideration for the club."

"The winner of the golf match determines membership, but if you can't control your caddie on the course it might have an adverse effect on your game," Mr. Smilodon said.

"Exactly my point, Smilodon. If my caddie misbehaves on the course, it detracts from my concentration and ability to remain competitive," the senator said.

"Apply the teachings we taught you this morning. Act like the alpha, and your caddie will obey," Mr. Smilodon said.

The senator, not satisfied with Mr. Smilodon's response, discreetly made faces at Wendingo and gave him the middle finger. Wendingo stood on the cobblestone path with outstretched arms for a hug. His red eyes conveyed confusion as to what he did wrong.

"Get away from me. You're covered in dirt; you don't deserve a hug," the senator said to Wendingo.

The other golfers continued toward the restaurant for breakfast. Their caddies followed with the curiosity of toddlers. They touched and smelled every object in their path without the destructive behavior of the senator's caddie. The three golfers sat at a circular table outside the restaurant that overlooked the golf course. The caddies sat next to their golfers at the table in the lotus position on their chairs.

The senator approached the table with an untucked shirt and his wispy comb-over hair was in disarray. He sweated profusely in the cool morning air and continued to berate Wendingo. Wendingo followed a short distance behind the senator and trounced through the numerous flower beds that lined the walkway toward the restaurant.

"It is about time you joined us for breakfast, Senator," the doctor said.

"Having difficulty with your caddie?" Tito asked.

"Do you have room for me at the table?" the senator asked.

"We can make room for you and Wendingo," Mr. Smilodon said.

"My caddie?" the senator groaned. "Why the hell would I eat with him at the table?" the senator asked.

"The caddies dine with their assigned golfers at the table, Senator. These are not pets relegated to another part of the room when they inconvenience you. Go clean yourself up; you're a mess," Mr. Smilodon said.

"He looks worse than his caddie," the colonel said.

"The walk from the barn to the restaurant is only about 500 feet. I can't begin to imagine what he will look like after eighteen holes," Tito said.

"I don't need to clean up. I'll join you guys for breakfast. Have you already ordered?"

"Breakfast is a buffet, Senator. Use the facilities inside the restaurant, or you will not have breakfast," Mr. Smilodon said.

"Fine. Will someone keep an eye on Wendingo for me?"

"No, Senator. Wendingo goes with you," Mr. Smilodon said.

"Well, save some food for me. This might take a while. Come on, Wendingo. I said move, Wendingo! You stupid beast," the senator mumbled under his breath.

Wendingo followed the senator into the restaurant and shredded white tablecloths with his razor-sharp nails as he walked by the tables in the restaurant.

"Mr. Smilodon, let's eat. We don't need to wait for the senator," Tito said.

"Patience, Tito; you have to see this. You don't want to miss the best part of the morning," Mr. Smilodon said. He checked his watch and donned a pair of sunglasses.

"The best part of the morning is breakfast, Mr. Smilodon, and I can smell the feast," Tito said.

"A few more minutes, and look east," Mr. Smilodon said. Mr. Smildon put on a pair of black leather gloves.

"Wow!" the three golfers gasped in unison.

The sun climbed higher into the sky and dispersed the natural light across the walls of the rock formation. The formation glowed with deep reds, browns and purple hues.

"A front-row seat to watch God paint. No artist can capture colors like these on their canvas," Tito said.

Mr. Smilodon moved his chair to another part of the table that remained covered in the shadows and away from Tito.

The tranquility of the morning was interrupted when the sun startled the caddies and they stampeded toward the shadows to avoid the sun. Pooka swatted a heating lamp on the patio that provided warmth for the golfers when he dove for cover under an adjacent table. The tall, narrow column of aluminum holding the heat lamp above the table bent from Pooka's arm and caused it to become unstable. The heating unit toppled over on an empty table and ignited the table cloth. The colonel frantically doused the fire with pitchers of water, but Mr. Smilodon told her to relax and let the table burn. It was a common occurrence at breakfast. The three caddies cowered underneath the tables of the restaurant, mesmerized by the table fire.

"What the hell happened?" the senator asked after he saw the table on fire. "Let me guess; Pooka did this, huh, Colonel?" The senator laughed.

"Shut up, Senator, and enjoy the sunrise," the senator glanced at the canyon walls and was unimpressed.

The other three caddies climbed out from underneath the tables and rejoined the golfers as the table fire smoldered.

"What time do we tee off this morning, Mr. Smilodon?" the doctor asked.

"Exactly 8:05, at the first hole. If anyone is late or you don't have your caddie, you will be disqualified."

"What about our golf clubs?" the colonel asked.

"Your golf bags are at the driving range so you have plenty of time to enjoy breakfast this morning," Mr. Smilodon said.

The golfers frantically called their caddies to follow them toward the buffet line, but not one budged from the table. The smell of freshly squeezed orange juice and crisp bacon enticed the golfers but not the caddies. Once the colonel managed to get Pooka to follow her into the restaurant, the other caddies followed out of curiosity.

"Amazing spread of food," Tito said. He retrieved a large white plate from the stack next to the buffet line and began to pile food on his plate. "I have conquered some great buffets in my time, but this has the best assortment of food I have seen. The lavish buffets of Vegas can't compare to these options."

"Tito, go around me; don't wait for me in line. And pile your plate to the ceiling with food," the doctor said. He encouraged Tito to load up on food in hopes it would affect his game.

The other golfers felt tempted to indulge in the variety of fresh and exotic offerings, but they did not want to risk their performance.

"Ah hell, can't I get any peace? Shampe is more destructive than a hurricane," Tito said. He dropped his plate of food as he waited for his fresh omelet when Shampe bumped into him. Shampe was startled by the flames from the range and dove for cover underneath a table.

"Wendingo, behave!" the senator yelled after he witnessed his caddie pick up a stack of plates and throw them across the room. The broken dishes smashed on the ground infuriated the senator. He picked up a plate and sailed it toward Wendingo. The plate hit the caddie in the head and caused him to topple onto the pastries section of the buffet.

Pooka burned himself on a heating unit underneath the serving containers and caused a batch of the freshly cooked turkey sausage to spill on the floor. Shampe plucked yogurt containers from a bowl of ice and squished each one between the matted fur on his hands before Tito could intervene. Yogurt exploded on Shampe and the other caddies who joined him in the assault on the yogurt containers.

The golfers managed to salvage some breakfast items and returned to the table, but the caddies' shenanigans continued with spilled drinks, sugar packets ripped open and some of the golfers' breakfast items tossed through the air.

"Doctor, I would not offer your caddie a piece of bacon."

"Why, Mr. Smilodon?"

"They don't consume human food. They feast on a different substance," Mr. Smilodon said.

His comment drew everyone's attention except Tito, who struggled to keep the secret of what he saw in the room to himself.

Azmur snatched the piece of bacon from the doctor and held it up above his head. Azmur's nostrils flared as he breathed in the scent of the bacon and threw it at the doctor. Tito noticed Mr. Smilodon did not eat any food with them.

"Do caddies drink human blood, Smilodon?" the senator asked.

"The caddies obtain their nutritional needs from goat blood and, on a rare occasion, cow blood—they don't consume any human food. When you offered your caddie the piece of bacon, I thought the caddie would recoil in fear because javelinas and domestic pigs terrify them," Mr. Smilodon said.

"Glad I chose a piece of turkey bacon," the doctor said. He took another bite of the bacon in front of Azmur.

The colonel inhaled her pork bacon and sausage before Pooka caught a whiff of the decadent morsels.

"Mr. Smilodon, here; have a piece of my bacon," Tito said.

"I'll pass, Tito. I had a light breakfast before we met this morning," Mr. Smilodon said.

"Damn it, Wendingo; get your fingers out my juice!" The senator covertly removed the butter knife from the table and stabbed it into the caddie's rib cage. He thought Wendingo would jump out of his chair in pain, but instead the senator felt the blade break. Wendingo looked at the senator and grunted while he poured a decanter of water on the senator. The senator, doused in cold water, tumbled backwards in his chair and reached for the table cloth to break his fall but instead caused his breakfast and the empty water pitcher to land on himself. The golfers at the table had a good laugh at the senator's expense.

"Enjoy your breakfast, and I shall see you at the first tee box at 8:05, ready for the game," Mr. Smilodon said.

The senator ignored Mr. Smilodon's departure and slid a piece of bacon toward Wendingo.

"I would not do that, Senator," Mr. Smilodon said.

The senator was startled to see Mr. Smilodon next to him, scratching Wendingo behind the ears.

"Be careful how you treat Wendingo," Mr. Smilodon said before he left the table for the main building. The golfers ignored each other after Mr. Smilodon was gone to mentally prepare for the match. They finished their meals in silence and left with their caddies to the driving range.

CHAPTER 29

SNAPPED IN HALF

EACH GOLFER WENT THROUGH their own practice routine, interrupted occasionally by the shenanigans of the caddies.

"Damn, Shampe, let me practice my chipping in peace!" A cloud of sand covered Tito after his caddie tossed clumps of dirt from the sand trap. "Shampe, get out of the sand trap!" Shampe shook off the sand and took his time to exit the sand trap. "Here, take my club and go clean it for me." Shampe snatched the club from Tito, sniffed it, grunted and threw the club at Tito. "Fine, I'll clean it myself. Go sit in the shade, and don't destroy anything," Tito said.

"May I chip a few from the sand?" the colonel asked.

"Go ahead, Colonel, plenty of room," Tito said. "What happened to your caddie?"

"What do you mean? I gave him my putter a few minutes ago. He is right behind me with my golf bag," the colonel said. She turned around, but he was not there. "Where did he go?" the colonel frantically called for Pooka. "We have to find him before the match begins. Otherwise, I will be disqualified," she said.

"Did you leave him at the putting green? Come on, Shampe, grab my bag. You can rake the sand trap later," Tito said. The caddie grunted, slung Tito's golf bag over his shoulder and followed the two golfers.

"I see him," the colonel said, relieved. "Pooka, no! Drop those flags!" the colonel scolded. Pooka ignored the colonel and continued launching the weighted golf flags from the putting green into the air.

The senator let out a loud stream of profanities as one of the weighted flags crashed into his golf bag.

The doctor found peace and quiet on the driving range as he practiced with his irons. He was oblivious to the mayhem with the other golfers and had no problems with his caddie. Disgusted with the interruptions from the other caddies, the senator left the putting green with Wendingo and found a spot on the driving range. He observed the doctor hit a few golf balls and noted how each swing was flawless.

The doctor will be a challenge on the course today. The colonel lacks consistency, and Tito has copious amounts of power and concentration but his short game will unravel on the back nine, the senator said to himself. He took note of the doctor's drive and corresponding yardage markers on the driving range.

"Smooth swing, Doc. You can unwind a few more yards with accuracy if you don't drop your elbow," the senator said.

"Save your tips for the beginners, Senator," the doctor said.

"Hand me the driver, Wendingo." Wendingo grunted and knocked over the golf bag. "Stupid caddie. Fine. I'll get it myself," the senator said as he picked up the golf bag and retrieved his favorite golf club. The senator felt envious of Azmur because he offered the correct club, cleaned each club after the doctor finished and left the doctor in peace to prepare for the match.

"Wendingo, notice how Azmur helps the doc on the driving range? Why can't you do that for me?" Wendingo looked up at the senator, grunted and flicked broken golf tees at him.

"Worthless caddie," the senator said. The senator's intense concentration and near mastery of the game did not resemble his state of mind in other areas of his life. He addressed the golf ball on the tee with intensive focus and visualized how and where he would hit the golf ball.

"What the hell, Wendingo!" The senator shanked the golf ball when a loud noise distracted him in mid-swing. The senator turned around to see the caddie next to a pile of golf clubs dumped from the senator's golf bag.

"You're a stupid caddie. Put those clubs in the bag!" the senator ordered. Wendingo grunted and reached for a club but instead kicked the senator's golf bag. The golf bag tumbled through the air and landed in the middle of the driving range.

"Wendingo, go pick up my golf bag!" Wendingo looked at the golf bag in the middle of the driving range and ignored the senator's command. Wendingo instead picked up a bucket of water for cleaning clubs on the driving range and dumped it on the senator's golf clubs.

This infuriated the senator, who charged at Wendingo with his golf club raised above his head. Wendingo did not move as the senator closed the distance and screamed profanity at his caddie.

The caddie retrieved the empty bucket next to him and hurled it at the senator. The bucket hit the senator in the center of his chest and caused him to stumble and fall. The senator struggled to get on his feet. With a look of fury in his eyes, he smoothed his clump of thinning hair to cover his bald spot and dusted off the dirt and sod. The senator charged Wendingo again and intended to hit Wendingo over the head with his golf club.

Wendingo stood motionless with a devious grin. The senator swung the club toward Wendingo like a makeshift battle ax, but Wendingo was too quick and snatched the club from the senator.

Wendingo unleashed a deafening growl that caused the other golfers to look toward him. The other golfers saw Wendingo poke the senator in his fat gut with the golf club. The senator thought the worst and pleaded with Wendingo not to hurt him.

Wendingo raised the club above his head in triumph and then snapped the club in two pieces over his furry leg and mangled the club head. Wendingo smiled at the senator, handed him the pieces of his favorite club and shuffled toward the shade of an oak tree on the edge of the driving range.

"A famous golfer gave me this club as a gift," the senator stammered. "It is one of the finest clubs on the market."

A loudspeaker ushered the players to proceed to the first tee box. The senator yelled at Wendingo to pick up his clubs and retrieve the golf bag. Wendingo took his time to retrieve the senator's bag from the driving range. He stuffed the clubs haphazardly in the bag and dragged it behind him as he followed the senator to the first tee box.

"Looks like you taught Wendingo how to organize a golf bag, Senator," the doctor said.

The senator cringed at the sight of his filthy golf bag with clumps of sod stuffed in between the golf clubs that poked out from the bag at odd angles. "Screw you, Doctor," he said. He glared at the doctor while the doctor scratched Azmur behind the ears.

Azmur stood patiently with the doctor's golf bag slung over his shoulder like a proper caddie.

The doctor's clubs were clean and well organized in the golf bag.

"Did everyone have a productive practice session on the range this morning?" Mr. Smilodon asked. No one saw Mr. Smildon approach the group.

"It would have been more productive without my caddie," the senator said. The senator suppressed his anger because of the destroyed golf club.

"How does he do it? He materializes out of thin air. Did you see him approach us from the driving range?" Tito asked the colonel in a hushed voice.

"I paid no attention to Mr. Smilodon. Too busy laughing at the senator and Wendingo," the Colonel said.

This is an easy match to win if Wendingo continues to distract the senator, the doctor thought to himself.

Mr. Smilodon noticed the senator's golf bag in disarray and asked the senator, "You had more issues on the driving range, Senator?"

"His golf bag could pass as contemporary art in some circles. A sculpture that reflects the challenges of the game," the colonel said with a wry smile.

"Smilodon, Wendingo's caddie skills are terrible. I want a new caddie," the senator said.

"Anyone willing to trade caddies with the senator?" Mr. Smilodon asked.

No one in the group offered to trade caddies.

"Senator, the other golfers do not want to trade caddies with you. You have two options: learn to get along with Wendingo or return to the lodge and pack your kit because you will be disqualified if you don't complete the round of golf with your assigned caddie," Mr. Smilodon said.

"I have no desire to quit before the first hole, Smilodon."

"Good. Then it is settled. Wendingo will continue to be your caddie."

"Mr. Smilodon, it is far from settled. I am at a disadvantage because of Wendingo's poor caddie skills. He is a distraction," the senator said.

"Senator, you must make the best of the situation. You are stuck with your caddie. Like I said, if you don't like the arrangement, quit and go pack your suitcase."

"You can't get rid of me that easily, Smilodon. I will win this match and the membership despite this freak show," the senator said.

Mr. Smilodon said nothing and continued to lead the golfers toward the first tee.

Tito noticed Mr. Smilodon sought to walk in the shade and avoid the sunlight at every opportunity.

CHAPTER 30

ELECTRIFIED FENCE

A PAR FOUR WITH A SLIGHT DOGLEG to the left flanked the edge of the canyon and greeted the golfers on the first tee box. Four banners with the lodge logo rippled in the breeze behind a table on the first tee. Two staff members of the lodge stood up behind the table when they saw Mr. Smilodon approach with the golfers.

"Good morning, Mr. Smilodon. A glorious day for golf," one of the staff members said.

"Yes, indeed. Please pass out the tablets to the golfers."

The attendants handed a tablet to each golfer personalized with their name and the logo of the lodge on the red cover.

"These are your digital score cards uploaded with the latest course data for the match. Your tablet also has detailed pictures of each hole along with the distance data for the pin and other information to aid you on the course. If you lose or damage your tablet before the tournament is complete, you will be disqualified," Mr. Smilodon said.

"What is the style of play for the game today?" the doctor asked. The doctor twirled a golf tee in between his fingers while he surveyed the first hole.

"The style of play will be stroke play for today. Your score is the sum of strokes for eighteen holes," Mr. Smilodon said.

"The lowest score wins, Colonel, not the other way around," the senator said in jest.

"I know why you enjoy golf so much, Senator." The colonel said as she took her tablet from the attendant.

"Why do I enjoy golf, Colonel?" the senator asked. The senator's bulbous nose was already buried in his tablet.

"A low score in golf is a good thing, unlike the low scores you received in your academic life."

"Don't forget the low approval ratings for Congress," Tito added.

"Excellent observation, Tito," the doctor said.

"Please put your tablets in your golf bag and pay attention to the next piece of the kit," Mr. Smilodon said.

"We can carry stun guns? No more problems with you," the senator said as he pointed his stun gun at Wendingo. The senator had tortured animals in his youth and the stun gun rekindled old memories. Wendingo's sharp claws and strength tempered the senator's harassment, but the stun gun leveled the field in the senator's mind.

"Yes, Senator, I thought you might enjoy this new addition to the game. Pay attention to the attendant's familiarization of how to use the stun gun, but under no circumstances will you taze each other. We modified the stun gun to work on the anatomy of the caddies. A few seconds of voltage is lethal to a human. Only use the device on a caddie when he threatens you, other golfers or the wildlife. Also, take one of the leather pouches from the table," Mr. Smilodon said.

"A leather pouch of tequila?" Tito inquired.

"Not exactly, but it might be a popular addition for the next round of guests," Mr. Smilodon said.

The golfers' leather pouches contained golf balls, tees, a divot tool, and a leather golf glove, each festooned with the course logo. On the table were four boxes of Snickers candy bars next to leather pouches.

"Any chance we can trade our Snickers for potato chips, Mr. Smilodon?" the doctor asked.

"The Snickers bars are to reward your caddie for good behavior on the course."

"You will not receive any candy from me, filthy demon," the senator said in a low voice to his caddie. Wendingo grunted and knocked over the senator's golf bag.

"Stupid caddie, pick up my bag!" Wendingo shrugged his shoulders and sat on the senator's golf bag.

"I thought caddies don't consume human food," the senator said in disgust.

"True, until we discovered their taste for Snickers by accident. A few years ago, a caddie discovered a Snickers candy bar, and pandemonium ensued. It is the only human food they will fight over or eat," Mr. Smilodon said as he handed Wendingo a Snickers bar.

The caddie sniffed the wrapper in front of the senator and extended one of his claws and peeled the wrapper from the candy bar like a banana. He took his time to chew the candy with his mouth open and devoured the wrapper after he finished the candy.

"The order of play for the first hole will be Colonel Askeri from the red tees," Mr. Smilodon said as he entered her information into his own tablet.

"I will not be playing from the ladies' tees! I will hit from the blue tees along with everyone else," the colonel interrupted. She had her hands on her hips in a defiant stance.

"I should hit first from the tee box because of seniority and importance of my position in society," the senator said as he snapped a cartridge with the electrode darts into his stun gun.

"Senator, shut up and let Mr. Smilodon finish," Tito said.

"Thank you, Tito. The rest of the order for the first tee will be Dr. Sean Matson, Tito Cruz and last will be Senator Jack Seavan." Mr. Smilodon smiled and moved the senator from second to last on his tablet.

"Saving the most skilled for last works for me," the senator said. He discreetly kicked Wendingo as his caddie struggled with the harness for the golf bag.

Mr. Smilodon adjusted the golf bag harness so it was more comfortable for Wendingo and spoke to him in a low voice that perked up the caddie's spirits.

"Let the game begin," Mr. Smilodon said.

"Pooka, hand me the driver," the colonel said. Her caddie reached into the bag and pulled out a putter instead and handed it to the colonel. The colonel suppressed her anger toward her caddie and casually walked over to Pooka.

"This club is a putter. I want the driver," she said as she pointed at the club with a black and gold cover with the Army logo.

Pooka grunted and pulled out the driver for the colonel. She removed the club cover and handed it to Pooka, who sniffed it and tossed it behind him on the tee box.

"It's not too late for the ladies' tees," the senator teased.

"Save your strength for the game, Senator. You are out of breath from the short climb to the tee box before your first drive," the colonel said.

The colonel plunged a white golf tee into the turf behind the blue markers on the tee box and balanced a golf ball with the club logo from the leather pouch on the tee. She surveyed the fairway with the club in her hand and squinted to see the pin on the green. The warm sun streamed in from the east and invigorated her while she addressed the ball.

She regretted her decision to play from the blue tees. Those extra yards would have offered her a much-needed advantage. She told herself to hit a clean shot in the middle of the fairway and let the rest take care of itself. She addressed the golf ball and noticed a number six printed on the ball.

How could they know I play golf balls with the number six on them? she thought.

With every promotion in the Army she played a different ball that corresponded to her grade. Each rank from second lieutenant to four-star general had a corresponding grade from O-1 through O-10. She took a deep breath and relaxed before a practice swing. The graphite club with an oversized club head sliced through the morning air.

Her transition felt good, and she made a mental note to move her feet. She swung the club and transferred the power from her legs and hips with precision for the downward momentum of the club. Like a hairspring in a watch that unraveled in increments, she transferred the rotational power with aplomb and kept the club aligned to hit the ball dead center on the sweet spot of the club face.

She might have hit the perfect golf shot, but Army life damages the mind, body and soul. To the untrained eye the shot looked flawless. The club head made the familiar *thwack* sound with a slight twang at the end that indicated the golf ball hit the bulls eye on the golf club. She held the swing for a few seconds and watched the ball soar into the air. Her ball landed on the fairway about twenty yards short from the ideal location for a second shot.

The other golfers clapped with approval, except the senator. Pooka snatched the club from the colonel's hand.

"Well done, Colonel," the doctor said as he took his turn on the tee box.

She glanced at Mr. Smilodon, who nodded in approval. The senator had a stoic expression and offered no praise. She retrieved her tee and strolled with confidence to the back of the tee box with the other two golfers.

"A well-played shot, Colonel," Tito said.

"Thank you, Tito," The colonel felt good about her drive and the prospect of a win today.

"Your caddie left this on the ground," Tito said as he handed her the club cover.

"Thank you, Tito," she said. She did not bother to correct Pooka for the discarded club cover.

These rare moments on the golf course where skill trumps any sexist remarks drove her to master the game. Despite her success and achievements in the Army, some would view her inferior to hold the job because of her gender. On the golf course skill leveled the field.

The doctor took his position on the tee box. His drive contained the same finesse as the colonel's, but with more precision that wrung an extra seventy-five yards from his swing.

The baseball player and the senator each launched their golf balls well past the Colonel's ball on the fairway. Tito out-drove the other three golfers.

"A good match is in store for us today," Mr. Smilodon said to the two staff members behind the table.

After nine holes, three of the caddies resembled PGA tour professionals from a distance, except for their awkward walk and hairy presence. Wendingo, however, continued to provide much frustration for the senator. He refused to carry the golf bag on his back but instead dragged it behind him across stone paths, sand traps and fairways. Wendingo never offered the correct club to the senator and the other golfers picked up the senator's discarded clubs Wendingo left behind on the course.

By the tenth hole the doctor had the lead by five strokes under par followed by the senator with three under par; Tito and the colonel both had four over par.

"Shampe, hand me the eight iron. Shampe, are you listening? What has your interest along the edge of the fairway?" Tito asked.

"It's your turn, Tito; hit the ball," the colonel shouted.

He could see the impatient colonel with her hands on her hips. The other two golfers and Mr. Smilodon waited on the green.

"Come on, Shampe, we don't have time to explore the woods," Tito said. He noticed the caddie's nostrils flared as he breathed in a scent from the woods.

"Shampe, I need my eight iron from the bag." Tito moved closer toward Shampe to retrieve his golf club and the caddie's demeanor changed.

"No, Shampe, don't move!"

Shampe, with a burst of speed, charged toward an innocent deer on the edge of fairway. Tito fired the stun gun at Shampe, but the two electrode darts missed the caddie. The deer saw the chupacabra and bounded into the dense woods.

"Shampe, stop!" Tito yelled while he reloaded another cartridge in the stun gun. The cumbersome golf bag slowed Shampe's speed and gave the deer a much needed head start until the caddie broke free of the golf bag. The contents of the golf bag spilled on the fairway. The caddie closed the distance between the deer once free of the golf bag.

"Come here, Shampe! Tito caught up with Shampe, who stood motionless. "Good, Shampe, I knew you would listen. Pick up my clubs and golf bag."

The caddie did not respond to Tito but instead stood in a trance-like state.

"Tito, hit the damn ball!" the senator yelled. The senator threw a clump of sod at Wendingo in frustration.

"Senator, shut the hell up. My caddie made a break for the woods," Tito said. Tito sensed someone next to him and turned to see Mr. Smilodon.

How can Mr. Smilodon move so fast? Last time I saw him he stood on the green with the other golfers, Tito thought to himself.

"What is wrong, Tito?" Mr. Smilodon asked.

"Sir, Shampe saw a deer and charged after him, but he does not respond to my commands. He appears hypnotized or in a trance."

"Do you see the obelisk the caddie stares at with intensity?" Mr. Smilodon asked.

"Yes, our driver told us they are artifacts from the ancient civilization."

"It is an ancient relic from the past, but it also marks the boundaries of the lodge. The caddies can't roam past these markers," Mr. Smilodon said.

"Same concept as an electric fence, Mr. Smilodon?" Tito asked.

"Fair comparison, but no electric currents emanate from the obelisks."

Tito observed Mr. Smilodon tap the caddie in between his shoulder blades and the trance dissipated. Shampe looked at Tito, grunted and shrugged his shoulders as picked up the discarded golf bag.

"Mr. Smilodon, have any caddies ever escaped from the lodge?"

"I am not aware of any stories about escaped caddies, not since my arrival at the lodge, but without the obelisk sentries the caddies might not find a way out of the canyon, anyway." Mr. Smilodon poured a liquid onto the obelisk from a small vial he removed from this pocket. Tito checked to make sure his bag contained every club.

"Keep your head down. You can reach the green from here," Mr. Smilodon said. Tito looked up from his golf clubs and noticed Mr. Smilodon had left him and Shampe.

"Come on, Tito, you have delayed the game long enough. We have already finished the hole," the senator said.

Tito ignored the senator and paid attention to Mr. Smilodon's voice in his head. "Keep your head down. You can reach the green from here."

Thwack! The club face smacked the white ball dead center on the sweet spot of the club for maximum distance and accuracy. The ball soared into the air and sailed past the sand trap. Tito heard cheers on the green, but groans of disappointment from the other golfers followed as the ball hit the pin but did not land in the hole.

"Excellent shot. You almost eagled this hole," the colonel said.

"What did you think of Tito's shot, Senator?" the colonel asked.

"Beginner's luck. Bet you could not do it again," the senator said.

"What did you shoot on this hole, Senator?" Tito asked. Tito turned away from the senator before the senator could answer his question.

"What happened on the last hole, Tito?" the colonel asked.

"I don't know. A relaxed state came over me and I hit the second shot," Tito said. He looked toward the obelisk, impressed with his second shot considering the distance to the hole.

"No, I mean with Shampe; I saw him run toward the edge of the fairway," the colonel said.

"He saw a deer and ran away with my golf bag," Tito said.

"Fine birdie, Tito," the doctor said.

"Hey, Doc, was Mr. Smilodon with you when Shampe gave chase after the deer?" Tito asked.

"Yes, we were on the green with the senator. Why do you ask?"

"No reason." Tito checked the distance from where Shampe saw the deer and the green after he recorded his score on the tablet. "How could Mr. Smilodon close the 200 yards in such little time?" Tito wondered.

CHAPTER 31

SETTLED DEBT

"TITO, YOU'RE UP, and I doubt you can birdie this hole," the senator said with impatience.

Tito chose a nine iron for the short par three with an island green surrounded by sand traps and ignored the senator. "Smooth swing and let the club take care of the rest," he said to himself. He hit the ball with enough distance to reach the green, but the ball drifted left and landed in the sand trap.

"Too bad, Tito. I thought you would be in a position for another birdie," the colonel said.

"One tiny variation in the swing mechanics can squander a great shot," the doctor said.

"I told you, Tito, you don't have it in you to play with consistency at a high level. Your game needs much work. Step aside and I'll show you how a professional would play this hole," the senator said with a smug expression.

Tito broke his golf tee in two pieces and flicked them at the senator. "You're a professional clown, senator."

The senator, immersed in concentration, ignored Tito's insult.

"Tito, one thousand dollars the senator drops the ball in the sand trap," the doctor said in a loud voice to disrupt the senator's practice swing.

"I'll pass, Doc. Either side of that bet is not helpful for me," Tito said.

"Hey, Doc, how about a thousand bucks I make a hole in one," the senator responded.

"He sounds confident—I don't think I would take the bet," the colonel said.

"The colonel is right. You have the lead. Why fuel his ego if he makes the shot?" Tito said.

The doctor ignored the others' advice and observations. "Senator, let's increase the risk and reward of the bet. If you don't make a hole in one on this par three, you owe each of us 5K."

"Each of you will pay me 5K when I make the shot?" the senator asked.

"Count me out!" the colonel said without hesitation.

"Relax, Colonel, I'll cover for you," the doctor said.

"Nope. I appreciate it, but I want no part of this male bravado," the colonel said as she distanced herself from the group on the tee box.

Tito thought about the bet and said, "Count me in, Doc; 5K the senator can't make a hole in one."

The doctor gave Tito a nod of approval and turned toward Mr. Smilodon. "Sir, do you want any of this action?" the doctor asked.

"No, thank you. I'll remain a neutral party," Mr. Smilodon said.

"Well, Senator, do we have a bet or do you lack the confidence in your own game?" the doctor asked.

The financial risk of the bet did not concern the senator because, if he lost, he would not pay the debt with his personal funds. Instead, taxpayer money would settle the bet through senate accounting shenanigans. The senator wanted the psychological advantage it would give him over the doctor if he made the hole in one. The senator heard a voice. *You can make the shot; take the bet.*

"Doc, let's raise the stakes to 10K," the senator said with a serious tone.

"Shit, I don't trust him for the money," Tito said.

"He will pay, but it won't be with his own money," the doctor said.

"Don't take the bet," the colonel said.

"Tito, are you in on the bet?" the doctor asked. The doctor avoided the colonel's stern look of concern.

Tito considered the odds for a moment.

"The senator is sweating," the doctor said.

"He always sweats, and I will take the bet," Tito said.

"Senator, we will take the bet," the doctor said.

"Good, and I want cash, Senator. I don't trust your checks," Tito said with a grin.

"Wendingo, hand me the nine iron. Stupid caddie, you handed me a six iron. Do you want me to hit over the green?" the senator asked.

Wendingo grunted, shook his head yes and tossed the nine iron at the senator.

The senator studied the pin location on the green, noted a slight breeze and closed his eyes to imagine the shot. Wendingo had ignored the senator's golf game up to this point but watched the senator address the ball with interest. The senator loosened the grip on his club and *thwack!* The ball launched into the air. Everyone's attention focused on the white orb as it cleared the sand and landed above the pin. The ball rolled toward the edge of a slight dip in the green with the pin at the bottom and picked up speed.

"Damn, he might make it!" the colonel said in disbelief.

"How the hell did he do it?" the doctor said.

"You owe me 20K!" The senator threw the nine iron at Wendingo. Wendingo caught the club with his quick reflexes before it hit him in the head. "You recommend the six iron, huh, stupid caddie?" the senator said.

"What were the odds the senator could make the shot?" the doctor asked Tito.

"It does not matter. They did not pan out for us. We owe him 10K each, but worse, his confidence received a jolt," Tito said as he looked at the senator with disbelief.

"He has a toxic personality, but his concentration on golf is intense," the doctor said.

"He is one cool cat on the course," Tito said.

"Hey, Doc, think you can follow his performance?" the colonel asked.

The doctor looked at the senator who savored his victory with a cigar and an arrogant, disdainful expression.

"Senator, double or nothing I can make a hole in one?" the doctor asked.

"Doc, don't do it. You already lost 10K. Let it go."

"Tito is right, Doc. Don't take the bet. The senator got lucky," the colonel said.

"Luck might be a part of your game, but my game is skill, Colonel. Luck has nothing to do with my success. Sure, Doc, double or nothing you can't make a hole in one under pressure," the senator said.

Silence descended over the group while the doctor addressed the ball and took one last look at the pin. He closed his eyes, took a deep breath, slowly exhaled and swung his bespoke golf club. The moment he hit the shot, he knew he had a chance because he felt nothing through the club. The only sensory input he received until he opened his eyes was the sound of the impact of the club face on the ball. He held the swing and watched the ball climb over the hazards of the hole.

"Hooah, Doc! You might do the impossible," the colonel said.

Tito and the colonel were euphoric when the ball hit the pin on the green.

"Yes!" the doctor said as he fought to control his emotions. "Oh crap!" he said before he threw his arms up in defeat.

The senator squealed with delight. "He missed, he missed!" the senator said as he trotted around the tee box.

The colonel saw the white ball impact the pin and roll toward the edge of the green. "Too bad, I thought you made the hole in one," the colonel said.

"That is one hell of a shot though, and you're on the green," Tito said.

"Thanks, Tito," the doctor said.

The senator won the hole, followed by the doctor with par and the colonel and Tito each with a bogey. The golfers recorded their scores while their caddies mimicked the colonel who repaired a divot on the green. The caddies caused more damage in their quest to repair the divots than the golf ball impacts on the green. Chunks of sod flew past the pin as the caddies impaled the green with their divot repair tools. A sizable portion of the green on the par three had now lost its smooth appearance.

"Mr. Smilodon, have you ever witnessed a bet won on a hole in one or anything else on the course that comes close to this extraordinary event? Tito asked as he closed the cover on his tablet.

"This is the first hole in one made on a bet I have witnessed, but it would surprise you what other things I have seen on this golf course, Tito," Mr. Smilodon said.

The senator had the lead by one stroke after sixteen holes until the doctor closed the gap with a birdie on the seventeenth hole. The colonel and Tito were no longer in contention, but each competed to avoid last place.

"Senator, pay attention to Wendingo," the doctor said with an amused look.

"Did the colonel hit her ball? She can't win, so why does she continue to delay the game with amateur play?" the senator asked. He ignored the doctor's comment about Wendingo.

"Senator, she will not quit the game to accommodate your schedule," the doctor said.

The senator cringed when he heard the unmistakable sound of an object landing in the pond. "Tell me he did not jump in the water," he said with clenched fists.

"He did, Senator, with your golf bag," the doctor said. Both Tito and the doctor laughed at Wendingo in the pond.

"Senator, the colonel hit her ball. It's your turn," Tito said. He enjoyed the senator's frustration with Wendingo.

"You know damn well I can't hit my ball without a club," the senator said as he gestured with his middle finger at Tito.

"Chill, Senator, I will hit so Wendingo can continue to chase ducks and scatter the turtles," Tito said as he removed a golf club from his golf bag.

Wendingo taunted the senator and ignored the profanity as he swam close to the edge of the pond.

"Easy, Shampe, you're not going for a swim," Tito said.

"Doc, watch your caddie. Mine wants to jump into the water with Wendingo," Tito said.

"Azmur is a professional and a well-behaved caddie. I doubt he would disrupt my concentration with such antics," the doctor said.

"Will someone help me get Wendingo out of the pond?" the senator pleaded while he paced frantically along the edge of the pond.

"Having more problems, Senator?" Mr. Smilodon said as he approached the water hazard.

"Smilodon, you know Wendingo is the problem! Since breakfast that stupid caddie has wreaked havoc on my game," the senator said.

"The caddie won't respect you if you don't respect him, Senator," Mr. Smilodon said.

"Mr. Smilodon, look out! Wendingo threw the senator's golf bag!" the colonel shouted.

Like a ballistic missile launched from a submarine, the caddie threw the golf bag straight up into the air. The golf bag trajectory changed when it ran out of momentum and crashed to the ground close to the senator. He forgot about Wendingo and scurried over to inspect his water-logged bag after it crumpled over from the impact.

"Is everything accounted for Senator?"

"No, it's not, Smilodon! The bag is ruined, and the way I see it you owe me a new set of clubs and a new golf bag because of Wendingo!" He hit his golf bag with a golf club and imagined it was Mr. Smilodon.

"Easy with the club, Senator. You don't want to damage the box of Snickers. Wendingo will be hungry after his swim," Mr. Smilodon said.

"You think this is a joke, Smilodon. You owe me a new set of clubs and a golf bag—What the hell! That hurt!" The senator turned around after Wendingo pelted him with a golf ball.

Wendingo dove under the water after he threw the ball at the senator.

"I hope he drowns," the senator said when he did not see Wendingo surface. A few seconds later the caddie appeared above the water with an armload of golf balls and continued his golf ball onslaught on the senator.

"Damn useless caddie!" the senator yelled as he dodged the golf balls. He picked up a few golf balls and hurled them at Wendingo but missed by a wide margin.

"Senator, go hit your golf ball. I'll handle Wendingo," Mr. Smilodon said.

"It's about time!" The senator placed a golf ball Wendingo threw at him in his pocket.

Wendingo slowly climbed out of the pond with his head lowered as he walked past Mr. Smilodon toward a pile of clubs and the senator's water-logged golf bag. Wendingo shook like a wet dog before he picked up the clubs. The senator drew his tazer Old-West-style and fired two electrode darts at his caddie as Wendingo lifted the golf bag. Wendingo dropped to the ground and convulsed from the electric current. Mr. Smilodon's hand closed around the senator's arm with immense strength and caused him to drop the tazer. Wendingo, released from the volts of electricity, was motionless on the fairway.

"Taze Wendingo again and I will tear your arm from your shoulder and beat you senseless with it," Mr. Smilodon said with a snarl.

The senator howled in pain and pleaded with Mr. Smilodon to let go of his arm and show him the proper respect for a senator.

"Your titles mean nothing at this golf club. You must earn respect. It is not an entitlement," Mr. Smilodon said. He released the senator's arm and went to check on Wendingo.

"Screw you, Smilodon. You are lucky you did not break my arm, but you will live the rest of your life in prison for your assault!" the senator said.

"How do you intend to explain the golf trip and the caddies to the court, Senator?" Mr. Smilodon said. He stepped closer to the senator and caused him to step into the pond with one foot. "Remember the information we have on your professional and personal life. How do you think your precious donors and constituents would act if we release this information to your enemies and the public?" Mr. Smilodon said as he poked the senator in the chest.

The senator knew Mr. Smilodon had the upper hand. "Do you want me to quit the game, Smilodon?" He asked as he stepped out of the pond.

"Of course not, Senator, but if you crave respect, you must show respect to Wendingo. I have seen your behavior toward your caddie since breakfast," Mr. Smilodon said. He stepped forward into the senator's personal space. The senator stepped into the pond with his dry foot.

Besides the numerous discreet kicks, jabs and harassment of his caddie out of sight of the other golfers, the senator had also teased Wendingo with a Snickers on the end of his stun gun.

"You can't prove anything I did to the stupid caddie," the senator said.

"Pick up the stun gun and hand it to me, Senator," Mr. Smilodon said.

"What if I decide to taze you, Smilodon?" the senator asked.

Mr. Smilodon laughed; his eyes narrowed as he focused on the senator's throat. "I don't think you have the reflexes to chamber another cartridge in the stun gun and fire at me, Senator, but I will take that chance," Mr. Smilodon said. The senator never saw the old man move until he felt the pressure around his throat. "Taze me, Senator, and see how it feels when I crush your windpipe," Mr. Smilodon said as his grip tightened around the senator's throat.

The senator struggled and hit the old man's extended arm with both hands to dislodge Mr. Smilodon's grip.

"Pick up the tazer and let's play golf," Mr. Smilodon said as he released the senator.

The senator picked up the stun gun and handed it to Mr. Smilodon as his hands trembled.

Mr. Smilodon took the stun gun from the senator. "You have no need for this anymore, Senator."

"What will I have to protect myself from Wendingo if he acts up again?" the senator asked.

"I suggest you don't antagonize Wendingo anymore because I will no longer intervene on your behalf. Excellent birdie on the fifteenth hole and the hole in one. Keep your concentration and you might win the match, Senator. Finish this hole and I shall see you on the eighteenth tee box," Mr. Smilodon said.

CHAPTER 32

STRICT USGA RULES

THE CANYON WALLS COLLECTED the last rays of the setting sun and shone with vibrant orange, reddish yellow and purple hues on the rock formation. The four golfers stood mesmerized by the classic 601-yard par five with the backdrop of the canyon walls and the lodge perched above the eighteenth green.

The eighteenth hole enticed many golfers to go the distance and reach the green in two shots, but without a powerful tee shot balanced with accuracy, many left befuddled in the rough.

A small peninsula of fairway jutted out from the rough past a set of ancient oak trees that towered over the fairway.

The ideal drive from the tee box to reach the green in two strokes required strength to hit over the oak trees and finesse to land the ball on the small patch of fairway. If the drive lacks the distance to clear the oak trees or the accuracy to land in the small patch of fairway, the ball will end up in the rough, or worse, out of bounds with an incurred penalty stroke added to the score.

If you hit the tee shot with precision, the second shot requires the proper amount of loft to clear a water hazard at the six o'clock position of the green and accuracy to avoid two sand traps that flank the green. The green has a steep downward slope that can add additional strokes to the score if the ball does not land near the pin.

"This will be the last time the three of us play this exquisite course with the majestic rock formation as a backdrop," the colonel said with a tinge of melancholy in her voice.

"Fine by me," Tito said.

"You're not disappointed this is the last time we will set foot on these emerald green fairways, Tito?" the colonel asked.

"Colonel, this place reminds me of a cemetery without the gravestones unless you count those sinister black obelisks," Tito said. He took a few practice swings to loosen up for the last hole but could not relax because of the darkness that would soon cover the canyon.

"I enjoyed my round of golf at this mysterious course, but this trip did not rejuvenate me like a vacation. I am exhausted because I could not sleep and I believe an evil presence walks the golf course with us," Tito said.

"The caddies are harmless—an oddity, a freak of nature from a genetic mutation science can't explain. You can't get comfortable here because of the silence, but I appreciate the tranquility of the place," the colonel said.

"I agree with the colonel. The solitude and the lack of self-absorbed people who chat about inane things on their cell phones adds to the appeal of this place. When I win the match, I might invite you guys to play a round as my guests without the senator," the doctor said.

"The membership is mine, and when I win, none of you will be on my guest list," the senator said as he removed a beer from the ice chest on the tee box.

"Why do you covet this membership, Senator?" the doctor asked. "You complain constantly about the austerity and the lack of connectivity with the outside world."

"Remember his classic phrase to Mr. Smilodon; his influence in DC slips away the longer he stays at the lodge," the colonel said.

"I will retire one day, and the exclusive nature of this place will be worth the victory, plus the satisfaction that you will never set foot here again makes up for the lack of CNN or access to my constituents," the senator said. He guzzled his beer and ignored the majestic views on the last hole.

"Too bad you don't appreciate this place for its true value instead of your small zero-sum mentality," the doctor said.

"What happened to Wendingo, Senator?" the doctor asked with a look of curiosity.

"Oh hell no, I don't need a lost caddie at this point in the game!" The senator called for Wendingo, but he did not see his caddie.

"Wendingo has your tablet with the score card, and if you lose your tablet, you lose the game," the colonel said.

The doctor turned toward Tito and the colonel with a serious look.

"Want a beer, Doc?" Tito asked as he handed a beer to the colonel.

"No thanks, I don't know if I can beat this clown. Every time I pour on the birdies, he executes a game-saving shot. He could have a dominant lead at this point if he had treated Wendingo better," the doctor said in a low voice.

"Doc, the colonel and I have no chance to oust this fool from the top spot on the leader board, but you can win," Tito said.

"Listen to Tito, Doc. Your game is better by most metrics. Don't overthink the last hole," the colonel said. She took a sip of her beer and wanted to believe the doctor could win.

"No pressure. Right, guys?" the doctor said.

"Hey, Senator, Wendingo is on top of the water cooler," Tito said. He pointed at the senator's caddie balanced precariously on the cooler.

They heard a loud crash as the thin aluminum legs of the container that held the water cooler three feet from the ground buckled under the added weight of the caddie. Wendingo howled in pain on the ground.

"Wendingo, get the hell over here," the senator said.

Wendingo deftly zipped up the pocket on the golf bag with the Snickers and finished the candy bar before he obeyed the senator's command.

"The winner of this hole will win the game and the coveted membership," Mr. Smilodon said as he removed his dark sunglasses.

"What happens with a tie?" the senator asked.

"We will have a playoff at first light tomorrow," Mr. Smilodon said.

"Good, and one of these losers can caddie for me instead of Wendingo, Smilodon," the senator said as he pointed at Tito and the colonel.

"You think your caddie causes trouble for you, wait until I carry your clubs. You will regret the loser comment," Tito said. He glared at the senator who avoided eye contact with Tito.

Shampe mimicked Tito's behavior and growled at the senator.

"Such a spirited group. Too bad only one membership slot is available today," Mr. Smilodon said.

"Senator, if a playoff occurs tomorrow, Wendingo will be your caddie," Mr. Smilodon said as he handed Wendingo another Snickers bar.

"Stupid caddie, I could have won this match, but you have cost me at least five strokes. Wendingo, get over here! I need my tablet," the senator yelled.

"Shhh, let the doctor hit his drive in peace," the colonel admonished.

"Oh, does the doc need precious silence, Colonel?" the senator asked as he retrieved his tablet from the waterproof pocket on his golf bag.

"Senator, shut the hell up and let the doctor hit in peace," Tito said as he cracked his knuckles.

"If you need a minute to collect your thoughts, go ahead," Mr. Smilodon said.

"I am good. His antics don't bother me, Mr. Smilodon."

The doctor's tee shot impacted the ball on target and traveled 300 yards in the center of the fairway. The ball landed in perfect alignment with the green for a second shot before the sand traps.

The doctor played it safe; it will take him three shots to reach the green and maybe more if he does not hit it over the oak trees, the senator thought to himself. He checked the eighteenth hole diagram on his tablet to confirm his assessment of the doctor's tee shot.

"Give me the three wood, Wendingo." Wendingo tapped each club with his sharp claw to annoy the senator. The senator scowled at his caddie. "Any day, Wendingo," the senator said. Wendingo settled on the golf umbrella in the bag and handed it to the senator.

"Imbecile! you handed me a golf umbrella. I want my three wood," the senator said. He removed the cover from the correct club and smacked Wendingo across the snout with it.

"Too bad Wendingo mangled your favorite club, senator. This hole will punish you if you lack confidence in your ability," the doctor said.

The doctor walked to the back of the tee box after his drive to watch the other three hit their tee shot. Did he make the right decision to play this hole safe, he wondered?

The senator would never admit it, but the doctor played at a level beyond his own game. He could compete in the PGA if he left the lucrative life of a plastic surgeon. The senator played against lesser mortals and sycophants who did not challenge him with intensity like the doctor did today at Goat Trails Golf Club.

"Tito, a thousand bucks the senator plays it safe and avoids the chance to reach the green in two strokes," the doctor said.

"Hell no, Doc; I owe him 10K, and I do not intend to add another pile of cash to the debt I owe him," Tito said.

"If he had his favorite club he would have a chance, but the drive is a challenge with a three wood, and I don't think he has the skill to execute the shot.

How about you, Colonel? Think the senator has the stones to go the distance?" the doctor asked.

"Count me out, Doc. I don't have your deep pockets," she said in disgust. *A disgrace the doc has piles of money, but the people who serve in the military to protect his freedom don't have his lifestyle,* she thought to herself.

"Too bad, Colonel; I don't think the senator has the courage or the skill to reach the green with two shots," the doctor said.

"If you're so bold, Doc, why didn't you go the distance? Shut the hell up while I hit my ball."

The doctor winked at the colonel. "I hope it rattled his confidence," the doctor said.

The senator attempted to stay calm and ignore the antagonization, but anger seeped into his golf stance. His grip tightened around the club the more he thought of his favorite club destroyed by his caddie. He could outdrive the doctor, but his long ball stats had diminished after Wendingo snapped his driver in half. He would take his frustration out on Wendingo later.

The colonel studied the eighteenth hole diagram on her tablet while she waited her turn to hit. "If the senator goes the distance and aims for the small patch of fairway past the oak trees, he will be in an ideal position to reach the green," the colonel said.

"Any deviation to his swing or if he hits the ball too hard, he will pull the ball to the left and lose precious yardage for the second shot. Worst case scenario, the ball lands out of bounds in the rough and he has to record a penalty shot," Tito said to the colonel.

"Mr. Smilodon, tell these amateurs to be quiet!" the senator said.

"Silence, everyone, so he can concentrate on his drive," Mr. Smilodon said.

The senator took a deep breath, exhaled and swung the club. The golfers did not hear the familiar *thwack* sound of a well-hit ball after the senator hit his drive.

"Damn, I should have taken the bet," Tito said.

"I don't think he hit the ball the way he wanted," the colonel said.

The senator's golf ball veered away from the fairway and crashed into the rough twenty yards short of the patch of fairway past the oak trees. The senator wiped his brow with dismay and knew his tee shot could have cost him this hole, or worse, the match.

Wendingo clapped with excitement at the senator's misfortune and this infuriated the senator. The senator threw his club at Wendingo but missed his caddie. His golf club, instead, hit the carved stone marker for the eighteenth hole and snapped in half.

"That is two golf clubs of mine Wendingo has destroyed, Mr. Smilodon," the senator yelled.

"I think you have a bigger issue than your damaged three wood, Senator. Your ball might have landed out-of-bounds, and you must record a penalty stroke," the colonel said.

"I know what it means, Colonel, and you should have played from the woman's tees. Next time, take any advantage offered because of your inferior gender," the senator said.

"Senator, show the colonel respect, and I'll invite you to the club for a second chance at the shot," the doctor said sarcastically.

The senator left the tee box and kicked Wendingo before he sat on a bench out of breath and frustrated. "Expect an IRS audit," the senator said.

"Don't let him rattle you, Colonel. You're next to hit," Tito said.

The comment stung like other barbs she experienced in the military, but she remained calm, visualized where she wanted to hit her ball and took a practice swing.

The senator slumped on the bench, disgusted with himself, and paid no attention to the colonel. He was distraught about his last drive of the match and a penalty stroke added to his score if he hit the ball out of bounds. He struggled to lift his weight from the bench and walked toward Wendingo and his golf bag. Mr. Smilodon stepped in front of the senator in anticipation he might lash out at his caddie.

"Don't worry, Smilodon; I will not hurt Wendingo. I only want my tablet," the senator said as he reached for the zipper pocket.

Wendingo moved to open the pocket for him when the senator yelled at him.

"I'll do it! I don't want any help from a filthy fiend." The sound of cheers caused him to look up from his tablet and see the colonel and the other golfers celebrate her tee shot.

"Hooah! Is that the shot you wanted on this hole, Senator?"

The senator stood up from the bench and squinted toward the fairway and saw her ball in the open space in a perfect position to reach the green in two strokes.

"You will squander the chance to win with your second shot or your terrible putting skills will ruin the hole for you," the senator said. *How could she have hit the ball so far and with such accuracy?* he thought to himself.

Elated with the shot, the colonel ignored the senator's comment and hugged Pooka. She gave him the rest of the Snickers and savored her epic tee shot. The colonel could not believe the shot she hit, but when a misogynistic clown played the gender card, she made the impossible happen.

"Fine shot, Colonel," Mr. Smilodon said.

"Why the celebration? She can't win the match," the senator said, disgusted with their praise for the colonel.

"She can win the hole, and you might lose the match," Tito said.

The doctor hit a flawless third shot on the green when the ball avoided the sand, water perils and the steep slope of the green.

The colonel approached her ball and studied its position on the fairway. She exuded confidence and knew she could reach the green.

"Pooka, give me the fairway driver." He handed her the sand wedge, but she did not care. She felt good about her near impossible shot. She retrieved the correct club from her golf bag and corrected Pooka on his club choice without malice. She saw the senator on the edge of the fairway and he had not found his golf ball.

"By regulation you have five minutes to find your ball," the colonel said.

"Where did you get that number, Colonel?" His voice conveyed the anxiety he felt about a lost ball.

"The United States Golf Association rule book is on the tablet," the colonel said.

"Go hit your ball, Colonel. I know the rules of golf," the senator said. He walked deeper into the wooded area along the edge of the rough in search of his ball. He struggled to think clearly with the race against the clock to find his ball. If he went with a lost ball, he could take a drop ball one club length or arm's distance from the last known point it entered the rough. He would have a difficult third shot regardless of where he dropped the ball because of the uneven rocky terrain. He reached into his pocket and felt the golf ball Wendingo had thrown at him from the pond. He gripped the ball in his hand and, with a cunning smile, he thought of a plan to tilt the game in his favor. The senator covertly palmed the golf ball and scanned the ground. *I need a good spot to drop this ball, somewhere on the edge of the rough free of branches and other obstructions,* he thought.

"One minute, Senator, to find your ball," Mr. Smilodon said.

The senator's eyes opened wide at the ideal spot to drop the ball.

"Perfect. From here I can reach the green, but I need to drop the ball so the other hacks or Mr. Smilodon don't notice me," he said to himself.

The moment came when Tito, on the green, yelled, "Hurry up, Senator, take the penalty and play a provisional ball!" The senator dropped the ball the moment the colonel and Mr. Smilodon looked toward the two golfers on the green.

"I found my ball," the senator said as he addressed the ball he covertly dropped on the open patch of rough. The senator swung his club before anyone questioned him. The shot felt good the moment the club impacted the ball.

"Fore!" the senator yelled to warn the golfers on the green that his ball was in flight and it could hit them. He did not care if the ball hit them. He wanted to regain the psychological edge. Neither the doctor nor Tito could believe their ears. They scanned the sky and saw the senator's ball clear the hazards and roll toward the pin.

"Shit, this clown dropped it on the green from the rough," the doctor said in disbelief.

"He might drop it in the cup," Tito said.

The ball rolled within four feet of the pin. "Colonel, that is how you hit your second shot," the senator said. He pumped his fist in the air and walked toward the green, confident victory was in his grasp.

The colonel took a practice swing. The weight of the fairway wood felt odd as it sliced through the air.

"I should have taken this out of the bag more often at the range," she said to Pooka. Her shot cleared the water hazard, but the ball did not bite the green. Instead, it picked up speed and rolled into the sand. Everyone groaned as they watched her ball roll past the pin and into the sand trap.

"Guess you called the right club, Pooka," she said. Pooka ignored her while he lounged in the shade, oblivious to the game.

"Storm the beaches of Normandy for your third shot, Colonel!" the senator said. He laughed at her when he passed by along the way to the green.

She did not offer a snappy response because she was demoralized he salvaged victory. The senator triumphantly marked his ball on the green with a presidential seal ball marker he had stolen from the president last year.

"No, Pooka, wait until I hit the ball before you rake the sand trap," the colonel said. She pushed her caddie away from her ball in the sand. The colonel hit a clean shot to set up a par for the hole.

The doctor finished with a birdie on the hole and was not assured of victory. Tito shot for par but recorded a bogey for the hole after incurring a penalty stroke when his ball landed in the water hazard. His fate on the leader board was contingent upon how the colonel finished this hole.

The senator placed his ball on the green after he removed his ball marker. The colonel noticed the senator's golf ball before he squatted on the green to read the hole. He panted when he got to his feet and took a practice putt. He closed his eyes, took a deep breath and exhaled as he swung his putter like a pendulum. He tapped the ball with the proper amount of force and sent the ball over the lip of the cup. The ball made the familiar sound as it hit the bottom of the cup.

The color drained from the doctor's face as he watched the senator sink the putt.

The senator yelled in triumph and raised his pudgy hands over his head. Wendingo mimicked his victory celebration and threw the senator's golf bag into the air, but the senator did not care as he walked toward the cup to retrieve his ball.

"How could any one man have such luck?" the doctor shouted in disgust. He took one last look at the fairway and tee box of the eighteenth hole and burned the image in his mind. He was crestfallen as he realized he would not play golf at this course again. "Damn fine course," he said to himself. He held his head low, and the weight of defeat slumped his shoulders as he recorded his score.

"Sorry, Doc, I thought you had this game in the bag," Tito said as he recorded his bogey for the hole.

"This is the best course I have played, Tito. It is tragic the senator will have access to the lodge," the doctor said.

"This is a place of evil, and best you didn't win, Doc," Tito said.

The colonel observed the senator dance around the green and shout like a fool in victory. She bumped into him and he dropped his ball from the impact. The colonel snatched the ball from the ground before the senator retrieved it.

"I knew it. The senator cheated! The senator cheated!" the colonel said as she inspected his ball. "Look, Doctor, he played the wrong ball," the colonel said. She held the ball in the air for the other golfers and Mr. Smilodon.

"Shut the hell up, Colonel, and give me my ball!"

"Guess you lose the battle of Normandy, Rommel," she said. She handed the ball to Mr. Smilodon so he could inspect it.

"Notice the senator's ball does not have the logo of the golf club," the colonel said.

"Senator, how do you explain this ball without the golf club logo? Did you play the wrong ball on this hole?" Mr. Smilodon asked.

"The lack of the golf club logo does not prove I played the wrong ball. I played this ball since the first hole," the senator said.

"Why this ball?" Mr. Smilodon said with a curious voice.

"It brings me luck. A corporate executive at the Boeing company gave me a sleeve of them when we played eighteen holes in Chicago," the senator said.

"So you have no intention to claim you played the wrong ball by mistake on this hole, Senator?" Mr. Smilodon said.

Wendingo plodded toward the senator's bag to retrieve the box of golf balls he had received that morning.

"Absolutely not, Mr. Smilodon. That has been my ball from the first hole," the senator said with no emotion.

"You have played this ball for the entire duration of the game, Senator?" Mr. Smilodon asked.

"Yes. It has served me well," the senator said. He noticed Wendingo had a soggy box of golf balls he carried toward Mr. Smilodon. The senator glared at Wendingo because he intended to show the box of golf balls contained one short of a dozen.

Mr. Smilodon removed his own tablet from his jacket pocket and, with a swipe of his finger, brought up a map of the eighteenth hole.

"Senator, if you did indeed play this ball for eighteen holes, how do you explain this?" Mr. Smilodon asked. He held his tablet toward the senator so he could see the display.

Three red dots near each other flashed on the screen. A fourth dot also flashed on the screen but it was 220 yards away from the green.

"Each golf ball we gave you had an embedded GPS chip in its core. You activated the chip when you hit it with a golf club. We recorded your every tee shot, chip, and putt with the associated data to offer you a complete picture of your golf game at the end of the round. Senator, the ball you played since the first hole landed out of bounds," Mr. Smilodon said. He zoomed in on the senator's flashing red ball on the tablet. "If you played the ball in your hand for the entire round, how do you explain the fourth activated golf ball in the exact location you hit your drive from the eighteenth hole tee box, Senator?"

The senator's eyes narrowed. He was ensnared in a lie and had no procedural process to hide behind or inane congressional inquiry to place the blame on someone else. He played the wrong ball on the hole and did not accept responsibility.

"This fiendish ghoul you call a caddie set me up. I won this hole and the match; look at my scores for each hole," the senator said.

"USGA rules govern this game. You didn't declare a wrong ball played before you recorded your score and left the green. You are disqualified, Senator, and the doctor wins the match," Mr. Smilodon said.

The digital leader board displayed the final scores for the round: the doctor with a score of 71, followed by the colonel with a score of 76, Tito with a score of 77 and a red "X" next to the senator's name for disqualification.

"Screw you and your conspiracy to deny my win!" the senator said. He noticed the red "X" by his name on the leader board and threw a golf ball at Wendingo. Wendingo caught the ball and hurled it at the senator. The ball hit the senator in the head. He cried out in pain and demanded a playoff because no one had informed him the match would adhere to USGA rules.

The golfers and Mr. Smilodon laughed at the senator's demand for a playoff.

The senator threw his tablet at the golfers in a fit of rage but missed by a wide margin. The tablet shattered when it hit the cobblestone path.

"No rematch for you tomorrow, Senator, since you broke your tablet. You are disqualified twice," the colonel said.

The senator lunged toward the colonel to choke her, but Mr. Smilodon intervened before he could reach the colonel. Mr. Smilodon gripped the senator's head with his hands.

"What the hell, Smilodon! Let go of me. I am a US senator."

"Relax, Senator," Mr. Smilodon said. A cool sensation followed by a warm sensation eliminated the pulsing pain in the senator's eye socket and the rage he felt.

"You have lost the match. Accept it with dignity," Mr. Smilodon said. He held onto the senator's forehead for a few more seconds and released his grip. "Take a drink of water. Your strength will return and you will appear different tonight."

The senator, in disbelief, felt invigorated after Mr. Smilodon released his forehead. The walk through the undulated terrain of the course and the repeated golf swings punished the senator's obese body for the last eighteen holes. He ached as exhaustion took its toll on him, but after Mr. Smilodon released him, he felt refreshed.

"Everyone will meet in the ballroom at 9:00 PM tonight to celebrate our new member," Mr. Smilodon said.

"What is the dress code for tonight, Mr. Smilodon?" the colonel asked.

"Formal attire, Colonel."

"I did not pack clothes for a black tie event. The invitation did not mention a black tie event. Did any of you pack formal attire?" the colonel asked.

"Of course, I always pack a tuxedo whenever I travel."

"You do, Doctor?" the colonel asked.

"I am kidding. I packed for a golf vacation, not an evening at the opera," the doctor said.

"Mr. Smilodon, you should have mentioned the formal event in the invitation," Tito said.

"Relax, everyone, we have made arrangements to have the finest formal attire for each of you in your rooms, compliments of the golf club. Please meet at the grand ballroom at 9:00 tonight, but before you arrive for the party, pack your bags for travel because tomorrow you leave early in the morning," Mr. Smilodon said.

"You would kick us out of the lodge so soon, Mr. Smilodon? We can't extend the accommodations one more night?" Tito asked with a sarcastic tone.

"Since the doc belongs to the club, maybe he can extend our stay one more night, and why does he have to pack his bags?"

Mr. Smilodon interrupted the senator. "Everyone, have your bags packed and ready for travel before the festivities tonight. Fine game, Doctor," Mr. Smilodon said. He shook the doctor's hand before he left the tee box.

"Smilodon!" the senator shouted. What do we do with our filthy caddies?"

"They are your dates tonight," Mr. Smilodon said as he left the group of golfers alone on the tee box.

"Don't bother, Senator," the doctor said. The doctor pointed at the caddies.

The caddies tore away their golf harnesses, threw the bags on the ground and trudged toward the lodge.

"Wendingo, come here and clean my golf clubs!" the senator shouted.

"Let him go, Senator. He never took care of your clubs on the course," Tito said.

"You're right. Useless creatures. I am glad I will not spend any more time with them, but the Doc will enjoy their company as the new member of the club," the senator said with envy.

"Senator, the caddies are okay once you get to know them," the doctor said as he marveled at his name on the leader board.

"He cost me the game!" the senator said in disgust.

"Why do you think the caddies left in such a hurry?" the colonel asked.

"Their meal beckons from the barn to quench their thirst," Tito said.

Tito felt relaxed after a round of golf, but his stomach churned with anxiety on this course. He clutched the crucifix around his neck and said a prayer thanking God for his blessings and safe passage home. He had not spoken to God since his adopted missionary parents found him on the streets of the Dominican Republic.

CHAPTER 33

RETURN OF THE ROUTINE

"Wow, check out the colonel. Dressed to kill tonight without her military gear. What do you think, Senator? How does she look in her gown?" Tito asked.

"Nice shoes, but she looks better in her drab Army uniform," the senator said.

"Ignore the senator. You look good, Colonel," Tito said. Tito offered his arm for her to hold on to before they walked the red carpet toward the ballroom.

The colonel gazed at her reflection in the hallway mirror and felt stunning. The turquoise gown imbued her with confidence.

"I can get used to this lifestyle and thank you, Tito, for the compliment. Your tux looks good on you," the colonel said. She adjusted his bow tie and took his arm.

"Well, find out what the chef has on the menu tonight," the doctor said.

White-gloved attendants greeted the golfers at the top of the grand staircase and offered them champagne flutes. The golfers could hear the deep rhythmic sounds of techno music on the other side of the ballroom walls as they approached the entrance.

"I hope they have a better selection of music, and it would also be enjoyable to talk to other people besides the staff tonight," the colonel said. The colonel glanced at her reflection in every mirror she passed on the way toward the ballroom. She felt like she had emerged from the drab Army cocoon of conformity and into her own unique form.

"You want other people to see you in your gown?" Tito said.

"Yes, I do, Tito!" the colonel said.

The music changed the moment an attendant opened the doors to the ballroom. A waltz performed by a live orchestra greeted the golfers when they entered the ballroom.

"You got your wish, Colonel," Tito said.

Hundreds of guests mingled, drank and danced in the ballroom. Lavish tables decorated with red orchid flowers in black crystal centerpieces accented each table. A thirteen-foot crystal sculpture of a goat stood behind the bar.

"Colonel, a DJ arrived next to the bar, and soon we will have better music," Tito said.

Tito surveyed the impressive selection of liquor on the bar shelves.

"Maybe they will play rap music," the colonel said. "Senator, do you enjoy rap music?" she asked.

"Only if the voters enjoy it," the senator said.

The music stopped when the doors closed behind the golfers and a spotlight from the ceiling illuminated them in front of the ballroom of guests.

"Ladies and gentlemen, a big round of applause for our guests and the new member of Goat Trails Golf Club," Mr. Smilodon said. His deep voice filled the cavernous ballroom without the aid of a microphone.

Cheers and claps of adulation from the guests in the ballroom welcomed the golfers. Four life-size banners with pictures of them taken on the golf course unfurled from the ceiling behind the main stage.

Two gorgeous women escorted the group to the head table through a sea of well-dressed guests in opulent gowns and classic tuxedos.

"Hey, Doc, how does this stack up with the Hollywood parties you attend?"

"An A-list event, Tito. What do you think of the ambiance?" the doctor asked.

"Any party I've ever attended looks like a middle class quinceañera compared to this event," Tito said.

Tito admired the beautiful women in the room, but none showed any interest in him.

"What about you, Senator? Inside the Beltway they must throw the most lavish parties with taxpayers' money," Tito asked.

The senator shrugged as a member of the staff pulled out the silk-covered chair for him. "This event is all right, but I have seen better," he said.

"Yeah, right, Senator. You're indignant from the loss on the course," the colonel said.

"Do you recognize anyone here, Senator?" Tito asked.

"I have paid no attention to the other guests tonight," the senator said. Mired in defeat, the senator did not enjoy himself.

"Do you recognize any of the other guests, Tito?" the colonel asked.

"It's odd. Some of them resemble famous people or people from the past who died, but their faces become distorted when I focus on them," Tito said.

"Hooah! One flute of champagne and you see dead people," the colonel said.

"Waiter, Johnnie Walker Black, on the rocks," the senator said as he snapped his puffy fingers at the waiter.

"As you wish, Senator," the waiter said. The waiter did not bother to ask the other golfers if they would like any drinks from the bar.

"Ladies and gentlemen, please take your seats," Mr. Smilodon said from the main stage. The music will continue after a brief presentation about our guests."

"Boo, your Eminence, let's drink and dance before the full moon!" someone shouted from the audience.

"In good time," Mr. Smilodon said. He glanced at the oculus in the domed ceiling above a polished black square on the dance floor. A colossal screen descended on the opposite end of the ballroom and displayed a brief biography for each golfer.

"Your Eminence, who cares about the losers?" a member of the audience shouted.

"We want to hear about our new member!" someone else from the audience shouted.

"This is bullshit!" the senator said. He took a drink of his whiskey and scanned the room for the people who were not interested in the accomplishments of his life.

"You're right, the night belongs to our champion," Mr. Smilodon said.

The screen changed to depict the results of the tournament. The detail of information displayed on the screen beside their final scores surprised the golfers.

"Colonel, did you know they recorded video and audio of our golf match?" the doctor asked. He placed his empty champagne flute on the table and scanned the room for cameras.

"I never saw any indication they recorded us or recall Mr. Smilodon mentioning their plan to record our game," the colonel said. Members of the lodge staff ignored her request for more champagne.

The room filled with laughter when the ballroom guests saw video footage of the senator and Wendingo on the golf course.

The edited video resembled a reality television show with the golfer's facial expressions, conversation and mannerisms captured in glorious high definition video. Different metrics recorded for each golfer on the course such as driving distance, putting accuracy and other information scrolled across the bottom of the screen like a stock-ticker tape.

"Senator, with the resolution on these cameras and multiple angles recorded on the course, I bet the guests will enjoy your covert attempt to cheat on the last hole," the colonel said.

"Shut the hell up, Colonel. Who would have known you talk to yourself so much on the course?" the senator said. He wiped the perspiration from his forehead with a silk dinner napkin.

The guests clapped in approval as Mr. Smilodon narrated the golf match and provided his own observations to the course shenanigans.

"It's about time," Tito said when he noticed a member of the staff arrive with the first course to their table.

"Mmm, smells amazing. I will miss the food here," the colonel said as she unfolded her napkin.

"Hey, guys, look around. Do you see anyone else with dinner at their tables?" Tito asked.

The golfers each glanced furtively to their sides, except the senator, who did not look away from the massive screen. The senator sat agitated and watched the video footage, oblivious to his surroundings. He cringed each time the guests laughed at him or when Mr. Smilodon made a comment about his behavior on the course.

"This is a *Three Stooges* flick with only one stooge!" someone shouted from the audience. The guests pounded on their tables in approval and roared with laughter. The senator pushed aside the plate of food the waiter placed before him and took another sip of whiskey.

"Tito, you're right, none of the other guests in the room have any food on their tables, only glasses of dark red liquid," the doctor said.

"Do you think the food is safe?" the colonel asked in a hushed voice.

"Let's ask the senator," the doctor said.

"Hey, Senator, how is the food?" Tito asked.

"What? I am not interested in dinner," the senator said.

"Senator, snap out of your foul mood and enjoy the gourmet meal" the colonel said.

"Fine, whatever," the senator said. He took a bite but did not shift his focus from the video on the screen.

The three golfers waited anxiously for his response.

"It's good, fantastic," the senator said. He took another bite and relaxed before more laughter from the audience rankled him.

"Satisfied, Colonel?" the doctor asked.

The three golfers raised their glasses in a toast to the game and laughed at the scenes from the video. When the video concluded, the guests in the ballroom chanted 'Senator, Senator' in unison.

"Doc, everyone in the room, including the staff, is fixated on the senator," Tito said.

"Guess they enjoyed his caustic behavior on the course instead of the skill and finesse of my golf game," the doctor said. He noticed the guests in the ballroom were looking at the senator, and no one was paying any attention to him.

The audience became quiet when the video screen retracted in the ceiling and theater-style lights illuminated three of the guests at the head table.

"Ladies and gentlemen, it is a sad evening because we have to say goodbye to three of our new friends."

"Who cares? Send the losers home! We want our new member!" the other guests in the ballroom shouted at Mr. Smilodon.

"Do you have the impression they care little for us?" Tito asked.

"It seems odd we are illuminated by the spotlight and the senator is not in the light," the colonel said.

"He is on the other side of the table," the doctor said.

"Screw the losers, your Eminence. We don't want them here!" the crowd shouted. Some members of the audience threw their glasses at the stage.

"Members of our venerable golf club, you are correct; we should not acknowledge the losers of the golf match today. We are a club of exalted members who have achieved impressive accomplishments in our lives. I will not besmirch our pedigree with a toast to the losers! Instead, a toast to our new member who shares our lineage traced to what once stood where this golf course is today. Ladies and gentlemen, may I present our new member, Senator Jack Seavan!" Mr. Smilodon said.

A thunderous applause echoed through the ballroom. Mr. Smilodon wiped the red drink from his lips and looked at the oculus.

The doctor stood up from his chair but sat down again when he heard the senator's name and noticed the spotlight shining on the senator.

"What the hell happened?" the doctor asked Tito with a look of confusion.

"You won the match, Doctor. I don't know why they called the senator's name."

"The fat fool bribed Mr. Smilodon or threatened him," the colonel said.

At first the senator did not notice his name called, but when he saw the doctor's face and listened to the crowd chant his name, he cracked a smile.

"The people have spoken," the senator said to the doctor. He buttoned his tuxedo as he stood up to the roar of the crowd and winked at the doctor.

"Thank you, thank you," the senator said. He stretched out his hands toward the crowd and beamed a broad smile as he pivoted to each corner of the room.

"Speak up! We can't hear our new member!" someone shouted from the audience.

The senator's voice lacked the strength to fill the room unaided. A member of the staff made their way toward the head table and handed him a microphone. "Welcome to the family," the staff member said as he hugged the senator and kissed him on both cheeks.

"I want to thank everyone here tonight," the senator said as he cleared his throat and tapped on the microphone. "I am humbled you chose me to join your extraordinary golf club," the senator said in a high-pitched voice amplified through the ballroom. The senator glanced at the three golfers at the table and smiled. "Let's not forget these three who made the win possible. Give a round of applause for Colonel Askeri, Tito Cruz and Dr.

Sean Matson," the senator said.

"Losers!" the crowd shouted.

"You're right. We don't honor the losers," the senator said as he dodged a deluge of glasses tossed at him from the crowd.

"Doc, don't make a scene. The other guests don't want us here," the colonel said.

The doctor ignored the colonel and snatched the microphone from the senator in mid-sentence.

"Mr. Smilodon, I won the round of golf. This membership is mine. Why did you announce this buffoon's name as the new member? Did he bribe his way into the club?" the doctor asked.

"Sit down, Doc. No one cares. We want the senator!" someone yelled from the audience. Mr. Smilodon approached the doctor with a scowl.

"You brought great honor to yourself and played the game with integrity. You carried yourself with aplomb, but the tournament was not the only element we evaluated for membership. We also considered your accomplishments in life, what you have done with your tremendous gifts and talents, and how you interacted with lesser mortals. We also observed your behavior from the day you received the exclusive invitation. Each of you possess the bloodlines we favor, so consider yourself a member of the elite in that regard, but Seavan has the qualities we want in a new member," Mr. Smilodon said.

"An arrogant sociopath who manipulates people and exploits them as pawns in his games of power and corruption. People are mere props in his life to be discarded when they no longer serve his purpose. This caricature of everything wrong with humanity is who you want for membership?" the doctor asked.

"Why, yes, Doctor, among his other traits," Mr. Smilodon said with a big grin.

Laughter filled the room and infuriated the doctor.

"I want nothing to do with this place or your members," the doctor said. The colonel and the baseball player both nodded in agreement.

"Members only! Members only!" the crowd chanted.

"Get rid of the losers!" another member shouted from across the room.

"Get lost, you three! The members have spoken, and make sure you mail the check you owe me to my capitol office," the senator said.

The doctor threw the microphone and hit the senator in his fat chin. The senator recoiled in pain and shouted at the staff in the ballroom, "Arrest that man! He assaulted a US Senator," the audience roared in laughter.

"We did indeed choose the right person to join our ranks," Mr. Smilodon said to the crowd.

Mr. Smilodon turned toward the three golfers and glowered at them.

"Leave us! Your bags and your vehicle wait for you outside the lodge. The night belongs to Senator Seavan," Mr. Smilodon said with malice in his voice.

"Tito, I'll take that as our cue to leave before the crowd turns violent on us," the colonel said.

"I agree. Stay close, Colonel," Tito said.

"Doctor, do you plan to stay with these monsters?" the colonel asked.

"Of course not," the doctor said, dismayed by the turn of events.

The crowd chanted in the ancient language Mr. Smilodon had spoken to the caddies. Tito pushed members of the lodge in a trance-like state out of his way and created a path for the other two golfers to reach the ballroom exit. The doors of the ballroom slammed shut once the golfers exited the room. The building shook when the doors closed behind them. The white-gloved attendants, polite in manner earlier in the evening, snarled with faces contorted from anger and pointed toward the staircase.

"Don't stop!" Tito said as the group approached the staircase.

"They extinguished the fireplace," the colonel said as they passed the massive stone fireplace.

"The doors to the lodge are wide open," the doctor said.

"Should we get into the SUV?" the colonel asked.

"We will be lucky if the SUV is outside instead of a group of angry caddies who want to shred us to pieces!" Tito said.

"What choice do we have?" the doctor asked.

"Maybe we should look for a phone and call someone," the colonel said.

"Do you hear the chants and the eerie sounds from the ballroom? We need to leave this building," Tito said as he clutched his crucifix.

The ornate wood doors slammed shut the moment the golfers exited the lodge. The three golfers turned around to see the entrance morph into the solid rock of the canyon.

"What the hell happened?" Tito said. He extended his hand toward the rock where the wood doors once stood.

"Don't touch it, Tito!" the colonel implored. She pushed his outstretched hand away from the rock.

The sound of a vehicle on the cobblestone driveway drew their attention away from the vanished entrance.

"Quick, get in the vehicle. Tito, you sit up front with the driver to keep an eye on him," the colonel said as she pushed him aside and moved toward the SUV.

The vehicle sped away with no headlights to illuminate the road. The bright moon above provided the only light in the canyon. Tito saw the lights on the lodge extinguish in the side view mirror of the SUV.

The driver of the vehicle turned toward Tito. "Guess you guys did not win the golf match," he said. The full moon illuminated his furry hands as he clutched the steering wheel.

The senator raised his hands in victory from the main stage and shouted, "Let the party begin!" The guests in the ballroom continued to chant and paid no attention to the senator. He shouted again but the lights in the ballroom went dark. The senator's eyes adjusted to the darkness aided by the full moon that poured through oculus. The senator bathed in the moonlight from above, stood motionless, waiting for the emergency generators to turn on the lights, but the darkness lingered. The air became stale and the atrocious smells from the barn filled his nose.

A red glow appeared on stage where Mr. Smilodon stood, followed by red orbs scattered across the ballroom. The senator rubbed his eyes to focus on the red lights, but they faded away simultaneously before the lights turned on in the ballroom. The senator's eyes, wide with disbelief, fixated on the chupacabra dressed in the same tuxedo Mr. Smilodon had worn with a red pocket square, standing where Mr. Smilodon had stood before the lights went out in the ballroom.

The senator looked around the room and the other guests appeared as chupacabras dressed in formal attire. The senator brought his hands to his face and screamed in horror when he saw his hands covered in the same matted fur of the chupacabras. He ran toward one of the massive mirrors in the room. He pushed the other chupacabras out of his way and stood before the mirror. He howled like a caddie and smashed the mirror after he noticed his bruised flesh replaced with fur in the reflection.

Mr. Smilodon stood behind the senator. His body was that of a chupacabra and his face, in human form, said, "Welcome to Goat Trails Golf Club. Your caddy apprenticeship begins in earnest tomorrow."

The senator collapsed on the black obsidian floor illuminated by the moonlight from the oculus.

Freeway traffic would crawl in gridlock an hour from now, but at this hour the colonel enjoyed the empty lanes. She usually listened to National Public Radio when most of the city was asleep, but today she listened to her foreign language lesson to prepare for her new assignment overseas. Bright halogen lights from the checkpoint on the military post greeted her. She noticed the American flag flying at half-mast when she stopped her car next to a soldier at the gate. She inspected the soldier's uniform and appearance before she opened her window.

"Identification, please," the soldier asked, barely awake as the long night shift took its toll on his mental faculties.

"Private, why is the flag at half-mast?" the colonel asked when she handed him her military identification card.

"Oh, a senator died in a plane crash yesterday in Arizona," the private said, his hand over his mouth to conceal a yawn.

Arizona? Must be a coincidence, she thought. "Private, you will address me as ma'am or colonel. Do you know the senator's name?" the colonel asked.

"Sorry, ma'am, I did not see your rank."

"My ID card has my rank. Did you check my ID to ensure it is authentic?" the colonel asked.

"Sorry, ma'am, it has been a long shift," the private said.

"No excuse. You need to remain vigilant while on duty. Do you know the name of the senator?" the colonel asked again.

"I think it was Senator Seavan, but I might be wrong. The announcement interrupted the game on television, ma'am."

The private handed the colonel her ID and saluted. The colonel took her ID and did not bother to return the private's salute before she rolled up the window and drove onto post. She considered turning on the radio for news about the plane crash but instead listened to the foreign language lesson. She wanted nothing more to do with the senator or the ghastly Goat Trails Golf Club.

The End

ACKNOWLEDGMENTS

Writing a book is like the perfect golf swing. It requires desire, concentration, discipline and fortuitous timing.

A special woman whom was the first to hear the whisper of the plot in the mountains above the desert believed in the idea instead of dousing the burgeoning flame of creativity with criticism. Thank you, Myrna.

A creative and talented writer of mystery novels whom made the daunting task of filling a blank manuscript with substance seem possible motivated me to coax the idea from the quintessence. Thank you, LC Hayden.

When the mind is quiet, the imagination flourishes despite the noise. I would be remiss for not mentioning an extraordinary woman whose creativity far surpasses my humble attempt at writing a story. Thank you, Ann, my SP, for revealing the world behind the noise.

Slay the tentacles that lurk in the shadow of the ego every day before they take hold of the idea and submerge it in self doubt. Thank you, Mom and Dad for your steadfast support.

Many thanks to Eric Padgett who motivated me to write during our lunch break when we were both working on our manuscripts at work instead of squandering the valuable time by plotting shenanigans in the shire.

A colossal thank you to Kim Hester for designing the intriguing cover and formatting the manuscript. And thank you to my ghost editor for helping me communicate with precision.

Most of all, thank you reader for going *Beyond the Goat Trails* with me.

Mike Sovelius

AUTHOR'S BIOGRAPHY

The author is a graduate of the University of Texas (Hook' em Horns!) and a former soldier. He enjoys a good walk unspoiled by the game of golf and writes in both time zones of the great state of Texas. This is his first book.

Pooches
Publishing

Evoke the Magic of Writing